The

Courting

Buggy

Fay Risner

Maybe it has something to do with our aging process, but eventually, we learn how important family is to us. Those of us who have been fortunate enough to have an Aunt Tootie in our lives decide to remember and smile fondly. Holidays seem to bring out the warm feelings for our extended family and memories of relatives that we wish were alive to enjoy a family gathering with us. In my case, my family often thinks about our grandmother, Veder Bright, and my mother, Sylvia Bullock. We invoke stories about them at gatherings. They were two great cooks that loved to feed their family any time, and we miss both of them very much.

That's why the following recipe seemed like a natural to add to this book. This was a recipe handed down through three generations of James Dustin Morrison's family. That's the best kind of recipe to share with others, because those recipes not only come through loving hands, creating the dish puts those special people that touched and formed our lives right there with us while we're cook.

Years ago, cooks didn't have published cookbooks. They kept handwritten recipes from relatives and friends in a drawer. The Party Potato recipe belongs to James Dustin Morrison's grandmother. She passed it on to Dustin's mother and his mother gave him a copy. He couldn't have picked a better time than Thanksgiving of 2013 to share his culinary efforts with John and Diana Bullock's family. That's because my husband, Harold, our son, Duane, and I were lucky enough to be a part of their holiday feast. We enjoyed Dustin's Party Potatoes, and the sentiment behind the dish made it even more special. I appreciate that Dustin was willing to share the recipe with all my readers so that you might enjoy his Party Potatoes, too.

4

Party Potatoes

Shared by James Dustin Morrison

From the kitchen of his Mom and Grandmother

Ingredients

5 pounds of potatoes
One large bar of Cream Cheese
One 6 oz. Tub of Sour Cream
Garlic salt or powder to taste
Squares of butter on top of finished potatoes (1 to 1½ sticks)

Instructions

Peel potatoes, cut in half and boil. Combine softened cream cheese and sour cream in a mixer. Add the cook potatoes and some of the potato water. Add garlic salt or powder to taste.

Oven temperature 350   Time 30-40 min   Serves 8-10

On November 1, 2013, I entered the National Novel Writing Month contest (NaNoWriMo). By the end of November, The Courting Buggy draft was pulled over the finish line by Mike, Jim Lindstrom's sorrel horse. You now have the finished project, my published book.

Enjoy

Fay Risner

Chapter 1

John Lapp stepped out of the barn and observed the sky. The west was dark from the recent rain, but the sun beat down overhead now. He felt the sun's warmth on his face. It felt good. He closed his dark brown eyes and threw his arms above his head, stretching the kinks out of his joints. The hour before, a black rain cloud poured large, cold drops on him as he ran into the barn. He was thankful to see the sun back. Even more thankful for peaceful calm times like these when all was right in his family's world.

Laugher from the end of the driveway caused John to glance toward the gravel road. His two sons sauntered toward him. Daniel's growth spurt had shot him up almost as tall as his brother, Noah. John's youngest son must have found something Noah said funny. He elbowed the grinning Noah who usually was the serious natured one of the two.

The boys acted like they were up to something. John waited for them to get to him. "How was your visit with Jimmie Miller?"

"Gute," Noah said.

"Jah, we had fun," Daniel replied. The eleven years old boy had his jacket buttoned shut. The black material moved in and out over his chest.

John pointed at Daniel's jacket. "What do you have rutsching around in there?"

1

Daniel asked, "Remember we talked about some day getting another dog?"

"Jah," John answered.

"Did you see Jimmie's dog and her litter of pups when we had the Sunday meeting at their farm a month ago?" Noah inquired.

"Jah. If I remember right, she was a black and tan coon hound with a mess of pups. Ain't so?" John recalled.

"Jah, and Jimmie is ready to wean the pups and give them away. He gave us one to bring home on approval." Daniel added reluctantly, "If you and Mama Hal do not like him we can take the pup back."

"Bring him out of your jacket before he suffocates, and let me see him," John said.

Daniel unbuttoned his coat and handed the fat, cream colored puppy to his father. "He's cute, ain't so?"

The puppy's spiked tail quivered back and forth. He let out a series of yips at John like a wind up toy.

"Right now he is. Is he pure coon hound?" John asked.

"Jah. Bred to, Jimmie's cousin, Morgan Miller's black and tan coon hound," Noah said.

"I take it you two are planning to take this pup coon hunting when he's older?" John surmised.

"That is the plan," Noah agreed.

"It is all right with me to keep him, but this pup is not the breed your Mama Hal might have had in mind when we talked about getting another family dog like Patches. You show her the puppy. If you get her approval then it is all right with me to keep him," John said.

"How about we let Mama Hal name the pup? Think she would like that gute enough to let us keep him?" Daniel asked.

"Might work in your favor. Give it a try," John agreed. "I'm headed to the house. No time better to show the puppy to Hal and Emma."

John trod behind the house and into the mud room with the boys right behind him. When John entered the kitchen, Hal marched at him, wringing a corner of her white apron. "I don't know how I could have done such a thing. This is awful. I don't know what to do about it."

John stopped short. Bewildered, he watched his wife pace around the kitchen. Daniel grabbed Noah's arm. He whispered, "We better stay out here until Dad gets Mama Hal settled down. This does not sound gute for our puppy."

"Jah," Noah hissed solemnly. "I have been pondering this. Maybe we should not bring up that our dog is a coon hound unless Mama Hal comes right out and asks its breed. She can not tell one breed from the other when they are puppies."

"Gute idea," Daniel whispered back. The puppy squirmed in his arms. He nearly dropped the pup before gathering him in a tighter grip.

Emma was mixing cake batter at the table. Her gray green eyes shifted nervously back and forth from the batter to her upset stepmother. Hal made a lap around the room and back to John. "This is just not fair. How could this happen? I don't know how I could have done such a dumb thing? Do you, John?"

"I can not answer that until you tell me what you did. What did you do?" John implored, wondering what could be so bad to cause Hal's face to flush as red as her hair.

"I got a letter from my parents today. They're coming to visit us, because I invited them," Hal groaned. She grabbed the letter off the table and waved the sheets of paper at him.

John looked confused. "What's wrong with that? I like your folks."

At that news, Noah and Daniel edged into the kitchen. Standing behind Noah to conceal the pup, Daniel said gleefully, "Dawdi Jim and Mammi Nora are coming. That is gute news."

"Nah, it's not gute news," Hal narrowed her eyes at the boys. They ducked their heads and studied their bare feet. Hal continued, "It's very bad news. Why did I do it, John?"

"The mystery of that will only be solved if you tell me the whole story. Come sit down." He grabbed Hal by the elbow and led her to the table. "You are all worked up, ain't so? Now tell me why is it not gute news that your folks are coming if you invited them?" John asked patiently. *What was I thankful for just a few minutes ago? So much for it being peaceful around here.* He took Hal by her shoulders and pushed her down into a chair.

"Because my mother asked Aunt Tootie to come with them, and Aunt Tootie is coming. Isn't that awful?" Hal cried, dropping her hands in surrender onto her apron.

"Who is Aendi Tootie?" Daniel asked.

"My mother's sister," Hal answered.

"Does she have a husband?" Noah asked.

"Not anymore. She's been a widow for years," Hal told him.

"If your aendi is anything like your mother we will be looking forward to her visit," John said truthfully.

"You hit the nail on the head," Hal barked at him. "That's the problem. Aunt Tootie is nothing like my mother. She will say or do something to upset people in the Amish community and get our whole family shunned. That's the way she is. She doesn't think what she's going to say. Words just shoot out of her mouth. She doesn't think before she acts. She just does things. Weird things."

Emma took a stab at placating Hal. "Hallie, I do not see how she can be that bad. We will be all right."

"Nah, we won't. I'm sure of it," Hal declared, rubbing her forehead to ease the throb.

"Consider the family warned and calm down, Hal. Surely nothing can happen to get us in trouble in the short time your relatives will stay," John reasoned.

"Wrong! They're going to stay a month at least, and maybe more if they think they're having fun," Hal groaned.

"Maybe it would have helped if Mammi Nora had given you a whiff of a warning they were bringing your aendi with them," Emma groused as she poured the batter in the cake pan.

"Nah, any other relative maybe, but it wouldn't have helped this time. Not when it's Aunt Tootie they're bringing," groaned Hal with both hands to her face.

John said, "Now, Hal, hospitality is a virtue commanded in

the bible."

"God never had my Aunt Tootie sit at his table! If he did just once, he'd have given asking her second thoughts when she showed up again," Hal fumed.

John spoke a cautionary slow, "Hal."

Noah interrupted. "When are they coming?"

"They will drive in sometime next Tuesday afternoon," Hal said quietly.

John rubbed the side of his face. "That is a week from today. That soon?"

"Jah, and there's so much to do. My parents can sleep in the spare room, but where are we going to put Aunt Tootie?" Hal worried.

"She can sleep with me," Emma offered.

"Oh, no! Trust me. You don't want Aunt Tootie to sleep with you," Hal declared.

"I do not understand why not. I am sure I will be able to endure her for the short time they are here," Emma said.

"Nah, you will not. Where do you think she got the name Tootie?" Hal exclaimed, slumping in the chair.

Emma looked puzzled then her eyes widen. "Oh."

Noah and Daniel put their hands to their mouths and giggled.

Hal leaned back against the chair. It appeared she had run out of steam.

This was as good a time as any to get Hal's mind on something else. John said, "The boys have something to show you."

Daniel stepped around Noah and stood in front of Hal, holding the wiggling puppy. "Jimmie Miller is weaning a litter of pups. He let us bring this one home on approval. If you like the puppy we can keep him. If you do not like him, we will take him back."

"I see. He sure is a cute little fellow," Hal said, holding her hands out.

Daniel gave her the puppy while Noah said, "If you like him, you can name him for us."

Hal studied the boys and then the puppy. "Let me get this

5

straight. If I name him, you get to keep the puppy?"

Noah wasn't sure what was the right thing to answer since Mama Hal hadn't been too happy. "I guess that is recht."

"What an honor to be able to name the puppy. Denki, boys. Emma, what do you think of him?" Hal asked. She twisted in the chair and held the puppy out where Emma could see him.

Emma put the cake pan in the oven, before she focused on the pup. "He is a sweet puppy right now while he is in your lap. It wonders me the bedevilment he will be full of when he is turned loose on us."

"Sister, that describes all puppies," Noah defended.

Daniel hissed at Emma. "It is either a puppy or another raccoon. Which would you rather we get for a pet?"

"No question. The puppy," Emma relented quickly.

Hal held the puppy up, inspecting his chubby body and long ears. The pup sniffed at her, gave her cheek a lick of approval with his pink tongue and yipped in her face. "He's such a pretty cream color. Reminds me of one of Emma's biscuits. I think I'll name him Biscuit."

Daniel's mouth fell open.

Noah looked helplessly at his father.

The corner of John's lips twitched in good humor at his sons' chagrin. Daniel opened his mouth to protest the puppy's new name, but John stopped him. "Boys, better find a place to settle the puppy so you can help me milk and get the calves bottle fed."

Daniel sounded dispirited. "Jah, Daed."

"Where are you going to put him?" Hal asked. "The nights are still chilly."

"In one of the pens in the barn with clean straw bedding to snuggle in," Noah said. "He slept in the barn at the Miller farm."

"By himself?" Hal asked.

"Nah, he was with the rest of the litter," Daniel told her.

"I thought as much. They kept each other warm at night," Hal said. "If you find a box big enough Biscuit couldn't crawl out of, he could stay in the mudroom for a couple of weeks. At least until it warms up at night. Think that would be all right, John?"

"Jah, that would be fine," John agreed. "Now we have work to do. Noah, you help me. Daniel, you get the box, put the puppy in it then bottle feed the calves."

As they walked to the barn, Noah said, "Daed, we can not name the dog Biscuit. That is not a fit name for a dog."

"Help us talk Mama Hal into a different name. One that is for dogs," Daniel said, tagging along.

"It will not be wise for you to back out on letting Hal name the puppy right now. She is upset enough about her aunt coming. She might not take kindly to hearing you do not like her name for the dog. Best stick to your bargain, and be thankful she is letting you keep him. I am hoping the puppy will give her something to think about instead of the company coming."

"But, Daed, how is that going to sound when we take this dog coon hunting with the other boys, and we're calling in the dark timber come here Biscuit," Noah groaned.

"They are all going to have a good laugh at us. That is what will happen," Daniel complained.

"I expect they will," John said, chuckling.

That night during supper, Hal silently worried about all that needed done before next Tuesday. She pushed her food around on her plate, hardly eating anything.

Daniel rose in his chair enough that he could reach across the table and pick up the butter dish. Hal frowned. On top of everything else, both boys needed to remember to use manners around her parents and aunt. "Daniel, instead of reaching across the table for the butter, the polite thing to do is say please pass me the butter."

Daniel bowed his head. "Sorry, Mama Hal."

"It's all right this time. It's just that I want us to use our best manners while we have company," Hal explained.

The next few days passed by in a fast whirlwind of activity as Hal and Emma rushed to clean the house and air out the spare room for Hal's parents.

7

When the boys came in one afternoon, Emma sent them to the basement to sweep and take down the cobwebs.

"We are sure going to a lot of work for company," Noah complained.

Daniel grumped, "You would think Aendi Tootie and Mammi Nora do not ever see a speck of dust."

"They do not from the way Mama Hal is acting," Noah replied as he swiped the ceiling cobwebs with the broom's straws.

When the boys appeared back upstairs, Emma cornered them again. "Make up the fly bags and put them around the doors and windows. We do not want a lot of flies in here."

Noah asked, "Mama Hal, you have enough pennies to put in the water?"

Hal rifled in her purse and gave the boys what pennies she had. Emma laid a box of quart baggies on the kitchen table. The boys put six pennies in each bag and filled them half full of water. Once they had the amount of bags they needed, they tacked the fly bags on the outside of the house.

Finally one morning after much thought, Hal announced as she wiped dishes, "Aunt Tootie is going to sleep in the clinic bed."

"Are you sure?" Emma asked. "The clinic is so far away from the rest of the family at night."

"There's nothing wrong with that. For goodness sakes! It's not like I'm sending her out to the barn to sleep. The clinic is attached to the house after all," Hal declared out of sorts.

"I know, but what if you need that bed for a birthing?" Emma considered.

"We will deal with that when and if it happens. Maybe we'll be lucky and not have a birth while our company is here. I can't think of anyone that's due this soon."

"Just the same we should treat your aunt like company. Besides, she is a lot older than me. She can have my bed. I can sleep in the clinic. That way if we have a birthing I will be the one without a bed which I will not need if I am assisting you," Emma declared logically.

8

Hal gave in. "All right, if that's the way you want it."

Emma fixed the mop bucket and mopped the kitchen's black and white checkered linoleum. She tossed the dirty water out the back door. As she hung the mop pail on a nail and the rag mop beside it, Noah and Daniel charged into the mud room. Emma eyed the squirming puppy warily in Daniel's arms as she snapped, "Watch your step! I just mopped that kitchen floor. It is slick."

"We will," Daniel said.

The boys tiptoed into the kitchen. Hal smiled at them as she dried her hands on her apron. "How's the puppy doing?"

"He is growing fast, ain't so?" Noah said to Daniel.

"Jah," Daniel agreed. "Want to see him come to you, Mama Hal." He put the puppy on the floor. "Now call him."

Hal slapped the side of her leg. "Come to me, Biscuit. Come here." The puppy slipped and sprawled out several times on the damp floor before he finally slid to a stop in front of Hal. She leaned over and patted his head. "You're so cute."

The nervous puppy licked her hand repeatedly. Suddenly, he squatted and relieved himself. The amber puddle spread out around his hind paws, ran under his front paws and flowed toward Hal. She stepped back to keep the pool from running under her bare feet. The puppy yipped as he pattered around her, leaving his wet tracks on the clean squares.

With her hands on her hips, Emma's disgust couldn't be missed.

With eyes on his sister, Noah said quietly, "Grab Biscuit, Daniel."

At the sound of Emma's heavy footsteps behind them, Daniel told Hal, "We need to go now."

Instantly, Emma was beside them, pointing to the puddle. "That is not a gute thing. I just mopped the floor. I did not want to do it over, but I will have to, ain't so?" Her stiff finger wavered toward the pup as she snapped, "Get him out of this house. He does not belong in here."

Noah rushed at the puppy. Biscuit dodged under the table. The puppy crouched down, shivering as he tried to figure out what went wrong.

Daniel told Noah, "I will crawl under the table on this side. You watch for him on the other side."

Daniel went at the pup on all fours. Biscuit scampered out of hiding and bumped into Emma's bare feet. She scooped squirming pup up and held him at arms' length. "I have him. Take him to the barn. He can not stay in the mud room anymore. Take the box away. It smells as bad as this dog does. They both need to be gone before company comes."

Chapter 2

Late Tuesday afternoon, Jim Lindstrom's car pulled into the driveway and parked. Nora patted down her gray streaked brown hair before she opened her car door. Tootie plastered her round, smiley face to the back window, waving furiously. Jim twisted in the seat and spoke to Tootie. She handed him a straw hat perched on top the back seat. He donned the hat before he got out of the car.

The Lapp family rushed to greet them. John hollered, "Wilcom."

Broad shouldered Jim Lindstrom gave John a hardy handshake. John said, "Looks like you got a new straw hat?"

Jim chuckled. "You bet. Didn't figure I should borrow yours anymore."

He gave Hal a bear hug. "How you doing, Carrot Top?"

"Oh, Dad," Hal scoffed, wishing he'd forget that nickname.

By that time, Nora made it around the car and headed toward them. Hal remembered when her mother was considered a looker with neatly trimmed short brown hair, warm eyes and curves in all the right places. Now her neat hair was streaked with gray and her curves were slightly larger. With the long times between visits, it was easy for Hal to notice the aging changes.

Behind Nora was her sister,Tootie. A shorter version of Nora except Tootie kept her short gray hair in a curly perm. Both women dressed in neatly tailored pantsuits which made Hal covetous since she had to wear long dresses.

The two women hugged everyone as Hal introduced the family to her aunt before she said, "We should go in and sit down for awhile before we unload the trunk. I'll bet all of you are tired after such a long trip."

"Been sitting all day," Tootie stated, rubbing her bottom. "Your father doesn't believe in stopping except in an emergency. I darn near was the emergency a time or two before he pulled into a gas station so I could use the restroom."

"Now, Tootie, it wasn't as bad as all that," Nora defended her husband.

John said, "Hal take the women inside while I help Jim unload the car."

Daniel tugged on Jim's shirt sleeve. "Dawdi Jim, we have a new puppy."

"That right?" Jim asked with interest.

"Would you like to see him?" Noah said, "He is in the barn."

"Sure, let's take a look. John, I'll be right back to unload." Jim turned to leave with them.

"Jim, you best get into your work shoes before you go to the barn. Those are your Sunday shoes you're wearing," scolded Nora.

Jim winked at the boys. "I'll be careful. We'll be right back. Won't we, boys?"

"Sure, Mammi Nora," Daniel said. "This will not take long."

"They have nasty chickens running wild," Tootie hissed at Nora's shoulder. "You know how chickens go everywhere." She tisked as she stared at the flock of hens, scratching in the barnyard. "I've never seen anything else like chickens that does so much strutting over so little to be proud of."

"I'll watch where I step and even rub my shoe soles in the grass on the way back," Jim promised. "Come on, boys. We can't stay gone long. I have to carry in the suitcases."

"We can help, Dawdi," Noah offered as he opened the barn's half door.

The puppy scampered to the side of his pen when he heard

their voices. He yipped an excited greeting, jumped up and planted his front paws on the side of the pen then bounced off. He twisted in a circle, chased his tail a moment and jumped up on the pen again to be patted.

"He's sure a cute fellow," Jim said. "What breed is he?"

Daniel patted the pup's head. "Black and Tan coon hound."

"You taking him coon hunting when he gets a little older?" Jim asked.

"Jah," Noah answered.

"You will have to train him. You know how?"

Daniel shook his head a slow yes. "We know how. What we do not know is if we will be able to do it."

Noah suggested, "We might take him out when it is just me and Daniel. We have not decided what to do yet."

"Why not? He should learn what he is to do easy enough. Be quick to train him I'd think since coon hunting is bred into him," Jim exclaimed.

"That is for sure and certain," Noah agreed. "You see Dawdi Jim there is a problem. We told Mama Hal she could name the puppy. We thought she would like him better if we let her name him." He paused to look at Daniel.

Jim looked down his nose at the boys. "And?"

Daniel said plaintively, "She named our dog Biscuit."

"No kidding." Jim chuckled.

"Dawdi, this is not funny. It is a big problem. Can you see us out with a bunch of boys, and we call for Biscuit to come to us. They are going to tease us something awful."

Jim rubbed the back of his neck and tried to put on a serious face. "You fellows have a problem for sure. Hallie wouldn't give the dog another name?"

Noah shrugged. "She might have, but Dad will not let us ask her. He said that would be welshing on the deal. She was to get to pick the name if she let us keep the dog."

"What can we do, Dawdi Jim?" Daniel implored.

Jim rubbed his chin as he thought. "Seems to me what Hal doesn't know won't upset her. Let her call the dog Biscuit. When you're alone with this pup and training him out away from the house call him Dog. He'll figure that's his name if you use it often enough. Actually, I doubt a dog really knows his name. They just know from the sound of your voice when you say something that's what you want. Any word you say will work for a name.

When you're among your friends call him Dog, and they won't think anything of it. If you slip up and say Dog in front of Hallie that will sound natural. Just remember to call him Biscuit where she can hear you once in awhile."

"Dawdi Jim, you are a genius," Noah praised, grinning from ear to ear.

"I knew you would think of something," Daniel agreed happily.

"Seems like a win win situation to me," Jim said. "Now we best go back and help your dad with the suitcases, or he will be giving all of us a hard time for keeping him from his chores."

"You bring that much stuff to carry in?" Daniel asked.

"Not me, but when you get a little older, you'll find out women can't go anywhere without bringing half of what they own along with them," Jim grumped. He looked at his wrist watch. "Besides, it will be time to milk soon. I want to help so I have to hunt up my old jeans and work shoes to put on. If I don't get out of my Sunday clothes before I come back to the barn, your grandma's going to have a cow."

Daniel's face scrunched up. He said in concern to Noah. "Mammi Nora would take one of our cows if Dawdi Jim doesn't mind her?"

Baffled, Noah shrugged.

Jim laughed. "No, I just meant she will be mad at me."

Once the men and boys left for the barn to milk, Emma and Hal started supper while Nora and Tootie sat at the table.

Tootie gave a faint sniffle to get attention. "Hallie, there are a few things you should know about my diet before you do a lot of cooking. In the morning for breakfast, I only like two kinds of juice – grape or apple. I can't abide tomato juice. The acid is bad for my stomach you know." She let out a plaintive sigh as she rubbed her midsection. "I have a lot of digestive

14

troubles."

Emma said kindly, "That will not be a problem. We have those juices on hand."

"I'm so sorry to hear you have stomach problems, Aunt Tootie. That can be miserable," Hal sympathized.

Tootie sniffed a little louder this time and studied the table top. "I'll be all right unless I need an enema. I hope I don't have to have one while I'm here, but if I do, it's a fortunate thing I have a niece who is a nurse."

Emma's mouth flew open as she looked from Tootie to Hal. Hal turned a distressed stare on her mother and mouthed the words, "Really, Mom?"

Nora shrugged, clearly powerless where Tootie was concerned.

At supper, John asked Jim if he had plans for the next day.

Jim said, "No, figured to do whatever you do."

"The boys and me were thinking about going to the Wickenburg salebarn tomorrow. There is a big horse drawn equipment sale before the livestock auction. It is always interesting to look at. Would you like to go?"

"Sounds like fun," Jim said enthusiastically.

"Well, if you are done eating, we might as well get away from the table. You remember we always have a time of devotion in the morning and the evening after supper," John said. "We can wait in the living room for the women to do the dishes and join us."

"John, why don't you take Redbird and Beth with you. They're restless now that we're all busy," Hal said.

"Give me one of those girls," Jim insisted.

John lifted Beth out of her wooden highchair and held her toward Jim. She squealed in discontent and hugged John's neck. "Sorry about that."

"No problem. I'm a stranger to these babies. Let me try, Redbird, and see if I have better luck," Jim said. He lifted the toddler out of her chair. Happy to be freed, she giggled and patted his cheek. "That a girl." He said proudly.

"Works that way most of the time, Dad," Hal shared.

"Redbird is too friendly, and Beth is too bashful."

Jim inspected Redbird as he carried her away. "Hallie, what do you expect from another Carrot Top. She's just like her mother was at this age."

Once the men were gone, Tootie stood up like she was heading a women's church group, folded her hands in front of her and announced, "Ladies, we really should be getting these dishes done as soon as possible."

"Don't worry, Aunt Tootie. John's in no hurry to do devotions. He doesn't mind waiting for us," Hal declared.

"That's not it. I just can't abide dirty dishes roosting on the counter and table. I want to wash. I always have liked to wash the dishes."

"Oh," Emma said. "Usually I wash, but that is fine. The tea kettle is simmering on the back of the stove. I can make the dish water for you. I will wipe."

"What do you want me to do, Emma?" Nora asked.

"Help Hallie scrape the plates and put away the leftovers," Emma said. "Stack the dishes and set them on the counter by Aendi Tootie."

"The slop bucket's in the mudroom. I'll get it." Hal brought back a plastic ice cream pail. "Scrape the scraps in this, Mom, and I'll feed the cats in the barn."

While they worked, Hal said, "Mom, I expect you and Aunt Tootie need a day to rest up after that long trip. So tomorrow how about we hang out here while you get acquainted with your little granddaughters. The next day, we're invited to the Yoder farm in the afternoon. I told everyone at the Sunday worship meeting you were coming. The Yoders women said to make sure we brought you to visit them first thing."

"Sounds good to me. Is that Margaret and Linda you're talking about?" Nora asked.

"Jah, that's the ones," Hal told her as she scraped a plate.

By the time, Hal and Nora had the leftovers in cartons, Tootie picked up the last stainless steel kettle and swiped it out. "Emma, clean kettles tell other women what kind of a housekeeper you are. So do clean kitchens." She put the kettle

16

in the rinse pan and wrung out the dishcloth so she could scrub the counter tops before she moved to the table.

Emma implored, "Aendi Tootie, you should let me wash the table."

"No, Dear. That goes with the dish washing job," Tootie declared.

Hal left for the barn. When she came back, she set the empty pail by the dishpan. "Aunt Tootie, wash this scrap bucket last."

Tootie scrunched her nose up as she finished the table. "I'm done with the dishes. Do I have to wash the slop bucket, too?"

"Jah, we don't want it to smell and draw flies in the mudroom," Hal said.

Tootie's face stayed unpleasant as she washed the pail, but she didn't say anything. As soon as she finished the distasteful task, she left Emma to empty the dish pans and joined Nora and Hal in the living room.

After the family gathered, Tootie said, "John, if we're going to have devotions, would it bother you if I sang a hymn?"

Nora snapped, "Now, Tootie, John's the one who leads the family devotions. You sit back and listen."

Tootie leaned back on the couch and pouted.

Emma placated, "It is all right, Aendi Tootie. We like to sing hymns, too. Can I sing with you when Daed says it is time to sing?"

"Oh yes, Dear. Sure you can," Tootie crowed with a smug look at her sister.

"We all will sing," Hal added, trying to be as nice as she could to her aunt. After the way she'd talked about Tootie when she knew the elderly woman was coming, she felt guilty now.

As soon as the devotion time was over, horse hooves and the crunch of rocks on the driveway put them on alert.

John answered the knocks. "Wilcom, Eldon and Jane. Come on in."

Hal asked, "What brings you over tonight?"

Eldon's smiling red face took in each of the Lapp's visitors. "We wanted to wilcom your parents and invite them to come to the next Sunday meeting with you."

17

John said, "Boys, get some extra chairs from the kitchen. Jim and Nora, you remember Bishop Eldon and Jane Bontrager?"

"Of course, we do," Jim said, and Nora nodded.

Hal said, "This is my mother's sister, Tootie."

"Wie bist du beit, Tootie" Eldon said.

"It's nice to meet you and your wife," Tootie replied politely.

The boys came back with chairs and sat down on the floor near the men.

Emma said, "I am going to pop us a big pan of popcorn."

"I'll help," Nora volunteered, following Emma to the kitchen. She set a stack of cereal bowls on the table while Emma shook a skillet of kernels. "So, Emma, when do we meet your boyfriend. Adam is it?"

"Jah, Adam will be over soon. We are very special friends," Emma said, blushing. She poured the corn in the dishpan and popped one more skillet full. After she melted butter in the skillet, she poured that on the popcorn while Nora stirred the kernels with a spoon. Emma picked up the dishpan. "Now we are ready."

Emma set the dishpan down on the table by the window. Nora filled each bowl while Emma served.

When Emma came to Tootie, the elderly woman said, "Don't you have bigger bowls than this? I just love popcorn."

"Of course, Aendi Tootie. I'll get you one." Emma brought back a vegetable bowl.

The way Tootie stuffed herself with popcorn made Hal wondered if the elderly woman really had stomach and bowel problems. If Tootie could eat that much popcorn her ailments might be selective. Maybe she wouldn't have to give her aunt an enema after all.

"I am going to have a quilting frolic soon. I hope you ladies will be able to join me. Several of the neighbor women will be there," Jane Bontrager invited.

"We'd like that," Hal said. "It will be something different for my mother and Aunt Tootie to do while they're on vacation. Sound gute to you, Mom?"

"Yes, it does. We'd love to come. Don't know how good we will be at quilting, but it will be fun to watch experts at work," Nora said.

Jane replied modestly, "I would not call any of us experts. We just get by is all."

After the company left, everyone took turns yawning as they wound down.

Finally, Tootie said, "I'm sleepy. Where's my room?"

Emma pointed at the stairs. "You are going to sleep in my bed upstairs."

"That won't do," Tootie said matter of factly.

"Why not?" Hal asked.

"I really need a place downstairs," Tootie said quietly behind her hand so only the women could hear.

"Oh, so you're closer to the outhouse?" Whispered Hal. "We put a commode by your bed so you won't have to go outside."

"That too." Tootie put her hand up by her mouth again and whispered, "But I have nightmares sometimes. Your Uncle Edwin used to tell me I make the most unnatural sounds in my sleep." She gave a forlorn sigh. "The poor man didn't get a wink of sleep some nights. So the farther away I am from all of you the better so I don't disturb you. Most of the time, I'm not too bad, but I'm really tired tonight after traveling all day."

"That's too bad," Hal said. *Nothing like getting to know all about my relatives. How many more revelations is Aunt Tootie going to confide while she's here?*

Thinking it might be better not to mention what the clinic bed was used for, Emma suggested, "Would you like to sleep in the room off the living room? That is where I was going to sleep."

Tootie looked that direction. "That will be perfect."

Nora spoke up. "Tootie, you forgot to tell them you sleepwalk."

"You do?" Hal regarded her aunt in alarm.

"Not real often, Dear," Tootie assured her. "If I do, the best thing you can do is bring me a glass of water. If I drink it that wakes me up."

19

"All right, I'll remember that" Hal said.

John over heard. "You are in different country here from what you are used to. Best stay in bed where you are safe."

"I'll try my best," Tootie said seriously.

The next morning, Nora and Tootie got out of bed when they heard Emma and Hal come downstairs just before daylight. They dressed and were in the kitchen before Emma built the fire in the wood cookstove. Tootie yawned as she rubbed her eyes and watched Emma tear an old Budget newspaper into pieces. She dropped the strips in, put on top the split kindling and lit the paper. Quickly, Emma clunked the lid into place to keep smoke from escaping.

Nora praised, "You certainly have this cookstove shiny clean, Emma."

"Denki, Mammi Nora," Emma said proudly. "It is a job that needs to be done after every meal."

"Emma rubs a greasy rag over the stove to clean it," Hal added.

Emma carried an arm load of wood from behind the stove and covered the crackling kindling. She said, "A rusted stove top can not be changed back to look like a new one."

"My goodness, I haven't seen a wood cookstove in use since we were small children, Nora," Tootie declared then she covered a yawn. "You people get up awful early around here."

When everyone was assembled, the family bowed their heads for a silent prayer. When John took a deep breath that was the sign that prayer time was over. He slid eggs and sausage onto his plate and passed the platters so he could take the biscuit plate from Hal.

After kitchen clean up was done, they all met in the living room. After John read two chapters from his German bible, he said to Jim and the boys, "Best get at the chores if we are going to the salebarn this morning."

Chapter 3

That Wednesday morning, chores were done a little quicker with Jim's help. John stuck his head in the mudroom door. "Hal, we are leaving for the salebarn. We will eat dinner there. Be gone most of the day."

"That's gute. Have fun," Hal called after him.

Around the house to the front came the two men and two boys. They climbed into the enclosed buggy and drove away.

"What are we going to do this morning now that the dishes are washed?" Tootie asked.

"What do you want to do?" Nora countered, expecting her sister had something in mind not to do.

"Not the cooking that's for sure," Tootie said. "I'm not very good at cooking."

"Aendi Tootie, I am going to work in the garden this morning. Come with me, and I will show you our garden," Emma said.

Tootie gave a half shrug of indifference. "I never had a garden so don't know anything about one."

"I started my own tomato and pepper plants from seeds in February in the house," Emma continued to explain. "Want to see how big they are now since I set them out?"

"Ah, I suppose if you've seen one tomato or pepper plant, you've seen them all," Tootie said lamely.

"Oh, pittle, Tootie. Just go look at Emma's garden. You

might learn something," Nora ordered. "Emma, if you have an extra hoe, give it to Tootie. Let her help you."

"Nora, you know I don't know a weed from a vegetable," Tootie barked.

"That's what Emma's going to show you," Nora replied.

"My back is bad. Doubt I'd last but a few minutes trying to hold onto a heavy hoe," Tootie whined, rubbing the small of her back.

Emma said, "It does me gute to hoe in the garden when I am thinking about things that are a worry. Weeding helps settle the soul, Aendi Tootie. I'll show you how it feels to work in my garden."

"I didn't know anything was really worrying me," grumbled Tootie.

"See you after while, Aunt Tootie," Hal said, trying hard not to smile as the elderly woman reluctantly followed behind Emma. She worried to Nora, "It really won't be too much for Aunt Tootie if she hoes will it?"

Nora smiled. "No! About time she did a little something, but knowing my sister, she'll figure out a way to get rid of the hoe and be back in the house shortly."

Meanwhile, Jim anticipated this trip to the salebarn with John and the boys. "Listen, what's that I hear?" He leaned forward to look out the windshield at the sky. A wild geese flock, on their return trip north in a gigantic V, honked with a clatter. The geese flew over the road in front of the buggy. Jim and John watched until the honks grew distant.

Other scenes came along to catch Jim's attention. A child worked in a garden with his mother, ankle deep in soft, moist topsoil. He hoed long trenches under tautly stretched string. His mother followed, dropping her spring seed crop; radishes, lettuce and spinach. Already in the garden were rows of milk jugs with the bottoms cut out to cover tender plants.

Jim pointed to the boy. "You boys help Emma and Hallie in the garden like that?"

"Jah," Noah and Daniel said in unison, peering out the back window.

"That's good. Nothing better than fresh food from the garden," Jim said over his shoulder.

"As soon as Emma gets around to cutting the potato eyes, we will help her plant them," Noah said.

"It will be time to plant the pumpkin, squash and sweet corn soon," Daniel added.

By the time they reached the salebarn, buggies, semi trucks and pickups were lined up to unload stock and find a parking place for the sale. John stopped at the end of the line. "Looks like a crowd today."

"Probably not much else to do until the farmers get into the field full time," Jim surmised. He chuckled as he pointed out the buggy in front of them with a hand painted sign on the back. It read Energy efficient vehicle: Runs on oats and grass. Caution: Do not step in exhaust. "Pretty cute."

John parked in the row of buggies at the back of the parking lot. They wove their way through the trucks and stock trailers to cross the street.

John had been right about the equipment sale. Jim glanced around in awe. "Where do they find all the different carriages? Look over there at that red stagecoach. It looks like it's right out of a western movie. Now who would want to buy that?"

"Can not say, but if no one bids, the buyer takes it home and brings it back to another sale," John explained.

They started between the two first rows. The boys quickly grew impatient. They had seen equipment like this many times before. Noah asked, "Daed, can Daniel and me go check out the small animal salesroom to see who all is there?"

"Jah. See you later," John said.

Jim watched the boys run to search for some of their friends. He shook his head. "Them two boys sure have an abundance of energy. Look at them scatter like quail."

"They do indeed. Them days are long gone for me," John declared, grinning.

"Me, too," Jim agreed.

John pointed as they approached the end of the first rows. "See that glass coach. Ain't that a sight?"

"Why, it reminds me of the one in the Cinderella story Hal used to read as a kid," Jim exclaimed. "I can't imagine who would want to spend money for that."

A man opened up the right side door to look in. John said from behind him, "Figure on buying this fancy coach, Bud?"

The blond haired man, in his thirties, turned around. "By golly, how are you, John Lapp?"

"Been a while since we met up," John said, shaking hands with the farmer. "Bud Carter, meet my father-in-law, Jim Lindstrom. He is visiting us."

"Nice to meet you, Mr. Lindstrom," Bud said politely as they shook hands.

"Call me Jim."

"Where you from?" Bud asked.

"Titonka, a small town in northern Iowa," Jim explained.

"Well, I hope you enjoy your visit," Bud said.

John's curiosity made him repeat, "Are you figuring on buying this glass coach?"

"Yeah, I am," Bud said, with a foolish grin.

"What use can you have for this?" Jim asked, amazed.

Bud gave them a sheepish grin. "The legion hall's having a Memorial Day dance. I figure on asking a woman to go with me. I'm going to show up at her place in this coach to impress her."

"That ought to do the trick," Jim said. "Women go for stuff like that."

"Anyone I know?" John asked.

"She's a newcomer in town. She's living in my old home place," Bud explained.

"That right. I thought the city man who owns the place only comes in the summer."

"He does, but Elizabeth Morris has lived there for a few months. As much as I hate to hear it, she claims she's leaving at the end of the month," Bud supplied.

"Looks like you've figured out a way to make her change her mind. Good luck," Jim told him.

John reminded Jim, "We better keep moving, or we will not

be done looking at the equipment before the livestock sale starts."

They strolled between small and large enclosed buggies that had seen plenty of wear. A surrey, with four seats, looked like the ones used to give English people tours of Amish country. From the worn look of the surrey, it was time to sell it and buy a new one since tourist trade brought in money to the area.

In the next line were the open buggies. Jim halted fast in front of one. "Will you look at that beauty?"

"It is called a courting buggy," John said.

"That bright red seat sure sticks out like a sore thumb," Jim exclaimed.

"It does at that." John studied the buggy. "Seems to me I have seen this buggy somewhere before. I can not think where."

"Suppose the horse hooked to it goes with the buggy?" Jim wondered as he studied the dozing sorrel horse, standing with one back leg cocked up.

"It does," came a voice behind them.

John turned. "Enos Yutzy, is this your rig?"

Enos looked rather sheepish as he admitted, "Jah."

That's when it came to John where he'd seen the buggy. "This was Eli's buggy, ain't so?"

"Jah, he will not ever be back to use it so I might as well get rid of it and the horse," Enos said sadly.

"That is not the horse that Eli always used if I remember recht," John said.

"Nah, I sold his black horse at the last horse sale before I decided to get rid of the buggy," Enos replied.

Jim's eyes sparkled as he circled the buggy. "Sure is a nice looking outfit."

"We better keep moving if we are going to finish looking before the livestock sale begins." John waved at Enos. "See you at the next Sunday meeting."

When they were out of earshot from Enos, Jim stopped short. "I want to buy that courting buggy."

John's mouth flew open. Finally, he got one word out.

25

"Why?"

"I can use it to get around in. With the high price gas is these days, it will save me money. Can't you see my neighbors eyeballs pop out when I drive by at home." Jim laughed as he pictured it."

"You have a car," John said bluntly.

"Sure I do. If we want to go any distance from home, I'll be glad to drive us, but that buggy looks like fun to ride to the Sunday meetings in. Nora and I could take it. That way your buggy wouldn't be so crowded."

"That is not a problem. We have the open carriage. The older children use it," John insisted.

Jim frowned. "Are you trying to talk me out of buying that buggy?"

John worried, "It just seems like something that could get both of us in trouble when you come home with that buggy. What is Nora going to say?"

"Don't know and don't care." John raised an eyebrow. "All right, I do care. Once I have the buggy bought and back to your place, I'll worry about getting Nora talked into liking it," Jim insisted.

"All recht. It is your money. We better go back and take another look at that horse. I know the buggy is practically new. The boy who owned it used to date Emma," John informed him.

"I noticed that man seemed upset at the mention of his son's name. Did the boy die?"

"Might as well have as far as the Yutzy family and the Plain community is concerned. Eli Yutzy left the Plain faith and is shunned by all of us. He will never be coming back," John shared.

"That's too bad. Well, I don't know much about carriage horses so you might be able to help me out," Jim agreed.

Enos Yutzy was talking to a very tall, thin man. When John and Jim approached, the man looked down his nose at Jim disdainfully and walked away.

John said, "Enos, we want to know more about the courting

26

buggy and horse."

Enos nodded at the tall man that stopped a few yards away. He had his back to them, but he was close enough to hear the conversation. "You should know, Laverne Rapp, is going to bid on the buggy for his boy, Jake."

"Denki for telling us," John said.

Jim eyed the man that was now watching them. "That man sure is tree tall."

"You will find that his bark is as rough as hickory. The man can be a bear if he does not get what he wants," John replied softly as he ran his hand along the spine to the back end of the horse. He moved his hand from the rump down the back leg and picked up the horse's hoof. After he felt of the hock, he placed the hoof gently on the ground and moved to the front leg and hoof. He opened the horse's mouth and checked the teeth. "How old is the horse?" He asked Enos.

"He is a strong five years old gelding."

John checked the other two legs and tapped the horse's rib cage, listening to the sound of the thumps. He turned to Enos again. " Is this horse a pacer or a trotter?"

"This one is a trotter."

"What's his name?" Jim asked, knowing that wasn't a very important question, but he wanted to ask something.

"Mike," Enos said.

"Jim, me and you should talk about this some more." John took him by the arm.

"The sale has started," Jim said anxiously. "See the auctioneer on the other end of the row coming this way."

John pulled Jim along until they were out of Enos's hearing. "We need to discuss this."

"What did you think of the horse?" Jim asked anxiously.

"He seemed sound enough, and he is young. Would last a gute long while," John surmised.

"What's the difference between a trotter and a pacer?" Jim quizzed.

"The gait. Pacers sway from side to side as they go down the road. Trotters hold their heads up high and put one foot in front of the other in a prance. If you ever noticed, my horses are trotters," John explained. "Are you really serious about bidding on that buggy?"

"I am," declared Jim.

"You have to get a number from the office. We better hurry inside so we can get back here in time to bid."

When John and Jim returned, they had a few minutes to wait for the auctioneer to get to the courting buggy. Laverne Beiler stopped other farmers to talk to them as they followed behind the auctioneer. Laverne's gray whiskered austere face looked stern as he spoke to the farmers. From the grave looks on their faces, Jim figured they didn't think much of the pushy man. He nodded toward the auctioneer, and they edged closer. Laverne Beiler continue to talk in Pennsylvania Dutch to the Amish men as he waved his hand toward the courting buggy. Jim asked John what the man was saying.

John listened. "He is telling other prospective buyers not to bid on the buggy. He says he will run the bid up on them if they do so they might as well not bid."

Jim said crossly, "He has his nerve doing that."

"The man has been that way his whole life when he wants something at one of these sales. He can afford to be."

"He hasn't said anything to me about not buying the buggy. Wonder why not?" Jim asked.

John hesitated before he said, "Laverne would not imagine you buying an Amish buggy. Probably he has not spoken to you, because you are English. Laverne Beiler does not speak to English people if he can help it."

"Well, doesn't matter what he wants this time. I'm buying that buggy," Jim vowed.

Soon the auctioneer was to the courting buggy. Jim went on the alert. The auctioneer called the starting price. Jim shook his finger in the air. The auctioneer said he had a bid and looked around the crowd. Laverne Beiler held up his hand. The auctioneer looked at Jim. He shook his finger again. The auctioneer looked at the others in the crowd as he waited for Laverne Beiler to bid. Beiler bid, glaring at Jim to scare him off. When the auctioneer had that bid, he looked at Jim. Jim upped his bid. The auctioneer tried to get a higher bid from the crowd, but the buyers avoided his eyes. They weren't interested if Laverne Beiler wanted the buggy. Beiler bid. Jim bid. The bidding war went on for several more bids.

John whispered out of the side of his mouth, "You should stop. You are paying too much."

"I'm buying that courting buggy. No matter how much it costs me I'm not letting that guy have it," Jim said through clenched jaws and upped the bid.

"What are you going to tell Nora when she asks what you paid?"

"Maybe she won't ask," Jim said as he watched Beiler struggled to make a decision.

"Good luck with that idea. She will ask," John hissed to deaf ears.

The auctioneer waited on Beiler. Finally, he shook his head no. The auctioneer said, "Sold to the guy in the straw hat next to John Lapp."

Excited as a kid with his first jalopy, Jim held up his number card for the auctioneer. When the crowd moved out of the way, he grabbed the lead rope and led his horse and buggy over to the hitch rack.

John tied the horse. "Almost time to watch the livestock sale." They went into the salebarn through the small auction so John could check on his boys.

Geese honked, ducks quacked, lambs and baby goats cried for their mothers. The babies didn't like to be contained in small pens. In front of them were cages filled with rabbits, cackling chickens and small turkeys. A rooster crowed as they passed his cage.

On a table, cartons of bright red eggs, small boxes of freshly hatched chicks, guineas, ducklings, and goslings shared the area with rhubarb and apple pies, packages of oatmeal cookies and saran wrapped bread loaves.

Noah and Daniel sat in chairs behind the partition. They were by an English boy holding some sort of flat square box with a screen on it. Noah and Daniel watched him with interest as the boy poked buttons below the screen. The boy gloated to them, "Don't you wish you had one of these games?"

Noah shook his head. "Nah, we would rather play kick the can. That game is more fun then sitting in one place poking buttons."

John smiled, pleased with his son's response.

Daniel waved when he saw them.

The boy looked John over. "Do all Amish wear beards?"

Daniel replied, "Nah, the women do not."

Jim cackled as he elbowed John.

John told the boys they were going to the other arena. The boys should come find them when it was time to eat.

In the large sale area, tiers of wooden seats built in a half circle around the sale ring were filled with English and Amish men waiting for the sale to start. The Amish voices rose and fell in the heavy accented German dialect which intermingled with English words. All the conversations had the same theme about farming and weather.

John and Jim watched the sheep and goats sell. In the afternoon, there would be the cattle auction. Jim admired the long, silky brown beard on a young farmer near them. He leaned over to John and nodded toward the man. "I grew a beard like his for the town centennial contest. After the contest, I couldn't stand to look at myself in the mirror. I looked so terrible I shaved it off."

John grinned. "I used to have a smooth face. When I saw how terrible I looked I grew a beard to hide my face."

Jim laughed.

When Noah and Daniel sat down by them, John said, "You ready to eat?"

"I'm starved," Daniel chirped.

John snorted. "What else is new?"

The diner filled up fast as the farmers hurried to eat so they could go back for the cattle auction. Behind the long counter, the young Amish women hustled from one end to the other, racing to keep up with the orders.

John pointed out to Jim the menu board on the wall. They gave the waitress their orders and sat down in one of the red leather booths to wait for their food and drinks. John nodded at English men and some of the Amish farmers while they ate. When they exited the diner, John bumped into Ben Krayman, an older Amish widower. He introduced Jim to Ben. They shook hands.

"How you and Susie getting along these days?" John asked.

"Since my wife passed away, she has been the next best thing to keep me gute company," Ben said with sparkling eyes.

As Jim noted the sparkle, Ben continued, "Susie lives with me but in another part of the house. She does not come over to my side when company comes to visit. Kind of shy that way."

John added, "She's much younger than Ben."

"Jah, and real gute looking," Ben boasted.

Jim couldn't fathom how an Amish widower got away with talking blatantly about living with a single woman. He couldn't imagine anything like that being stood for in the Amish community.

John said, "It is my understanding if a person really wanted to meet Susie you would be glad to oblige."

"Jah, I would introduce her to anyone that wants to get to know her. She has never minded that. Jim, you want to meet my Susie?" Ben asked.

"Guess that would be all right if we was to drop in on you sometime."

"She is with my buggy in the parking lot recht now if you want to meet her. She does not let me come to town without her. Goes everywhere I do," Ben said. "Follow me."

Jim looked at John.

John nodded. "Sure, we might as well go with Ben so he can introduce you to Susie before she decides to head home and hide out again."

John, Jim and the boys walked along with the elderly man. Ben stopped near the front of his buggy and patted his red horse on the rump. Jim eyed the enclosed buggy, trying to see movement inside. He didn't. His thought was, *Susie must be*

31

taking a nap in the back.

Ben cleared his throat. "Jim, meet my girl, Susie." He walked along the horse, extended his hand toward the mare and rubbed her face.

Jim did a double take at John, the horse and Ben. "All that time, you were talking about a horse?"

The men broke out laughing and Jim right along with them. He had fallen for that joke hook, line and sinker.

Later that afternoon when the sale ended, they made their way through the traffic to the line of parked buggies. John and the boys stopped at their buggy. Jim marched on.

"Where is Dawdi Jim going?" Daniel asked.

"Oh, I forgot to tell you. He bought his own buggy," John said.

"Why?" Noah asked.

John parroted Jim's reasoning. "He wants to drive around in it while he is here, and after he goes home just like we do."

Daniel was confused."But he has a car."

"I pointed that out to him, but I could not talk him out of it," John said.

Jim untied the horse, backed the courting buggy up and walked the horse toward them.

Noah blew out a breath. "That is what he bought?"

"Afraid so," John said.

"That is a courting buggy!" Daniel voice filled with wonder.

"Eli Yutzy's courting buggy to be exact," John informed them.

"That ain't Eli's horse," Noah remarked.

"Nah, Enos sold the black horse already so he hooked this one to the buggy," John explained.

Daniel said softly, "Mammi Nora is going to have a cow."

Noah nodded solemnly.

John looked at his son. "What did you say, Daniel?"

"Mammi is going to have a cow."

Noah explained, "That wondered us, too, at first when Dawdi Jim said it. That is how he says she is going to be mad at him."

John chuckled. "Jah, I am afraid it might be more like two cows this time. What worries me is your Mama Hal is probably going to have a cow, too, because I didn't stop your dawdi from buying that buggy. One of you want to offer to ride with him just in case he gets into trouble. Buggy driving is new to him."

"I can do that," Noah offered.

Jim stopped the horse beside them.

John said, "Looks like you have everything under control."

"I think so. You lead the way so I don't get lost," Jim suggested.

"Jah, I will do that."

Noah stepped forward. "Dawdi, this is a really nice buggy. Can I ride with you and try it out once?"

"Sure can. Meet my horse, Mike," Jim said with pride and climbed up to perch on the flashy red seat.

Chapter 4

John looked behind him in the rearview mirror often to see if Jim was keeping up. As they made their way to the edge of town, the pace was slow in the traffic. Jim's horse stopped several times when he didn't need to. Maybe Jim was pulling the lines too tight, sending mixed signals to his horse.

Once they were on the highway, the traffic was light that time of afternoon. Jim flicked the lines so his horse would trot. A car whizzed by, and Jim's horse stopped. John was a quarter of a mile down the highway when he looked back and saw Jim flicking the lines over the halted horse. Another car went by. The horse didn't budge.

"Look, Daed, Noah had to get out and tug on the horse to get him started." Daniel watched in his rearview mirror and continued the play by play, "The horse started again. Dawdi is going slow so Noah can grab hold and hop in. Noah is in the buggy now."

John was forced to slow down to keep an eye out behind him. "I do not like Noah running along side the buggy to jump in. That is not safe."

A pickup came by them. When the pickup passed the courting buggy, Jim's horse stopped. John pulled over and turned his buggy around. "We better see what is wrong with that horse."

Noah was out of the buggy, talking to the horse. John drove

across the highway, parked and walked to the front of the buggy. He looked from the horse to Jim. "You seem to be having trouble."

"I can't figure out why this horse stops and starts on his own so much. We'll never get home by chore time at this rate," complained Jim.

Noah observed, "The horse stops when a car or truck goes passed us. Suppose he is afraid of traffic?"

"Might be that is it," John said.

"What can we do about getting him to change?" Jim asked.

John thought a minute. "Usually tying a horse to a fence next to the road helps. Gets them familiar with traffic by doing that."

"Blinders might help. He does not have any on," Noah added.

"I'll buy some first chance I get," Jim said.

"No need. We have blinders in the tack room. You can use a set to see if that works once," John offered as he looked at the sun sliding down the western sky.

Jim read his mind. "You go on. Noah and I will be all right."

"Daniel and me should get home and start milking."

Jim said, "I know. Sorry about this. I didn't know I'd be holding you up."

John said, "Can not be helped. We did not know how the horse would be in traffic until we tried him once."

At home, John stopped the buggy by the barn. "Daniel, you put the buggy and horse away. As bad as I hate to have to do this, before I milk, I should smooth the way for Dawdi so it is not such a shock to the women when he drives in."

In the living room, Tootie watched Emma sew a dress for Beth on the treadle sewing machine. Hal and Nora played with Redbird and Beth. When the girls saw their father, they squirmed to be placed on the floor and crawled to him. John picked them up and kissed their cheeks as they gave him a welcome hug.

"Where's Jim?" Nora asked.

"He is down the road a piece. He will be here soon."

Hal looked at John sideways. "He didn't ride home in the buggy with you and the boys?"

"Oh, my goodness! What did that man do to make you kick him out of the buggy?" Nora cried, bolting to her feet with Hal beside her as they confronted John.

Tootie and Emma joined them. Tootie grabbed Nora's arm. "Holy Buckets! I told you I should have brought my book *All You Need To Know About Amish Customs.*"

Nora flushed as she glanced at John's surprised face. "Tootie, watch your mouth."

Tootie eyed them all in a wide sweep. "I'm sorry, but Jim could have avoided the walk home if he'd read the book when I told him to."

"Why did you not bring it along?" Emma said with her mouth twitching at the corners.

Tootie nodded sideways at Nora. "My sister wouldn't let me. She thinks she knows all there is to know about the Amish I guess."

John shook his head. "Now hold on, all of you, I did not make Jim walk home." He had trouble pulling the words out of his mouth as he said slowly, "He and Noah are coming in his own buggy."

"Whose buggy?" Nora asked.

"Isn't that nice. Noah bought himself a buggy," Tootie prattled to Emma.

Hal was surprised. "John, you let Noah buy a buggy?"

"Nah. It was Jim that bought the buggy," John blurted out.

Nora patted her chest as she slumped back on the couch and went on a tangent. "Be still my heart. What has that man gone and done now? I can't let him out of my sight for a moment. Bought a buggy for goodness sakes."

"If Dawdi Jim started for home when you did he should have arrived when you did, ain't so?" Emma asked, worried.

John nodded his head. "Maybe we better go into that later."

Emma clammed up and busied herself brushing lint and thread pieces off her apron.

"I know why, Emma," Tootie said knowingly. "Jim gets lost

easy. Aways has. Doesn't matter if he's driving a car or buggy, I'll bet he took a wrong turn somewhere."

"Nah, Noah is with him. Noah knows the way home," John assured her, putting his weight from one foot to the other. He didn't like being the center of attention with all the female eyes staring at him, some puzzled, some wondering and some suspicious.

The clip clop of hooves alerted the women Jim had arrived. They rushed out the door, letting it bang behind them as they lined up on the porch. Nora put a hand over her puckered mouth when she saw the buggy.

Tootie clapped in glee. "That sure is a fancy buggy."

"Just what I was thinking. What could that man have paid for such a contraption?" Nora grumbled.

John backed up to lean against the porch wall out of the way. Jim and Noah climbed down and came cautiously toward the women. Noah said excitedly, "Dawdi Jim bought a courting buggy. It is a looker, ain't so?"

"It is that, Dear," Tootie agreed gleefully.

"Is that what it's called? A courting buggy?" Nora asked no one in particular as she stared irritably at Jim's contraption.

Emma said softly to John, "It looks just like the one Eli Yutzy had."

"It was his buggy," John said as he shifted the wiggling girls to get a better hold on them. They wanted down to explore. He said louder, "Go see the buggy up close all of you. Jim is sure proud of it."

Nora, with the other women a safe distance behind her, marched past Jim. He turned around and followed his wife. When Nora was as close as she wanted to be, she stared at the buggy a long moment and wheeled around. "What have you done, Jim Lindstrom?"

"What's it look like? I want to drive the same kind of conveyance everyone else around here does so I bought me a buggy," Jim excused, sticking his hands in his jeans pockets.

"That doesn't look like the average Amish buggy to me. It doesn't look practical at all," Nora stormed.

Jim asked, "How about getting in and going for a ride with me? At least try it out before you make up your mind one way or the other."

"What! Ride in that thing?" Nora gasped.

"Sure, Mom. It will be fun," Hal said, trying not to smile. "I do it all the time."

"Mammi Nora, I rode home from Wickenburg with Dawdi, and it was fun," Noah encouraged with two of his fingers crossed behind his back.

Nora put her hands on her hips. "What I want to know is how much did that thing cost you?"

"About the going price a buggy and horse goes for I guess," Jim hedged, glancing at John.

John studied the sky above the barn roof. He didn't want involved in his in-laws argument.

"What do you plan on doing with that buggy when we go home?" Nora interrogated.

"I'm driving it home," Jim said, gleefully. "I'll sure get a lot of looks by the neighbors when they see this gem. They will be wanting a buggy just like mine."

"If you think I'm going to follow you with the car six hundred miles home behind a buggy and horse you're crazy. You can't drive that buggy home," Nora declared.

"We aren't ready to leave yet. For right now, we can drive it around here until we get used to it," Jim reasoned.

"Oh no." Nora wagged a finger at him. "There is no *we* to it."

"Ah, Nora. Come on. The buggy is already bought and paid for. Go for a ride with me to give it a try," Jim wheedled.

"Jim, why not let Noah hook up our horse, Molly, to the buggy for right now?" John suggested.

"Why?" Nora focused sharply on her son-in-law.

"Well," John paused. His eyes darted back and forth as he licked his lips.

Noah supplied, "This horse is tired, Mammi Nora."

"That's right. We need to give poor Mike time to rest up and get something to eat after he came out here all the way from town. He's been hitched to that buggy all day," Jim excused. "I'll pull over by the barn. Noah can help me change horses. I'll be right back."

As he led the horse and buggy away, Nora patted her chest. "Jim has done some crazy things, but this tops the cake."

Jim and Noah hooked up Molly, and Jim led the horse back to where his wife stood with the other women. For a few minutes, she stared at the red buggy seat with her hands on her hips. Finally, she admitted, "I can't get in this contraption. I don't know how Amish women are able to do it."

"I'll help," Jim said. He came up behind her. "Hike your foot up on the step and get hold of the seat." Nora did as he told her. "Now give a hop up with the other foot." As she hopped, Nora felt firm hands on her bottom as she rose fast in the air. She reached out to grip the back of the seat to keep from going off the other side head first, plopped down and scooted to the left side.

"Jim Lindstrom, that was a pretty sight for everyone to see. What must they think of us?" Red faced Nora scolded, afraid to look at her family.

"That I succeeded in getting you in the buggy," Jim said, grinning at her and winked to the good humored faces watching.

Nora grunted as she folded her arms over her chest, determined not to enjoy the ride.

Jim climbed in and picked up the lines. "Listen, I didn't come up with that idea on my own. I happened to see an old Amish man help his wife in their buggy that same way while we were at the salebarn. She was a lot older than you. I just figured the knowledge might come in handy sometime or other." Everyone waved while Jim called to John, "What did you say the horse's name is?"

"Molly," John answered.

"We're off." Jim said, touching the brim of his straw hat. "We'll just take a short ride and be home way before dark." He flicked the lines. "Get up, Molly."

The horse took off at a walk. In the waning sunlight, the clip clop of her hooves had a rhythmic sound that pleased Jim even more than other times he'd heard it. Maybe because this was his own buggy he was driving. He glanced sideways at Nora. She didn't look at all pleased.

At first, Nora gripped the seat as if she was going head first out of the buggy any second. After awhile, she relaxed and put her hands in her lap.

"Isn't that a pleasant sight?" Jim pointed to some red cattle that scattered away from the road fence when they drove by. The frisky newborn calves scampered after their mothers, bawling about being left behind.

In another pasture was a herd of red mares with new colts romping beside them. "Down right pleasant ride in this buggy with sights like these to see."

Stone faced, Nora paid attention, but she didn't reply.

Jim decided to try another tact. "This buggy sure does ride smooth as all get out. I guess you can tell it's almost new so the springs are good."

Not bothering to respond, Nora focused on her side of the road.

Jim tried again. "Just listen to the hooves of this horse hitting the road. Like music to my ears."

"That's what the radio in our car is supposed to be for," Nora said dryly.

"Want to drive for awhile?" He asked, extending the lines in outstretched fingers toward her.

Nora hid her hands under her armpits. "No, I don't want to drive. I wouldn't know how. Where we going anyway?"

"Just around the section ought to do it for the first time," Jim said. They came to Bender Creek Road turn off just as the sun set. "Think this must be the end of the mile at this intersection." He turned onto the dirt road. Behind the dense stand of trees, Bender Creek ran close enough they heard the water mummer. The thick tree cover swallowed from view anything else on both sides of the road.

As they rode on the twisting road, Nora fretted, "This is all a timber wilderness. How do you know where we are?"

"I don't, but I'll just follow the road. It has got to lead somewhere," Jim reasoned.

"Oh, sure! Most roads do, but it's going to be dark soon."

A raccoon bolted out of the underbrush and scurried across the road in front of the horse. Molly nickered and shied sideways.

Jim pulled back on the lines. "Easy, Molly."

As the horse calmed down, Nora cried, "That thing scared the horse. What was that?"

"Looked like a coon. Probably headed to the creek for a drink. The horse is fine now as you can see," Jim surmised.

"It's getting too dark to see anything, especially the road much less animals? Does this buggy have headlights?" Nora quizzed as the daylight faded to dusk.

"Of course, it has a headlight. You sound like this buggy is a 1800's model or something," Jim said defensively.

A quarter moon rose above the tree tops and shifted behind raggedy clouds. As a warm, gentle night wind blew around them, Nora said nervously, "You better turn on the headlight."

Jim searched in front of his feet and flicked a switch. Nothing happened. "Huh!" He grunted as he felt along the back of the foot board. "I sure thought that was the light switch. It's the only switch on here. Battery must be run down."

Nora made disapproving tisks. "You should have checked to see if the headlight worked before you bought this contraption."

"We'll do fine. The horse can see, and she knows where to go. Never seen a horse yet that didn't know the way home night or day," Jim assured her.

"Oh, that's real encouraging since you're such an expert on horses," Nora said dryly. "How long has it been since you helped your father with his work horses? Sixty years maybe?"

Jim thought he should change the subject. "The sky sure is dark. Getting overcast. I expect that means rain."

"I hope not before we get home. This buggy doesn't have a top," Nora fussed. "It seems to be lacking a lot of accessories. You don't even have an umbrella in here and no flashlight."

"The buggy has four wheels, a horse to pull it and a snazzy red seat," Jim said, trying to sound positive.

"You left the horse by John's barn, and the red seat is not a deal sealer for me," Nora brooded. "This seat is almost too small for two people."

"This is a courting buggy," Jim stated with meaning.

"I heard that before. Now tell me why you needed a courting buggy at your age. Looking for a younger woman to ride with you? Maybe one in a long dress and prayer cap?" Nora complained.

"You know better than that. I just thought this was a fun idea. Maybe we could pretend we're courting again," Jim said, chuckling.

"You are half a century too late for that," Nora scoffed. From a distance in the timber on Nora's side came a string of yips. She stiffened but relaxed somewhat when the noises seemed to travel away from them. "Jim, what is that?"

"Coyotes."

Nora gasped. "Mercy! Sounds like a whole bunch of them."

"They do tend to run in packs," Jim cracked.

A little farther on, large tree limbs hung in a canopy over the road, creating a tunnel that was very dark. Right above them came rattling leaves, beating wings and loud hoots, three in a row.

Nora shrieked as they drove out from under the branches.

"Relax before you scare the horse. That was just a hoot owl," Jim growled.

"I know a hoot owl when I hear one, but I've never had one right on top of me. He sounded like he wanted to make me his next meal," Nora snipped. "How soon are we getting on the road that goes back to the Lapp farm?"

"Soon." Jim uttered softly, "I hope."

"You don't know where we are, do you? I might have known. Fine thing. You get lost in the car and a buggy all in a couple of days. That's a new record for you, Jim Lindstrom," Nora chided.

Suddenly, the black shape of a stop sign appeared. They had

a cross roads in front of them. Jim sounded relieved. "We made it back to the main road. Guess I'll turn this way."

"You're guessing? You're turned around. Heaven help us. We may be out in this wilderness all night," Nora grumbled.

"Ah, I think John would come looking for us before morning," Jim said to reassure her.

"I'm not so sure. He doesn't know you as well as I do," Nora grouched.

As Jim listened to Molly's hooves on the packed gravel road, Nora heard cre e eak, cre e eak, cre e eak off to the side. "What is that?" She asked in a hushed voice as she stared into the darkness.

"Really? You don't know?"

"Sounds like a giant tree frog," Nora said nervously. "Mercy, I didn't know Hal moved to such a wild jungle."

"All you're hearing is a farmer's windmill. There's just enough breeze to get the blades to turn slowly so they squeak," Jim told her.

"Oh, well, how was I supposed to know that. I haven't heard a windmill since I was a kid," Nora excused sheepishly.

"Listen once in awhile to the Lapp windmill. It sounds the same way," Jim stated.

They traveled by large black shapes, cattle or horses, snuffling as the animals nosed the tender grass they grazed. Jim said hopefully, "That looks like the cattle and horses we rode by earlier."

"Cattle and horses all look alike in the daylight. For the life of me, I don't know how you can tell it's the same ones when it's pitch black out here." Ahead of them, Nora saw house lights. "There's a house. I pray it's Hal's house so I can get out of this contraption. Tootie and Hal must be worried sick about us."

Meanwhile some time ago, John and the boys finished the chores. They waited in the living room. The women had supper ready. The kettles were on the back of the cookstove, staying warm until Jim and Nora came back.

Hal paced from the living room to the kitchen and back.

Emma fed Redbird and Beth so they could stick to their schedule. It would soon be their bedtime. Tootie stared out the living room window on watch.

Hal fretted, "John, Dad said they would be back before dark. Something must have happened."

"I told you Jim gets lost easy," Tootie declared. "No telling where they ended up, and my poor sister's out there in the dark. They might be all the way back to Wickenburg by now. Poor Nora is going to be beside herself. That brother-in-law of mine is crazy."

Hal stopped pacing to give her aunt a cautionary look.

"Sorry, Dear. I know he's your father," Tootie relented.

"You want us to go look for them?" John asked Hal.

"Jah, I do," Hal said.

"Yes, she does," Tootie added her opinion.

"Boys, get the lantern and hitch Ben to the open buggy so we can go look." John and the boys were on the porch when they heard clopping and saw the buggy's dark shape turn in. John said through the door screen, "They are home."

"Thank goodness!" Hal exclaimed.

Tootie and Hal rushed to join John and the boys to meet the buggy as Jim parked.

John observed, "It was dark out there to be driving without the head light on."

"It doesn't work. Must be the battery is dead," Jim said softly to John as he hopped down.

Nora demanded, "Get me out of this buggy, Jim Lindstrom."

Jim held his arms up to his wife to help her down.

"Have any trouble other than the dead battery?" John asked.

"No, the horse did just fine" Jim said.

"He got us lost," groused Nora.

"The horse got you lost," Hal echoed.

"No, your father did," Nora complained.

"How lost could we have been. We're back to John and Hal's, aren't we?" Jim defended.

Tootie whispered in Hal's ear, "I told you Jim was lost. Never fails." The next sound was her clucking tongue.

"Dawdi Jim, did you stick to this road or turn off?" Noah asked.

"I turned off and went through a bunch of timber," Jim said. "It was a winding dirt road, and your grandma got a little nervous."

"A little! This country is like living in a zoo. I didn't realize so many wild creatures ran around out here at night," Nora complained as she went to the house with Hal and Tootie. "Hallie, you must be more careful when you're out at night alone."

"Hallie rides in a enclosed buggy, Sister. That's safer than Jim's open buggy," Tootie surmised.

"Denki, for the observation, Aunt Tootie," Hal said.

The men trailed along behind. "Don't know which made Nora more nervous. All the wild animals she heard, or me mentioning my buggy is a courting buggy."

John chuckled. "Sounds like you might have been in the right place with that line of thinking. If you were on Bender Creek Road, it is the local lover's lane."

"Didn't know that, but I tried my best anyway. Nora wasn't in the mood," Jim replied with a grin.

"I heard that, Jim Lindstrom. You aren't funny," Nora snapped as she stomped up the porch steps.

As he followed Nora into the house, Jim retorted, "Fine! Next time I'll take Tootie for a ride."

Tootie declared, patting her chest. "Holy Buckets! I don't think so."

Noah and Daniel giggled.

Nora snapped, "Watch your mouth, Tootie. Children are listening."

"Sorry about that, Nora, but I'm not going anywhere with that husband of yours. At least, I wouldn't consider it until he knows the roads better and how to get home before dark," Tootie groused. She turned to Jim. "For sure, I wouldn't let you take me for a ride on lover's lane in the dark or daylight. Forget that kind of nonsense, Jim Lindstrom."

Chapter 5

That evening, John said the supper prayer out loud. "I come before you in the name of Jesus Christ our king. Bless this family and keep us peaceful and thoughtful of each other. Bless me so that I can do your will in the coming days. Amen."

As they focused on eating rather than talking, Hal was glad that supper seemed to please everyone. Of course, the silence might have been because supper was later than usual so they were hungry. Hal feared it was more likely due to the fact that Nora was unhappy with Jim. Everyone thought they should keep quiet until she calmed down.

Finally, Daniel broke the ice. "Aendi Tootie, please pass me the butter."

"Sure, Dear," Tootie said as she handed the round glass dish full of homemade butter across the table.

Daniel made a face as he took it and set it beside his plate. He grumbled to Noah, "I would rather have had seconds from the green bean bowl. They sure were gute."

Tootie gave him a vexed stare. "Why on earth didn't you say that in the first place if you wanted green beans?"

"Mama Hal said while you are here I am to watch my manners and say please pass the butter," Daniel complained.

Jim and John burst out laughing. Emma put her hand over her mouth to keep from giggling. Hal looked upset at all of them for finding Daniel amusing. Nora and Tootie looked confused.

Jim said to Daniel, "Don't stand on good manners with us. We're family. If you want the green bean bowl, I can help you out there." He handed the bowl to Noah to pass to Daniel.

When everyone finished eating, Tootie hustled to the stove for the tea kettle, ready to make up her dish water. The other women settled into the routines that were left.

Hal left for the barn with the scrap pail. While she was gone, Tootie finished the last stainless steel kettle and tossed her cloth into the dish pan. "Emma, it's your turn to wash the counters and table off tonight," she ordered.

Tootie focused out the window while she wiped her hands on her apron. Yanking on the ties, she removed the apron, tossed it over a chair and hurried from the kitchen.

"Looks like I've done all I can," Nora said and followed her sister.

When Hal came back, Tootie and Nora were gone. Hal put the slop pail in the pan and fished around in the murky water for the dish cloth.

Emma whispered, "I think Aendi Tootie was trying to keep from washing the pail. She washed the dishes as fast as she could to get out of here before you came back from the barn."

"Did she now? Well, I'll just have to hurry faster to get ahead of her next time," Hal hissed.

The next afternoon, Noah and Daniel hooked up the manure spreader. Daniel stopped cleaning the sheep pens in the barn long enough to hitch up Ben and drive the enclosed buggy over by the house for the women to take to the Yoder farm.

The boy was on his way back to the barn when the women walked to the buggy. Suddenly, a loud clatter, horse screams behind the barn and stampeding hooves caused everyone to look that direction. The team bolted around the barn with the empty spreader careening from side to side behind them.

Startled by the sight, Daniel froze as the frightened horses and spreader came at him. Hal ran toward Daniel as the boy took a step backward. She grabbed his arm. "Move," she screamed. Daniel leaped with her, and they just barely made it out of the horses' path. A fearful dread welled up in Hal at what a close call that had been as she hugged Daniel.

Emma asked frantically, "Where is Noah?"

Daniel gulped. "I do not know. He was with the horses and spreader while I hitched the buggy up."

Hal, Emma and Daniel took off. Noah came to meet them from behind the barn with a staggering gait. They all turned their attention to the sounds in the pasture lane. The swerving spreader hooked onto the fence. Posts snapped, livestock panels clattered to the ground and strands of wire caught on the spreader and flying harnesses. The horses finally halted in a tangle of wire and fence posts.

Noah said to Daniel, "We have to get the horses unhitched quick before they get hurt."

Hal grabbed his arm. "Are you hurt, Noah?"

"Nah, I just twisted my ankle some."

"I want to look at that ankle," Hal insisted.

"You can look at it later, Mama Hal. We have to get those horses unhitched before they get hurt if we are not too late all ready." Noah limped after Daniel to free the horses.

The boys unhitched the horses and led them to the barn. When they came back, Hal said, "Noah, sit down on a porch step. I'll get an ace wrap from the clinic to bind that ankle so it's easier to walk on."

She was back in a few seconds. Noah had his shoe and sock off and his trouser leg rolled up. She felt the swollen ankle. Noah sucked in air when pain seared through his leg from her poking. "I don't think the ankle is broken. You're putting some weight on it."

"Jah, it is just sprained," Noah assured her through clenched teeth.

When Hal finished winding the ace wrap around Noah's ankle, she said, "We can soak that ankle in Epsom salts tonight after supper. That will help the swelling go down. As soon as you can, you need to get off your feet. Put the ankle up so it won't throb as bad. If we don't see an improvement in a couple of days, you may need an x-ray to see if the ankle bone is cracked. Did the horses step on you?"

"Nah, I twisted my ankle in rutted tracks the spreader wheels made," Noah said.

"What happened behind the barn?" Emma asked.

Noah explained, "I tied the horses to a fence post while I worked on the spreader. A bolt was missing I had to replace. I heard a loud buzzing. Yellow jackets were flying around the horses' heads. There must have been a nest in the fence post. The horses panicked and started backing up to get away from the wasps. I just barely got out of the way before they broke loose and took off."

"Thank God, you aren't badly hurt, Noah," Nora said, giving him a hug.

"That was too scary for words," Tootie declared.

"Is there anything I can do to help you before we leave?" Emma asked.

"Nah, you go on," Noah said. "The horses are calming down already. They only have a few scratches we need to put some liniment on." He looked down the lane at the tangled panels and wire laying in the grass. "We will be patching up the fence the rest of the afternoon to keep the cattle and sheep in the pasture."

Hal did the driving to the Yoder farm with Nora in the front seat beside her. Tootie and Emma sat in back and held the toddlers.

As they left the driveway, Nora pointed to the pasture road fence. "Isn't that the horse your father bought tied to the fence?"

"You never know," Emma commented smoothly. "Horses all look alike."

"That's true," Hal agreed.

Nora mused, "I wonder why John left the poor thing there like that?"

"Hal, you know where you're going I hope," Tootie interrupted much to Hal's relief.

"Aunt Tootie, I know this country like the back of my hand. Remember I'm a midwife and nurse around here. Don't worry.

I'll get us to the Yoder farm and back home before dark."

"Sure you will. I've heard words like that before from your father," Tootie said with little confidence. "You know what they say. An apple doesn't fall far from the tree."

When they arrived, Hal announced, "Aunt Tootie, we have arrived."

Linda and her mother-in-law, Margaret Yoder, came out of the house to greet them as they pulled up by the porch. Margaret, a middle aged woman with silver streaked brown hair and a warm smile that reached her brown eyes, called, "Wilcom, Sisters. Get out and come in."

Linda, with her quiet unassuming air, added, "Do join us, Sisters."

They gathered in the kitchen. Hal unfolded a quilt and laid it on the floor for the little girls to nap on. They curled up with their thumbs in their mouths. Emma knelt beside them and rubbed their backs until they were asleep.

The women settled at the table. Linda poured hot tea, and Margaret passed a plate of fresh baked oatmeal cookies.

"We'd have been here sooner, but the work horses ran away with the manure spreader," Hal said, taking a cookie.

Margaret quickly set the plate down. "Anyone hurt?"

"Nah, except for Noah's sprained ankle. "The team ran over the pasture lane fence and tore out a few posts and wires before they stopped. The boys had them untangled by the time we left."

Tootie said excitedly, "Daniel would have been trampled by those old horses if Hal hadn't saved him."

"Oh, my," Linda gasped.

Hal shrugged. "Daniel froze. I got him out of the way."

Margaret patted Tootie's hand. "These things happen more than we would like when we work with horses." She turned to Nora. "I'm glad you made your journey to the Lapp farm safely."

"Thank you. The trip does seem to take longer the older we get," Nora replied.

"Wouldn't be near as long a trip if Jim didn't get lost so

often," Tootie said with a put upon sigh.

Linda saw Hal nod her head at her aunt. Hal had forewarned Margaret and her about this odd relative. Linda thought it might help if she changed the subject. "Hal, did you know that Amy Zook's boy, David, fell off his horse and broke his arm last week?"

"Jah, Amy brought David over to see me. I told her to take him to the hospital. He needed more help than I could give him and a x-ray to see how bad the break was," Hal said.

"Was it a bad break?" Nora asked.

"We heard the break was serious enough to have a cumbersome cast on his right arm," Linda replied before she took a bite of cookie.

"I'm sure it was then," Hal agreed. "Usually a plaster cast has to be worn for six weeks."

Margaret said, "Someone told me Jacobus Stolfus is poorly."

"Poor old fellow," Hal said. "He never has very many gute days in a row."

"His wife told me he has not very many days left," Margaret told her.

"Wonder why Jeannie didn't come get me to take a look at Jacobus?" Hal asked.

"I think he is bad enough that she did not want to bother you. It is in God's hands now," Linda said.

"I feel sorry for that kind old man. He was given a tough life with all his ailments," Hal said sympathetically.

Margaret shook her head no as she rebuked, "Jacobus would say to you that God gave him the life he was supposed to have."

"Jah, I should be more mindful of that." Hal conceded to the Amish way of thinking and concentrated on her cookie.

"Nora, are you enjoying your visit?" Margaret asked.

"We are. I'll hate to go home once I've had this time with my daughter and her family."

"Maybe you will change your mind after Jim talks you into a few more of those awful buggy rides," Tootie quipped.

Linda and Margaret gave Tootie a quizzical stare.

Hal figured she better explain fast before the Yoder women thought Tootie was bias against Amish buggies. "My father bought a courting buggy at the salebarn yesterday."

"And he has tried it out I take it," Margaret said, smiling.

"He sure did," Nora told her. "With me in it."

"He got them lost in the dark last night," Tootie continued.

"Where were you at?" Linda asked Nora.

"I don't know. We could hear running water so must have been a creek close by and lots of trees on both sides of the road. Wild animals and birds were all around us." Nora cringed as she relived the moment. "We drove under some tree branches and woke up a hoot owl. Scared the daylights out of me when he hooted right over my head. I was afraid I was going to be his supper."

Margaret chuckled.

"I think it was Bender Creek Road," Hal supplied.

Margaret and Linda nodded agreement.

All too soon, the afternoon was over. Linda said, "Have a safe trip home. See you all at the next worship service at Jonah Rogies's farm, ain't so?"

"Yes," Nora agreed.

"We will we there," Tootie chipped in.

When Hal turned into the Lapp driveway, she parked behind Adam Keim's buggy. "Emma, Adam is here."

Adam came out of the barn with Daniel. Adam walked toward Emma, carrying Redbird. Daniel leaned up against the barn. Emma said, "Adam, do not tell me. Let me guess. You came to see the new dog."

Adam held out his right hand and wavered it back and forth. With a teasing grin, he pointed toward the barn, made a plus sign with one finger over the other and pointed at her.

"Nice to know I fit in there some place. I do not think I will ask where I rate, above or below the dog," Emma quipped as Adam made a face at Redbird.

The little redhead held her arms out to Adam and giggled. He gave her a pleased smile and took her. She paid him with a slobbery kiss on the cheek and patted the top of his head.

Emma grinned. "Maybe I am lower down the rating poll than I thought. Looks like I have to put Redbird on your like list ahead of me."

Adam shook his head yes and teasingly hugged the little girl. "Come with me. You should meet the relatives. Hope you plan to stay for supper. They are curious about you. It is time for them to get to know you," Emma said.

Adam nodded slowly, dusted himself off and straightened his gallouses.

Emma lowered her voice. "Don't worry. They are all nice and very friendly. Aendi Tootie's a little plumb off center, but she is harmless." She whispered as an after thought, "I think." When Adam arched an eyebrow, she grinned. Peering over Adam's shoulder, she said to Daniel, "How is Noah?"

"Sitting on a bale of hay with his foot up, talking to Dawdi Jim."

"Put the buggy away and unhitch Ben. We are going to start supper," Emma told Daniel. Nora and Tootie were waiting beside Hal for their introductions. Emma said, "I want you to meet my very special friend, Adam Keim. Adam, this is my Mammi Nora and my Aendi Tootie."

Adam shook hands with them.

"I take it you met my father in the barn," Hal said, repositioning Beth on her hip.

Adam shook his head yes and poked Beth gently in the arm. She smiled weakly at him and laid her head on Hal's shoulder.

"Now we women better head for the kitchen," Hal said. "Adam, are you staying for supper?"

He nodded yes.

"Gute, it has been a while since you last ate with us. I was beginning to think you had grown tired of our cooking," Hal teased.

Adam gave a silent laugh and took out his notepad from his shirt pocket. He wrote the word NEVER and turned it for Hal to see.

"Glad to hear that. We *all* like your company," Hal said as she nodded at Emma and winked at him.

Daniel came up behind Adam. "Want to go back to the barn with us men?"

Adam grinned about the men reference and nodded yes. He gave the protesting Redbird back to Emma. After a small wave of his hand, he followed Daniel, leading the horse and buggy away.

After supper, the men and boys went to the living room. In a few minutes, Tootie filled the dishpans herself and was washing dishes. Emma had to wipe fast to keep up with her. Hal scraped all the plates. She left her mother to put the leftovers in containers and store them in the gas refrigerator. She was determined to get to the barn and back before Tootie finished washing the last kettle.

Hal rushed to the barn with her skirt and apron flapping against her legs. She scattered the cats with her bare feet to get to the old cake pan she fed them in, dumped the pail and hurried back to the house.

She burst through the mudroom door out of breath. Her face fell in disappointment when she realized Emma was the only one in the kitchen, waiting for her. She hadn't beaten Tootie again.

That night in the bedroom, Hal slipped under the covers by John. "Wasn't there any way you could have talked my dad out of buying that buggy? Mom is still fuming about it."

"I tried, but he wouldn't listen to me."

Hal continued heatedly, "Well, I guess Mom is going to have to live with his purchase. Honestly, my family can be so irritating sometimes. I didn't realize Aunt Tootie was such a shirker until now. Odd yes, but lazy no.

Aunt Tootie was the one who picked the dish washing job for herself. Now would you believe she refuses to stick around long enough to wash the slop pail. That's part of the dish washing job! Aunt Tootie knew that from the first night."

"You should not get so worked up. Pray for a peaceful solution to all these problems," John said softly, hoping that wouldn't be the wrong thing to respond with.

If Hal wanted sympathy from him, she wasn't going to get it.

John rolled over on his side, baffled by all of Hal's fussing. She shouldn't get so aggravated over something as simple as who should wash the slop pail. After all, there were four females in the kitchen during the clean up. Why weren't they taking turns? It was as simple as that. He intended to go to sleep. Hopefully after a good night's sleep, Hal would be in a better mood tomorrow.

Chapter 6

Sunday morning, worship meeting day, started at four-thirty
as every other morning did, but the Lapp household hustled
around much faster, getting the chores done, eating breakfast
and cleaning up. Once everyone had on their for gute clothes,
they were ready to leave for church. John pulled the enclosed
buggy up by the house.

Noah offered to hitch Molly to Jim's buggy. Jim followed to
see if he could help. The boy lifted each of Molly's feet to
inspect them.

"What are you doing?" Jim asked.

"You need to check your horse before you start out. A horse
can lose a shoe, and you might not know it if you do not look,"
Noah said seriously. "It is one of the things you must learn,
Dawdi Jim, now that you own a horse."

"You're right. Until now, all I had to do was walk around the
car to see if I had a flat tire and kick the tires occasionally to
see if they had enough air in them."

"Jah, the two are much alike, but I would not try kicking the
horse if I were you," Noah warned.

"Oh, no! I wouldn't do that," Jim said.

The women came outside. Jim parked his buggy behind
John's. Nora declared, "Oh, Hallie, I don't think I can stand
another ride in that buggy."

"Mom, you will get used to it if you do it a few times. I did,"

Hal said.

"Yes, but you're a lot younger than I am," Nora shot back. "Besides, you have to ride in one now that you're Amish. I don't have to."

"It would make Dad so happy. He thinks this is going to be the best vacation ever, driving his buggy everywhere. He'll have so many stories to tell his friends when he gets home. Don't mess it up for him," Hal encouraged.

"Look on the bright side, Sister. If he follows right behind John's buggy you won't get lost again anyway," Tootie suggested.

Nora let out an exasperated sigh. "That's true."

"Come on, Nora. We better get a move on," Jim called. "We don't want to be late for church. It would make the Lapp family look bad."

"We wouldn't want to be the cause of that." Nora rolled her eyes. With a huffy breath, she went to her side of the buggy.

"Want me to get down and help you get in?" Jim asked.

"I don't want you helping me your way again ever with people watching. You stay put, and I'll get in by myself somehow," Nora hissed.

She took a tight grip on the seat and hopped. Jim grabbed her arm to steady her until she turned around and perched. "Good job, Nora," he praised.

A mile from the Rogies farm, the Lapp family found themselves in a line of buggies going to the same place they were. The wind billowed the dust up into John's buggy.

Tootie coughed. She pulled a hanky out of her green dress pocket, put it over her nose and gave a haughty sniffle. "Inhaling all this dust can't be healthy. I don't know how you Amish do this all the time."

Emma patted her hand to soothe her feelings. "We are just used to it is all."

John pulled into the Rogies's pasture parking lot. Jim pulled in beside him. Daniel and Noah got out of the buggy. They unhitched the two horses and turn them loose in a pen by the barn. The horses trotted to the full hay manger and wedged in among the other horses.

Most of the congregation had already arrived. Men gathered in one area of the yard. The teenage boys leaned against the barn, and teenage girls stood near the front porch, giggling behind their hands about the boys. The smaller school age boys and girls stayed in their groups. The three ministers were by themselves, working out which one would speak first, second and third and discussing what their sermons would be about.

The Lapp women entered the house and walked down the aisle between the benches to the kitchen. The bench wagon was parked by the barn. The men put their black felt hats on the now empty shelves. They spent the idle time talking, each with an eye on the ministers.

Finally at eight-thirty, Bishop Bontrager led the other two ministers to the house. They sat in the three chairs up front that faced the congregation.

The young girls sat on the women's side of the aisle. The women and smaller children up to the age of nine sat down in front of the girls. The oldest men came first, and the others entered the house according to age down to the younger men. Cooner Jonah Rogies went outside to call in the teenage boys. The boys combed their hair and dusted off their trousers before they filed inside.

"Page two hundred and twenty," announced the song leader, Lawyer Jeffrey Peifer. So nicknamed because he had some legal knowledge. There was a hushed stir as everyone picked up a songbook and searched for the right page. Lawyer Jeffrey began the song *Salve Regina,* and everyone joined in.

The morning sun slanted in the windows, casting its warmth on Tootie. She enjoyed singing so she tried to hum along. She hated it that she couldn't sing the words, but she didn't understand German.

Before the song ended, her mind flitted like a butterfly in a marigold bed, darting from one thought to another. *The bench is hard. How am I ever going to stand sitting here for three hours? Wonder what they fix for lunch at a worship service? Sure hope there's some food I can eat that will agree with my poor digestive system.*

Deacon Yutzy read scripture in High German as Tootie stared at a black widow spider descending on a web attached to the bench in front of her. Just watching the large spider made her shudder in disgust. She hated creepy bugs. *Amish women should be better housekeepers than this. Anna Rogies should have done a better job cleaning, especially when she knew she had a lot of people coming for the service.*

Tootie wiggled her shoe under the web. The spider inched back up toward the broad backed woman in front of her. *Oh, that poor woman. The spider might bite her.*

The spider crawled on top of the bench. Tootie leaned forward and raised her hymn book. She came down with a hard swat, missed the spider and clobbered the heavy set woman's behind. The loud splat resounded throughout the room just as Deacon Yutzy sat down. Minister Luke Yoder, Margaret Yoder's son, stood up, ready to give the opening sermon.

The whole congregation looked around, trying to see what made the noise. Hal turned red. She was dumbfounded that her Aunt Tootie, out of the blue, hit a Plain woman in the backside for no reason with, of all things, a hymn book. That embarrassment turned to horror when she realized the woman was, of all people, Stella Strutt. Stella twisted around and gave Tootie a very harsh stare then an equally mean glare at Hal. She said dummkopf sharply in German and looked like this assault was proof that Hal's queerness ran in her family.

Hal snatched the hymn book away from her aunt. She hissed, "Aunt Tootie, why did you hit Stella Strutt?"

Tootie whispered, "I'm very sorry. I was trying to kill a black widow spider. I was afraid it was going to bite her. I missed the spider, and now it has gotten away." She studied the floor around her feet, looking for the insect to make sure it wasn't on her. She blushed when she realized Stella was still glaring at her. Tootie said, "I'm so sorry, Mrs. Strutt. I tried to stop a spider from getting on you. It was a black widow. That's the worse kind you know."

That was enough to suffice for the moment. Stella shifted

59

around on the bench to face the front.

Hal patted Tootie's arm to get her attention. She whispered, "Perhaps you should just sit quietly now before you get into anymore trouble. You don't want to get us kicked out of here, do you?"

"Of course not, Dear. Never that," Tootie said meekly.

On the other side of Tootie, Nora leaned across Emma and whispered, "Tootie, this is their church. Act like it."

"I said I was sorry," hissed Tootie.

Minister Yoder crossed his hands in front of him, taking in the commotion in row four on the women's side. "Is there something wrong, Stella Strutt?" He asked.

The elderly woman puffed up like a toad. "It is all right now. The English woman behind me hit me in the back with her hymn book. She says she is sorry so I forgive her," Stella said in a tone that didn't sound forgiving.

Even more curious now, Luke turned his attention on Hal. "Was there a reason your aendi hit Stella Strutt?"

"Jah, a black widow spider crawled up its web and right behind Stella on the bench. Aunt Tootie was afraid it was going to bite her. She meant to kill it, but her aim was bad. Aunt Tootie is very sorry," Hal said with a heavy sigh.

"I see," Luke said. "Can I start my sermon now?"

"Aunt Tootie has promised to pay close attention to the front of the room from now on," Hal said solemnly.

"Gute to know. Instead of what I was going to preach, I am reminded of a parable that might fit this moment. Today I will recite it in English. It is about a spider web in a household that had a mother with several daughters. The mother had the daughters take turns cleaning the house from top to bottom.

One day, the daughter in charge of cleaning that day saw a spider web. It hung in the top corner of the door that went from the kitchen to the living room. It was up high so she could not reach it. She decided she was not going to worry about it. She had all she wanted to do to make the house look tidy when it was her turn to clean. She was not going to all the hard work to make the house look immaculate. After all with such a large family, the house would soon need cleaned again. If she was lucky, it would be one of her sisters' turn. That sister could take the spider web down.

When company came to visit, a woman noticed the spider web. She said to another woman someone should do something about that web instead of letting it hang there for all to see.

The other woman said in order to take care of the problem someone needed to kill the spider. The two women stood under the web looking for a spider but did not see one. Another woman came from the kitchen. They pointed at the web. She said she was amazed that there would be a web in this clean house. Someone should do something about the web she told the other two. They all agreed and just walked away.

Six months later, the worship service was in that house again. The house had been cleaned from top to bottom except for the spider web which now held the dead spider.

One woman took the time to look for the web she saw at the last Sunday service in that house. She whispered to her husband, as she nodded above them, that the web was still there. Someone ought to do something about that web she said to her husband, hoping he would take the hint. Another man stopped to speak to her husband, and the men went outside.

One woman pointed the dusty web out to another. Soon all the women took turns saying something should be done about that web. One woman pointed out, they were at the Sunday service in someone else's house. What could they do? None of them had a dust rag. It bothered all the women now to look at that web, but look at it was all they did.

The women of the house were really bothered by the web after they heard all the talk that day that cast aspersions on their cleaning. By the time all the company left that evening, the tired woman and her daughters had forgotten about the web. All the talk didn't bothered them enough to remember the web again.

Another six months went by. The Sunday service was again at that house. First thing the visiting women did on the way to the kitchen was to look up. Each commented she was bothered that the same old cobweb still dangled there after all this time. They all agreed that something should be done about that web.

One said, "We need to get rid of the cobweb." A couple of them went for the broom and dust mop. Others asked the woman of the house for dust rags. They stood looking up at the cobweb, complaining at the poor sight it made but doing nothing.

A deacon came over to see what the women were doing. His wife mentioned the cobweb to him some time ago. He thought by now one of the women in the house had taken care of the problem. "What's wrong?" He asked.

His wife said, "We are looking at that cobweb. It bothers all of us to see it still there. Someone should do something about it already."

The deacon looked at the dusty web. "How long has that cobweb been there?"

"For over a year," replied his wife.

"That long," he said. "All of you women have fussed about the web that long, but not one of you cleaned it down."

All the women burst forth at the same time with excuses. They wanted to do something about getting rid of the web. They gave reasons why they didn't, including the woman who owned the house and her daughters. They each ended their excuses with they agreed someone really should do something about that web.

The deacon took the broom out of his wife's hand and a dust rag from a woman. He threw the dust rag over the broom straws and lifted the broom up to the door facing. One swipe took care of getting rid of the web. The deacon was able to do something about it, and it took all of four seconds.

The lesson is we should all know not to leave something that we think is important to be done for someone else to do when we can do the job. If everyone does nothing, the job may never get done.

As for what happened today, anyone that sees that spider in here during the service or his web under a bench, I say do not wait for someone else to take care of it. Do what Nurse Hal's

Aendi Tootie attempted. Take care of the problem right away yourself, before that spider bites someone or builds a web." Minster Yoder said, "Now for the silent prayer. Und wann dir einig sin lasset uns bede."

At the minister's bidding, the congregation slipped off the benches onto their knees. After they were seated again, Hal vowed to keep a better watch on Tootie. She kept only partial attention on Deacon Enos Yutzy. He read scriptures about Aquila and Priscilla's lives as tentmakers and how they moved about the country.

When he finished, he turned the preaching over to Bishop Bontrager for the main sermon. "Dear Brothers and Sisters, blessed be the God and Father of our Lord Jesus Christ. Let us pray *The Lord's Prayer* together. Und wann dir einig sin lasset uns bede."

Everyone went from the benches to their knees to pray the prayer out loud. After the Bishop said amen, they rose and sat again.

During Eldon Bontrager's sermon, Hal heard familiar giggling. She looked beside her. Beth was on the bench, but Redbird was missing. Hal leaned over to look in the aisle. Mortified, she saw her redheaded toddler crawling toward the bishop. What more could this family do to interrupt this day's worship service?

Redbird made it as far as the bishop's feet. She sat up and giggled which caused a few snickers from the congregation. The bishop stopped talking. He stood very still and watched the child. Redbird pulled on his shoestring and untied his shoe. Giggling, she grabbed his pant leg, raised herself up and patted his knee. She smiled up at him, wanting his attention.

Bishop Bontrager smiled kindly at the tot and lifted her into his arms. He gave her a hug. "That what you wanted?"

Redbird cooed at him.

"If it is all right with you, Redbird, I will finish my sermon so we can call dinner. You must be hungry." The bishop turned to his congregation. "There is a saying. Nothing proves one's character quite like his kindness to children and animals. When we go about our daily life remember that saying when you are with a child or taking care of your animals. Remember not only the people you walk around see how you act, but God is watching you. Proverbs tells us train a child in the way he should go, and when he is old he will not turn from it. Redbird is here at the worship service to be trained in our ways. I do not want to be the one to do anything that would turn her away from us, including telling this tiny child she can not interrupt my sermon."

Redbird laid her head on his shoulder and blinked her eyes, fighting sleep. She dozed off. The bishop glanced at her and said softly, "In Matthew scripture says, Come unto me, all ye that labor and are heavy laden, and I will give you rest."

Eldon looked down at the sleeping toddler and smiled. "I hope my sermon wasn't so boring that I almost put all of you to sleep like Redbird." That brought some giggles and chuckles. "Now we will sing, *Amazing Grace* in English."

When the hymn was over, Minister Bontrager said, "As for announcements, if the Lord wills and we live, in two weeks the worship service will be held at Adam Mulenburg's farm. On Saturday evening in one week, there will be a free will donation supper at the school to raise funds for school supplies for the coming term. That starts at 7 P.M. There is not a member meeting this Sunday and no disciplining needed. Now it is dinner time. As you all already know the smells coming from the kitchen are voonderball gute."

Chapter 7

After the men turned benches into tables and placed benches around the tables for seats, they passed around the light lunch of bread slices with spreads of cheese, jams and applebutter. Relish plates full of pickle spears, red beets, radishes, and carrot sticks. Dessert was cookies and snitz which were fried apple pies.

John Lapp sat down next to Peter Rogies, father of Cooner Jonah. The elderly man stared at the wall. After awhile, he looked beside him. He said in a cracking voice, "Do you know who I am?"

"Of course, I do," John replied.

"That is gute that you do. At this moment I do not," Peter said wearily.

"Peter Rogies is your name," John said, wondering if this was the elderly man's dry wit at play. "Everyone knows who you are.

Peter nodded agreement. "I expect they do." He took the bread, served himself and handed the platter to John.

Conversations flowed at all the tables as the men caught up on the news of the last two weeks. After they ate, they made room for the next diners by going outside to get a breath of fresh air. The service gatherings every two weeks were much better than the Budget newspaper when it came to catching up with what was going on in the Plain community.

John Lapp sat on the edge of the porch with Cooner Jonah Rogies. Cooner Jonah's father, Peter, walked down the driveway in front of them. He had changed out of his black suit to his every day blue shirt, trousers and gallouses already. He padded along barefoot with his straw hat perched on the back of his head which was how he always wore his hats. Peter was talking to an empty space beside him, and his right arm was outstretched with the hand closed.

"What is Peter doing?" John asked.

"His chores. Recht now Daed is taking his horse out to pasture," Cooner Jonah replied with a furrowed brow.

"Who is he talking to?"

"His dog, Pet."

John rubbed his beard. "I do not recall the last time I saw Peter's old sorrel."

"The horse died of old age several years ago. Daed does not remember that anymore. So did his dog die," Cooner Jonah said with a heavy sigh.

"You mean he thinks he is leading his dead horse and walking with his dead dog?" John gave Cooner Jonah a quizzical look.

"Jah, pitiful it is when a man as sharp as my father once was has lost his mind," Jonah said with teary eyes. "Sometimes, it is a tough day like this one for Daed. He does not remember anything except in snatches. I think having so many people he can not remember around him at the Sunday meetings makes him more ferhoodled. My family has faced the fact that he is old and sick. I know we can not help him get better. All we can do is take care of him and know whatever happens to him it is God's will."

"A shame. Know that Peter will be in our daily prayers along with your family for what you are going through," John said as he watched the elderly man walk up behind Tootie and stop her. The two of them seemed to be getting along all right. Since he didn't know what to say to Cooner Jonah, he changed the subject. "How you coming with the spring work?"

"Coming right along. Hope the weather holds for a while.

Seems every year we get started gute and get one rain storm after another that stops us from working," Cooner Jonah complained, still keeping a watch on his father.

After she ate, Tootie felt as if she was in the way in a room full of efficient Amish women as they cleaned up Anna Rogies's kitchen. What she needed was some fresh air with some peace and quiet. Tootie edged her way through the chattering women and went outside.

She came around to the front of the house. John was talking to a man on the porch. Other men were gathered by the front of the house. A group of boys stood by the barn, and teenage girls sat under a shade tree, watching the boys. Tootie turned in the only direction left that she could be alone which was toward the road.

She clasped her hands behind her back and strolled slowly, taking in the scenes this farm had to offer. Good fresh country air. She breathed deeply and appreciated hearing only faintly the chatter and laughter.

"What are you doing out here alone?" Peter Rogies asked from behind her.

The old man was dressed in chore clothes and barefoot. Tootie tilted her head over one shoulder as she curiously checked him out. He had one arm outstretched. His hand was a fist. Perhaps, he had a disability from a farming accident.

When he caught up with her, he said, "You were at the service today?"

"Yes, my name is Tootie."

"That can not be your given name," Peter said matter of factly.

"No, my given name is Dolly," Tootie answered.

Peter studied her face a moment as if he was trying to pull a memory from the depth of his mind. A glimmer of recognition came over his face. He smiled. "I thought I knew you. Where are you living now?"

"I live in northern Iowa, but I'm visiting John Lapp and his family. His wife, Hallie, is my niece. You are Peter Rogies, and you own this farm?"

"You should know," Peter said with meaning. "Are you still married?"

"My husband passed away a few years ago," Tootie replied. "Are you still married?"

He nodded no as he looked off into space. "My Sara died." He seemed uncomfortable dwelling on the subject of his wife. "What are you doing out here by yourself?"

"I needed some fresh air. All the chatter of so many people was getting to me," Tootie said truthfully.

"I know just what you mean. So many people around me makes me verhuddelt," Peter said.

"Excuse me, what does that mean in English?."

"It means I get confused. Wait a minute, and I'll walk with you." Tootie liked Peter's husky, cracking voice and his friendly manner so she waited. He walked over to the fence and made a circling motion with his hand around the top wire. "Now I am ready."

They continued their walk together toward the road. Not talking. Just enjoying quiet companionship until Peter looked down between them and said, "Heel."

Tootie didn't know what Peter meant. She remembered Edwin said heel when he trained a birddog he wanted to follow him. *If that is it, Peter must want me to walk a few steps behind him. Is this what Amish women do, heel like a dog when they are told to be submissive?* She slowed down and trailed behind him.

Peter looked back. "Sorry if I am walking too fast for you. I will try to slow down so you can keep up."

Tootie smiled. Amish men were truly strange, but she liked this man with the kind eyes anyway. She didn't want to hurt his feelings. *If only I had brought that Amish book with me. Maybe I'd have a clue what Peter Rogies meant by heel. I should have hidden that book in my suitcase so Nora didn't know I had it.* "I just need to get some walking practice in, and I'll do better," she excused.

"Dolly, you want to see the day old colt behind the barn. He is a nice looking fellow already," Peter said proudly.

"I'd love to see him," Tootie exclaimed. As they rambled along beside the fence line, she looked out over the cornfield filled with neat green rows. "The corn is coming up I see."

Peter gave the field a wistful regard. "Growing corn is a treat for these old dim eyes." Tootie edged closer to him with a scrunched up face, trying to avoid a large black and yellow spider creeping down a blade of grass. Peter looked at the grass and back at her with a youthful grin. "I see you still do not like spiders even after listening to the worship service this morning."

Tootie's face heated up. "If you think I'm going to step on that spider to kill him you're mistaken. As for this morning, I did try to kill that spider to keep that woman from getting bit. What happened is too embarrassing to talk about except to say I'm so sorry I caused such a ruckus at your worship service. What horrible things must your family and that poor woman think of me?"

Peter snickered. "That whop on the bottom is just what Stella Strutt has deserved for a long time, but no one has tried to do it. I am not sure how Moses puts up with her. The rest of us just avoid her as much as possible."

"Still I hate that I caused such a disturbance in the church service over a spider," Tootie declared.

Peter stopped at the pen fence that adjoined the back of the barn. His gaze didn't budge from her face. "That was not the first disturbance you made over a spider as I recall, and I doubt that it will be the last."

Tootie started to ask what he meant by that remark, but he turned his attention to the pen and whistled loudly. A red mare and leggy colt lifted their heads to find the source of the whistle. The mare took one more mouth full of hay from the manger and came running.

Peter stuck his hand through the fence to let the mare nuzzled it. The colt stretched its neck and sniffed Peter's hand.

"It's amazing that the colt isn't scared of you," Tootie said quietly.

"He was not born with fear. We want to keep him gentle, and

at his age, he is naturally inquisitive."

Tootie stuck her pale, smooth skinned hand through the fence beside Peter's larger calloused hand, darkened by years of work in the sun. The colt sniffed her hand and licked it. Tootie giggled.

"You used to like kittens. We have a litter. Want to see them? They are just big enough to open their eyes and be sassy," Peter said.

One more peculiar statement from this man, but Tootie didn't want to dwell on why he kept assuming what she liked and disliked. She clapped. "I do love kittens. Show me."

Peter pointed to a side door on the barn. "We can go in there, Dolly."

Tootie wouldn't have had any trouble finding the noisy kittens by herself. The mother had left them to take a break, and they didn't like her being gone.

Peter opened a horse stall. "There they are."

The six fuzz balls were crawling over and under each other in the loose straw as they cried for their mother. Tootie bent down and picked up a hissing kitten speckled with every color a cat could be. "This is certainly a brightly colored one. He's so pretty."

"That is a she," Peter said, stroking the fussy kitten on top the head with one gentle arthritic finger.

"How do you know that?" Tootie said, doubting him.

"Calico cats are always females," Peter said.

"Really! I didn't know that," Tootie declared.

"Now you do, Dolly."

Tootie put the kitten gently back in the pile of churning fur. "I should go to the house. When my family can't find me, they might be worried. I didn't tell anyone I was going for a walk."

As they stepped out of the barn, Tootie wanted to tell Peter she enjoyed their walk. She felt a flutter in her stomach that stopped her from speaking.

Peter gave her the most intense look as if he was reading her mind. "Maybe we could do this again sometime. We used to enjoy long walks together."

Tootie wasn't sure why this man thought she liked to take walks with him, but he knew about calico cats, didn't he? Maybe Amish men just sensed things about others. No matter. She knew she was born a romantic, but she was too old to be doing anything about it. "Thank you for showing me the colt and kittens. I must go now. This has turned into a pleasant afternoon indeed thanks to you."

"Sure, now I will get back to my chores." Peter walked away.

Cooner Jonah and Anna walked with the Lapp family to their buggies. Soft spoken Anna said to Hal, "Next Wednesday is Peter's birthday. We are having him a small celebration that evening. Just cake and homemade ice cream. We would like your family to come and bring your company. That should be enough visitors to make it look like we are celebrating Peter's birthday."

"Sounds gute," Hal said. "We accept."

"Nothing more fun than a birthday party," Nora said.

Tootie smacked her lips. "With homemade ice cream."

That night after supper, Noah got out the battleship game for Daniel and him to play.

Jim said in a low voice with his eyes on the kitchen door, "John, how soon do you think my horse will be ready to pull my buggy? Is he learning anything tied to the road fence every day?"

"We will not know until you try him and find out. When you do we will put blinders on him which should help," John said.

"I want to use my own horse. I think tomorrow I'll try him out by myself, or maybe one of the boys would like to ride with me. I don't dare ask Nora to go with me until the horse knows what he's supposed to do," Jim whispered.

"I understand," John said knowingly.

Meanwhile in the kitchen, cleanup went as usual. Before Hal could get back from the barn, Nora and Tootie were on the couch, waiting for Hal to join them. Hal sunk the slop bucket into the dish water and gave the bucket more of a scrubbing than a slop bucket deserved.

Emma heard Adam drive in to take her to the youth singing. She threw her dish towel over the line, said good bye to everyone and rushed to clamber into the buggy. "I could hardly wait for you to pick me up."

Adam flicked the lines over his horse's back. Once they were on the road, he wavered his hand.

"It is a mad house at our place with company around," Emma replied. Adam raised an eyebrow at her. "Oh, do not get me wrong. I like Hallie's folks and aunt, but it is different when they are there all the time. I never know what is going to happen." She paused then blurted out, "Take the slop pail."

Adam's head jerked back as he stared at her.

"Silly, I did not mean you should take it home with you literally, but if you want to rescue my sanity, it might come to that to get some peace at our house. Hallie and Aendi Tootie are feuding about who should wash the slop pail. Aendi Tootie wants to wash dishes, but she does not want to wash the nasty pail. She hurries through the dishes while Hallie empties the pail to the cats in the barn. Aendi is on the couch looking innocent by the time Hallie comes back, all worn out from running."

Adam grinned.

"I would not find this funny if I were you. Especially if it is Hallie telling you this story. Let me tell you, she is not too agreeable recht now when it is time to do dishes," Emma said. She tipped her head back and welcomed the faint breeze over her face and neck. "That is not all that is wrong. Dawdi Jim and Mammi Nora are having words over that courting buggy Dawdi bought. She does not like the buggy at all. She would be even more upset if she knew what was wrong with the horse that came with the buggy."

Adam raised his eyebrow again.

"The first time Dawdi drove the buggy, he found out he did not buy the best horse for road driving. The horse stopped every time traffic went by him on the highway. Noah had to get out of the buggy and get the horse going each time then hop back in the buggy. Daed thought it might help if he tied the horse to the road fence so it got used to the traffic."

Adam wavered his hand.

"We do not know if it helped. Dawdi has not tried the horse yet. He has been using one of our horses. When the time comes, Daed is going to loan him a pair of blinders. We are all hoping that the horse works well soon. Mammi noticed the horse tied to the fence, but so far she has not realized something is wrong," Emma related. "So help me enjoy our evening at the singing. Cheer me up before I have to go home and face whatever comes up next." She looked sincere then she giggled.

Adam grinned back as he turned into the Rogies driveway. The sun's golden light slid slowly below the horizon. The glow tinted the grass and parked buggies. The rays dotted the laughing and chattering teens, waiting for everyone to arrive. Two hours later the singing ended, and all the Plain teenagers left for home.

Adam let his horse go at a slow walk, prolonging their evening together, while Emma and he enjoyed the pleasant ride. When they neared the turn off for Bender Creek Road, Adam turned onto the dirt road. The deeply shadowed trees flickered past on both sides of the buggy until Adam stopped. He took Emma in his arms, gave her a hug and a gentle kiss.

"Denki, Adam. I needed that," Emma said softly.

That same evening, Redbird and Beth crawled over by John's rocker, pulled themselves up and jabbered at him. John swept them up on his lap and rocked them.

Jim offered wistfully, "I could rock one of them babies. Wouldn't be any trouble at all."

"I know," John said. "But they like me to do it every night before they go to bed. He hummed *Sweet And Low.* Soon the girls drifted off to sleep.

Hal brought a chair from the kitchen and placed it beside the couch. She sat down with a sigh.

"You look tired, Hallie," Nora surmised.

"For some reason I feel tired. I think Sunday is the hardest day of the week. Makes me tired doing nothing. Noah, do you need to soak that ankle again tonight?"

"Nah, the swelling has gone down. It's just a little stiff. No need to bother. I'll walk the stiffness out of it."

"If you say so," Hal said.

Nora commented, "That Adam sure is a nice young man. Emma got herself a fine pick."

"We sure like having him around," Hal agreed.

Tootie mused, "Too bad he can't talk."

"Tootie, I declare, you know what not to say and just go ahead and say it anyway," Nora scolded. "Your brain is as scattered as ashes blowing in the wind."

"It's all right, Mom. Aunt Tootie, Adam has been that way since birth so he's not bashful about it. Besides if you noticed, he communicates just fine with all of us. Emma has been with him so much I think they can read each other's mind," Hal said.

"I noticed that," Nora agreed.

"Their love is a sign of true love if I ever saw it," Tootie added dreamily.

"Tootie, are you feeling all right?" Nora asked.

"I'm fine. Why?"

"You have been so different this evening. Quiet and sort of … ." Nora searched for the right word. "Well, out of it."

"Guess I'm tired," Tootie excused.

The boys gave up their game and went to sit on the floor by John and Jim in the rockers to listen to their father read the bible for devotions.

When John stopped reading, Noah said, "Some of the boys are going tomorrow night to practice with their coon hounds. Daniel and me want to go."

John stood and put his bible on the shelf above his rocker. "Where do you plan on going?"

"Bender Creek timber. Should be coons prowling in there all the time. We figure Dog ...," Noah paused, rolled his eyes toward the ceiling and amended, "Biscuit should start his training."

Jim smiled at Noah's slip in front of Hal and rubbed his chin. "Gonna be good and dark in that timber. Don't you worry about

74

getting lost, or better yet what might be out there in the dark with you like ghosts or boogie men?"

"Nah, not us," bragged Daniel. "We do not believe in such things."

"Good thing you live this far away from the timber that's near my farm," Jim baited the boys.

"Why is that?" Noah asked.

"I could tell you the story of old Jasper Newcomb, but are you sure you want to hear it?"

Nora scolded, "Maybe you shouldn't be telling such things to these boys."

"We want to hear, ain't so, Noah?" Daniel said eagerly.

"Don't say I didn't warn you. This story isn't for the weak hearted," Jim warned.

"Maybe I'll take the girls upstairs and put them to bed before you start," Hal said."

Nora asked, "Can I help with one of them?"

"Sure you can. They're a load to carry up the stairs at the same time. I usually have Emma here to help me."

As Hal and Nora left with the sleeping girls, Jim commenced with his tale. "Well now, old Jasper said he didn't believe in ghosts just like you boys did. His very words a matter of fact.

Everyone in our part of the country knew that two hundred acres of timber was haunted. Plenty of folks talked about glowing lights bobbing around when hunters weren't in the timber. Some folks claimed on full moon nights, human like figures, dressed in white, appeared out of no where and stood in the moonshine for a spell. They disappeared before folks' eyes. Jasper laughed when they talked about it.

Finally, a friend of Jasper's, Andy Brown, and a bunch of other coon hunters dared Jasper to spend the night in the woods by himself if he was so brave. If he stayed until dawn, the men said they would buy him a cart load of watermelons. Jasper was delighted. Watermelon was his favorite fruit. He accepted the dare, packed some matches, his pipe, and a bedroll. He went right to the middle of the timber to camp for the night."

Jim looked around the room. He had everyone's attention.

Poor Tootie scrunched down with her arms folded over her chest. Her skittish mind filled with thoughts of what it was like out in that dark timber among spirits. Jim could tell she was all ears. The effect his story had on her tickled him, and he was just getting started.

Hal and Nora came downstairs as Jim leaned forward. He folded his arms across his legs so he'd be closer to Noah and Daniel. In a lowered voice, he said, "Jasper started a campfire, lit his pipe, and settled on a stump by the fire with yesterday's newspaper. As he read, he heard a creaking sound close to what a tree frog might make. He looked around right quick. He saw a gnarled little creature with glowing red eyes on the log beside his stump. The creature had showed up without Jasper hearing him. This critter had a long, forked tail, two horns on its head, claws where fingers should be at the ends of its hands, and sharp dirty teeth.

'What are you?' Jasper asked in a quivering voice.

'I'm called Sneak Upon, because I sneak upon humans that trespass in my territory. Ain't nobody here tonight except you and me. You're trespassing,' the creature informed old Jasper. Sneak Upon's voice gave Jasper the creeps. It sounded like the hiss of fiery flames coming from a saline torch.

Poor old Jasper's heart nearly stopped with fright. He leaped to his feet and backed away from Sneak Upon. 'Ain't going to be nobody here but you in a minute,' he told the gnarled creature. Jasper leaped over the fallen log and hightailed it through the trees lickety-split. He ran so fast he overtook two rabbits being chased by a coyote. The animals all veered out of his way, but it wasn't long before Jasper heard little hooves pounding back of him.

The ugly creature caught up with him and stayed right behind him. 'You're making pretty good speed for an old man,' taunted the creature.

'I can run much faster than this if I'm of a mind to,' Jasper told Sneak Upon. He took off like a bolt of lightning, leaving the gnarled creature in his dust. As he past his friend house, Jasper hollered as loud as he could. Andy came outside to see what was wrong.

'Never mind about buying me them watermelons. You can keep them,' Jasper shouted without breaking his stride. He ran all the way home, locked his doors and hid under his bed for the rest of the night.

After that, he was a firm believer in ghosts and spooks. He refused to go anywhere near the woods at night to coon hunt unless some of his friends were with him."

Daniel gave Noah a wide eyed look. Noah scoffed, "Dawdi, that sounds like a real wild tale but a gute one. I do not think we will ever see one of those Sneak Upons this far south so we have no need to worry when we are in the timber."

John teased, "I think it might be time for the two of you to go to bed while you are still all in one piece."

"Ah, Daed," Noah scoffed.

"Maybe we all should call it a night," Nora suggested. "I agree with Hal. It does seem like it has been a long day."

"Do you lock the doors at night?" Tootie asked in a shaky voice.

"Not usually," Hal said to her. "Why?"

Tootie gave a sniffle. "I just wondered is all."

Daniel said, "Do not worry, Aendi Tootie. We know there are no Sneak Upons around here."

"Could we lock the doors tonight just to be on the safe side?" Nora asked, watching her jittery sister.

"Mom, you don't actually take that story Dad told seriously do you?" Hal exclaimed.

"No, I've heard it many times before, but I should have sent Tootie to bed before Jim told it. It doesn't take much for her to have nightmares. That brings on the sleepwalking. I'd hate for her to get outside and wander away," Nora said.

Daniel commiserated, "You are just like me, Aendi. I used to sleepwalk, but I outgrew it."

"I think it's too late for me to outgrow it, Dear," Tootie groaned.

"Jah, we will lock the doors tonight." John went to the front door. "I will do it right now, Aendi Tootie."

"Thank you, John," she said. "That makes me feel better."

After John and Hal were in their bedroom, they heard Nora in the spare bedroom scolding Jim. "What were you thinking when you told that awful story in front of Tootie? We're in for a sleepless night I'm afraid."

"Sorry," Jim's hushed voice answered.

John climbed into bed and put his hands behind his head. "Hal, have you paid any attention to Peter Rogies lately?"

Hal slipped her nightgown over her head before she answered. "Nah, is something wrong with him?"

"His mind is failing fast. This afternoon, Peter walked along the driveway talking to himself. Cooner Jonah says it is his dead horse and dead dog he is talking to. He does it all the time. Peter thinks he is taking his horse to pasture, and the dog is walking along with him. The strange way he acts must come and go. Peter was walking with Aendi Tootie, and he seemed fine. At least, Aendi Tootie was smiling," John said.

"I wonder how that happened. My Aunt Tootie went for a walk with Peter. Really?"

"That's what I said. Just thought you being a nurse, you might be able to help him," John said. "I think the Rogies family might be a little bashful about asking since it embarrasses them when Peter says the wrong things in a gathering."

"I know how they feel. I feel the same way with Aunt Tootie."

"Hal, Aunt Tootie is not so bad," John defended.

"Her mind is fine. She just doesn't think before she does the dumbest things.. Now I understand why Anna didn't want a big gathering at Peter's birthday party." Hal hung her dress on a wall peg.

"Cooner Jonah said large gatherings like the Sunday services make Peter verhuddelt," John relayed.

"If Peter is confused that is not a gute sign. When we go to the birthday party, I'll see how he acts." Hal blew out the lamp. She got in bed, pulled the covers up over her and turned on her side toward her husband. "I noticed Peter is not the only one who is verhuddelt. The boys have trouble remembering the dog's name. Is there a reason for that?"

"Might be," John said. "You want to know the truth or not?"

"You can tell me. I'm a big girl now," Hal said, grinning.

"The boys remember the dog's name just fine. They have trouble referring to their coon dog by the name Biscuit."

"Oh, I see." Hal giggled.

"What is so funny?" John asked.

"I thought that might be what's wrong," Hal said. "They thought they had to give me the privilege of naming their dog so I'd let them keep him."

"Jah."

"It serves them right for letting me pick the name to bribe me into letting them have a puppy," Hal said.

John's eyes widened. "You gave the dog the name Biscuit for that reason. That was mean."

"If you remember I was feeling mean that day anyway."

John chuckled. "Real out of sorts as I recall. How long are you going to keep the boys on the hook about the dog's name?"

"I haven't decided yet," Hal said with a soft laugh. "Besides, they seemed to have found a way around their problem."

"They have. Your father helped with that," John shared.

"I might have known," Hal said drowsily.

It was the middle of the night when a piercing scream broke the silence. John and Hal bolted upright in bed.

Hal said, "What was that?"

"You have two choices – a Sneak Upon or your Aendi Tootie," John grumbled.

"If it was Aunt Tootie she must have dozed back off. I don't hear anything now so I'm not getting out of bed to go downstairs to see about her." Hal turned on her side to get comfortable again.

About an hour later, loud moans and groans came from downstairs. Hal rubbed her eyes and stared at the dark bedroom door. Down the hall she heard her mother grumble, "You and your monster stories. See what I told you. When are you going to learn not to tell scary tales around my sister?"

79

Disturbing sounds carried up the stairs for a minute then quiet reigned again. Hal listened for footsteps. Sure enough she heard the patter of bare feet downstairs. As much to herself as to John, she said, "I better go see about her."

Hal met Daniel coming out of his room. "What are you doing up?"

Daniel sounded concerned. "I thought Aendi Tootie might need me. I understand what she is going through."

"Gute thinking," Hal said. "You can get the glass of water she said wakes her up."

"You want me to come with you, Hal," Nora's sleepy voice called.

Hal answered, "It's all right, Mom. Stay in bed. I'll go take care of Aunt Tootie."

Hal and Daniel eased the clinic door open and peeked in. Tootie was pacing back and forth, mumbling and groaning. Hal eased over to the elderly woman and took her by the arm. She directed Tootie toward the bed.

Daniel came with the water. "Come on, Aendi Tootie. Get back in bed and warm up. I brought you some water."

Tootie laid down, and Hal pulled the covers over her. Daniel started to give her a drink. He brought the glass back in a hurry to keep the elderly woman from spilling it. Tootie tossed and turned in a dreaming fit as she fought to kick the covers off. "Get away from this bed, Sneak Upon. Get out of this room."

"She's still asleep," Daniel said.

"She thinks you're the monster. We better wake her up, or she's going to be the only one that gets any sleep for the rest of the night," Hal said. "Keep the glass close so we can get water in her." She patted Tootie's arm. "Wake up. Wake up now."

The elderly woman sat up in bed. "Wh – What is going on?"

"You're having a bad dream," Hal said. "We didn't want to disturb you, but we thought it would be better for you to wake up and go back to sleep."

Tootie patted Hal's hand. "You're so thoughtful, Dear."

"Here is a glass of water to drink. It will help," Daniel said.

Tootie patted his hand on the glass. "You're thoughtful too,

Dear." She took the glass from him and drank half of it.

"You go back to sleep, Aendi Tootie. You are all right now," Daniel said to comfort her.

"I know I am with a brave boy like you in the house to take care of me," Tootie said. "Good night."

By the time Hal and Daniel made it to the door, Tootie filled the room with snuffling snores.

Hal softly shut the door. "Maybe that will muffle her snores so we can sleep."

Chapter 8

The next morning was wash day. Hal carried buckets of water to the washing machine while Emma fixed breakfast. Once Hal had the clothes sorted in piles in the mudroom, she threw in a load of shirts, started the machine and listened to the swish swish of the agitator a minute before she added the soap.

"Good morning, Hal," Nora said. Tootie shuffled in behind her sister, wearing her fuzzy pink slippers.

"Morning, Mom. Morning, Aunt Tootie," Hal greeted.

They all found something to do to get breakfast ready. After a silent prayer, Jim announced, "I'm going for a buggy ride this morning to Wickenburg and back. Anyone care to go with me?"

Nora and Tootie chased their eggs and sausages on their plate instead of answering Jim. Daniel looked around the table. No one else offered. "I would like to go. Is that all recht, Daed?"

"All recht with me," John agreed. He was glad someone wanted to ride along. He didn't like the idea of Jim on the road by himself.

Hal said, "I have some things you can get me at the grocery store while you're in town."

"I could use a bottle of hand lotion," Tootie said, giving a disgruntled sniff. "My hands are drying out from washing so many dishes."

"I need a bottle of no scented bath soap as long as you're going," Nora added. "Mine's about gone."

"Better write that stuff all down, or I'll forget half of it," Jim told them.

After breakfast, Tootie started for the tea kettle. Hal stopped her. "This morning, Emma's going to wash dishes, Aunt Tootie. You and I are going to hang out the basket of clothes I washed. That will give your poor, dry hands a rest."

"I don't know if I can," Tootie groaned. "My knees are bothering me this morning."

Nora said, "Tootie, you might find your knees won't hurt as bad if you exercise them. Standing at the sink in one place won't do the trick."

"All right," Tootie said. "Let me get my shoes on."

When they came back to wring out a load of dresses, Hal asked Tootie and Nora to bring their dirty clothes. After she threw in another load, she said, "Let's go hang up the dresses, Aunt Tootie."

Hal pointed to a wren hiding in the new leaves on the maple tree. "Listen to that wren. He loves to sing to us. Follows me around the place all the time."

"Cute little bird," Tootie said approvingly as she reached into the basket. She shook out a dress and pinned it to the line. Her mind kept going back to her Sunday walk with Peter Rogies. She smiled pleasantly as she picked up another crumpled dress.

They had just about emptied the last basket when an open buggy came down the road and turned into the driveway.

Tootie nodded behind Hal. "You have company coming."

"It's Peter Rogies. Wonder what he wants this morning?" Tootie edged along behind Hal and waited for the elderly man to stop.

Hal greeted him. "Morning, Peter. Get down and come in."

"No time for that," Peter said curtly as he looked around. He focused on Tootie. "Morning."

"Morning, Peter," Tootie responded brightly.

Peter pulled his attention back to Hal, "I came to talk to John

Lapp."

"He's in the field. He won't be back until dinner time."

"I will come back," Peter replied flatly. He flicked the lines over his horse's back.

Disappointed, Tootie watched as Peter drove away. He should have been nicer. She couldn't help some tongue clicking. "He wasn't very friendly, was he?"

Hal wondered what Peter's visit was about. "Nah, he wasn't. We should go in and help Emma and Mom now."

Daniel and Jim were on their way to Wickenburg when Peter Rogies's buggy passed them on his way to the Lapp farm. Daniel waved, but the elderly man stared straight ahead.

They passed a barefoot child by the side of the road, watching the family dog jump through the ditch weeds. Daniel waved at him.

"Know that fellow?" Jim asked.

"Jah, I go to school with Andy Stoll."

They crossed the bridge over Bender Creek. Child like laughter echoed under the bridge. Daniel straightened up. Boys his age were wading along the edge of the creek. Wistfully, he thought that looked like fun.

When they reached the city limits, Jim blew out a sigh of relief. Mike had trotted the whole way without paying any attention to the traffic. "I believe we have Mike cured of his highway fright."

"Jah, he did gute," Daniel agreed.

"Where do we go to find hand lotion and no scented bath soap?" Jim wondered.

"The Walmart is close by," Daniel said.

Jim stopped at the Walmart hitch rack. He climbed down and tied the lead rope in a double slip knot. "Okay, now let's see if we find what we came for."

"Will we have time to look around a little for ourselves?" Daniel asked.

"I don't see why not. Half the fun of shopping is the looking," Jim said.

An hour later, they came out of the store. Each was carrying a sack. "I sure hope I bought the right stuff," Jim worried. "Women are particular about their personal stuff you know."

Daniel replied, "Nah, I do not know. I am not particular, Dawdi. I like very much the candy in my sack."

"I thought you might," Jim said, winking at him.

An enclosed buggy had parked next to their space. They walked around it. Their parking space was empty.

"Where's my horse and buggy?" Jim exclaimed.

Daniel glanced around the parking lot. "I do not see them anywhere."

"Someone stole my rig!" Jim declared.

"I would not think that happened," Daniel said.

"We better call the sheriff's office and report this anyway. Come on back to the store with me."

Jim wasn't sure where he could find a phone. Along the side of the store were shops, but one heading said Exchanges and Returns. "Think we could ask the woman behind that counter if we can use her phone to call for help?"

"Jah, but if she can not help us, ask her where we can find a phone," Daniel said uncertainly.

Jim went to the counter. "Good Morning."

The middle aged woman asked, "You want exchange or return?"

Daniel spoke up. "We want return. My dawdi's buggy is missing."

The woman peered down her nose at him. "That's too bad. Now how can I help you."

Jim said, "I want to report my buggy stolen to the sheriff department. I need to find a phone."

The woman peered closely at the English man and wondered if he was mentally stable, but she wordlessly handed him the phone so he could make the call. *If he has a problem whether it is about his buggy or not, let the law handle it. Just so he isn't my problem anymore.*

Sheriff Dawson pulled up by the entrance doors in a few minutes. Jim and Daniel went to meet the car before he could get out. He rolled down his window. "You the one called in you had some trouble?"

"My buggy and horse have disappeared. I want to report them stolen," Jim said.

"I see," Sheriff Dawson said slowly, inspecting Jim's manner of dress and noting it was peculiar that this English man had an Amish boy with him. An English man owning an Amish buggy and with an Amish boy didn't exactly add up. He opened his car door and stepped out so he was eye to eye with Jim. "What's your name?"

"Jim Lindstrom. I'm John Lapp's father-in-law."

The mention of John Lapp gave Jim some credibility with the Sheriff. "Who is this boy with you?"

"I am Daniel Lapp son of John Lapp. This is my dawdi," Daniel supplied.

"Well, get in and come to the office with me. You can fill out a missing buggy report. After that, I'll take you home," the sheriff said and slid back behind the wheel.

"Your grandma is sure going to be tickled the buggy and horse are gone. You wait and see," Jim moaned to Daniel as they slid into the back seat.

A couple blocks down the street, the dispatcher blared on the radio.

"Go ahead," the sheriff said into the mic.

"We have a report of a buggy and horse without a driver trotting down Main Street."

"Ask if the buggy has a red seat," Jim said excitedly.

"Tell him it does," the dispatcher responded.

The sheriff aimed his car that direction. They found the horse and buggy parked at the end of Main Street.

"That's my rig, Sheriff," Jim cried.

"That's a courting buggy," the sheriff said suspiciously.

Jim looked sheepish. "I know it is, but it's mine."

"It is, Sheriff. I was with Dawdi when he bought it at the salebarn," Daniel confirmed.

"All right, I'm glad to be of help to you." The sheriff stopped by the buggy to let them out, and Jim thanked him.

On the way to the grocery store, Jim worried about his horse and buggy. "You think someone was playing a trick on us? Let the horse go on purpose I mean."

"I do not know what happened," Daniel said.

The boy knew his way around the grocery store so he helped Jim find the items on Hal's list. When they came out of the store, Jim stopped short and shifted his sack of groceries. "Oh, no! My buggy is gone again."

"How can this be?" Daniel asked.

Eldon Bontrager was walking toward them from where he just parked at the hitch rack. He overheard some of what Jim said. "You have trouble?"

"Good morning, Bishop," Jim greeted. "Did you happen to see a horse and buggy wondering down the street without a driver."

"Nah," the bishop answered.

"This is the second time today my buggy and horse have vanished while we were in a store. We can't figure out what is going on. Unless we find my rig we're on foot. I hate to call the sheriff again to report this. Makes me feel foolish. He just helped us find my rig about forty-five minutes ago."

"I will drive you around to look," Eldon said. "Hop in with me."

They drove around town for almost an hour. As they passed the tree nursery at the west edge of town, Daniel said, "There is the buggy and horse."

"Where?" Jim asked.

Daniel pointed between two of the neat rows of young trees.

Eldon pulled near Jim's buggy and let them out. "I will wait until you catch the horse. Maybe he is skittish."

"Thanks for all your help, Bishop." Jim started to the buggy then he turned back. "I know it's against your belief to be anything but completely truthful, but could we keep what happened this morning to ourselves? My wife isn't too happy about me buying this horse and buggy. This will just be fuel for the fire, as they say, if she knew Daniel and me have been afoot today."

"I understand," Eldon said, grinning at him.

Daniel carefully reached for the horse's bridle, got a firm hold and waved the bishop on. Jim looked to see the two sacks were in the buggy before he stuck the grocery sack beside them. Nothing was missing. "Daniel, I can't for the life of me figure out what went on this morning."

Daniel shrugged. "I do not know."

"Are we done shopping?"

"Jah, and we might be late for dinner. We should go now," Daniel urged.

By the time they reached the Lapp driveway, Jim had time to do some thinking. "I have an idea I want to try."

He tied up the horse with the double slip knot to the hitch rack by the barn. "Daniel, back up with me. We're going to watch what happens when Mike's alone."

The horse took the rope in his mouth, lifted his head up and down, pulling until the knot turned loose. Mike backed up with the lead rope dangling and walked away as Daniel grabbed the lead rope.

"Now we know," Jim said, rubbing his jaw. "I feel bad. Here I was accusing somebody of stealing, and all the time it was this horse doing the mischief."

Daniel giggled. "He is pretty smart, ain't so?"

"We're going to be smarter than him from now on," Jim said.

Nora yelled from the porch, "You two better get in here. We're thinking about eating without you. John wants to get back to work."

"Remember, Daniel, not a word to Grandma about this morning," Jim said.

Daniel nodded.

At lunch, Hal told John that Peter had been by to see him.

"He did not say what he wanted?" John asked, puzzled.

"Nah, but he did say he'd be back," Hal replied.

"We passed him on the road when we went to town," Daniel said. "I waved at him, but he did not wave back."

"How did the trip to town go?" John asked.

"Fine," Jim said quickly.

"We were ready to go hunt them they were gone so long,"

Nora said.

"We just knew Jim was lost again," Tootie supplied.

"I was with Dawdi Jim. How could he be lost?" Daniel defended.

"That's right," Jim said and winked at Daniel.

That afternoon, Nora and Hal were constantly interrupted by Tootie as she took the conversation off in a direction that centered on her ailments. Emma decided it would be a good idea to get her out of the house so Nora and Hal could visit. "Aendi Tootie, how about going for a walk with me? It is such a pretty day."

"No, I don't think so. I can't do much walking. Bad knees you know, and I already did plenty of walking this morning when I helped Hal hang out all those clothes," Tootie complained, rubbing her knees.

"Oh, pittle," Nora said. "It would do you good to get a little exercise and some fresh air."

Memory of the walk she enjoyed with Peter came back to Tootie. She remarked to Peter she needed to walk more. Maybe she refused Emma's offer too quickly.

Nora was saying, "If you get some exercise, you might rest better so the rest of us can sleep."

Tootie thought about her restless nights. That was as good a reason to use as any to change her mind. She relented sheepishly, "All right. If you think a walk will help me sleep, I'll give it a try if we don't go too far." She felt she had to add that part. There was just so much she was willing to do in the name of exercise.

"We will not go far," Emma promised.

As they left the house, Emma heard Mammi Nora praise her. "Emma is as dependable as that rooster of hers that crows so loud at daylight to wake us up."

They stopped for Daniel. The reel mower clacked noisily as he rushed by them on another round. The clippings sailed around them and on their shoes, putting the scent of new mowed grass in the air.

Tootie noticed the glinting copper pennies in the fly bags

tacked by the door and windows. "What are all the bags filled with water and pennies for?"

"The flies see their reflection in the water, and the sparkle the pennies make. They will not come past the bag to go in the doors or sit on the windows," Emma said.

Tootie scoffed, "Does that really work?"

"Have you seen many flies in our house?"

Tootie thought a moment. "No, I guess I haven't."

"So there you have it," Emma said. "We can go this way and walk down the lane between the cornfield and the pasture. It is a pleasant walk."

"If you say so," Tootie said, pushing her lower lip out in a doubting pout.

"Look over that way. I hear Daed's tractor coming over the hill. He's planting corn with Dawdi Jim sitting on the fender of the tractor." Emma shaded her eyes with her hand. Tootie did the same thing. When she saw Jim, Tootie waved, and Jim waved back.

Emma said. "I think our farm is one of the prettiest around. I love watching the animals with their young in the pasture. Ahead of us is the hayfield, growing fast. Daed will have the seeds planted soon, and we will be able to row the corn when the plants come up."

Tootie pointed at Noah hoeing in the cornfield. "What is Noah doing?"

"Along the fence at the field gate hole, Noah is planting pumpkin and squash that will vine into the corn. We sell what we raise in our roadside stand in the fall," Emma explained.

"I see," Tootie said as she stepped close to the opposite fence to look at the sheep, cattle and horses in the pasture. A pheasant burst out of the dead grass. With a great flapping rush, the bird soared away and lit beyond the grassy swells strewn with cedars and multiflora rose bushes. The elderly lady hurried back by Emma. "Gracious sakes! That scared me."

"Pheasants do have a way of surprising us. All the other birds that live around us are back from their winter home," Emma pointed out. "See the red wing blackbirds in the trees. If you watch, you might see cardinals, mourning doves and blue birds."

"That's nice, Dear." Tootie said, sounding like she was trying to appease. Huffing and puffing, she had all she could do to keep up. Emma chose to ignore her until they reached the hayfield gate hole. "This is the end of the lane."

"Good! Can we go back to the house now?" Tootie squeaked. Her face had turned a fire engine red.

"Sure, stop and rest a minute. When we get back, we will have a cold glass of lemonade. How does that sound?"

Tootie's head shot up. "Is it homemade? I don't like canned or bottled lemonade."

"My lemonade is homemade. I would not drink any other kind," Emma declared.

In the kitchen, Emma was pouring the lemonade around the table when she heard hooves on the driveway. She pushed the bushy parsley plant pot over so she could look out the window. "Hallie, Peter Rogies stopped in front of the house. You said he was here this morning, ain't so?"

"Jah, he wants to talk to your dad. He did say he'd be back. I just didn't expect it to be this soon," Hal said, getting up from the table. "I'll go talk to him." She met the man on his way to the house. "Afternoon, Peter. What can I do for you?"

The screen door squeaked. Hal looked back. Tootie was edging up behind her.

"I want to see John Lapp," Peter said hoarsely.

"John's in the field. He will be here in time to milk," Hal said. "Would you like to come in for some of Emma's lemonade? We were about to have a glass."

"Nah! You tell John he might as well quit avoiding my visits. I will catch up with him sooner or later." Peter looked over Hal's shoulder at Tootie and nodded before he walked back to his buggy.

The elderly woman stared at the leaving buggy. Hal fleetingly wondered what was running through her aunt's head, before her mind shifted back to Peter. From what John said about him, she worried that Peter soon might not be capable of finding his way home.

The next morning, John sat down at the table. "Aendi Tootie had a good night."

Hal agreed, "Not a peep out of her."

Emma winked at her father. "It wonders me how a long walk can help someone get a gute night's sleep.

When John and Jim were going to the tractor, Peter Rogies drove in. John greeted, "Morning, Peter. How are you doing?"

"Have been better," Peter said shortly. He glared sullenly at John as his horse pawed the driveway with a restless hoof.

Finally, John cleared his throat and spoke. "Hal said you stopped to see me when I was in the field. What can I do to help you?"

"I want you to give back the post hole digger I loaned you last year. I think you have borrowed it long enough, ain't so?" Peter demanded in an acid tone.

"I did not borrow your post hole digger. It must have been someone else. I have always had my own," John said calmly.

"If that is true where is your digger," Peter retorted testily.

"In the tool shed. Have not used it for some time. My fences are all in gute shape as you can see," John declared. He was suddenly grateful the boys fixed the pasture fence before Peter had a chance to see the mess it was in.

"Can I see the digger?" Peter demanded.

"Jah, but will you recognize your own if you saw it. I thought diggers all look alike," John said, trying to reason with the man.

"Mine has a nick in one of the handles about half way down. I will know it when I see it," the old man said.

"Get down and come to the tool shed with me."

The two men went to the shed with Jim following them. John opened the door, stepped in and looked around. He spotted his digger in a far corner, picked it up and held it outside the door for Peter to inspect.

The old man looked up and down the wooden handles and ran his crooked fingers over them. "You sure you did not sand the nick out?"

"Nah, Peter. I did not," John declared.

"And is this the only post hole digger in there?" Peter looked around John to search the insides of the shed for himself.

"Jah, You can see that. This is the only digger I have," John said solemnly.

"Someone must have stole my digger. I will go home and tell my son to help me hunt the man who stole from us," Peter said angrily. "Gute day to you." He hesitated when he saw Tootie swaying back and forth in the porch swing. He walked past his buggy and across the yard to the edge of the porch.

He took off his straw hat and smiled. "Morning, Dolly."

"Morning, Peter. It's a beautiful day," Tootie replied softly.

"It is that. Praise the Lord."

Tootie patted the swing seat. "Would you like to sit with me a spell and visit?"

Peter shook his head no and blurted out, "Would you like to go for a ride with me?"

Tootie's heart beat faster in her chest as she smiled at him. "Where would we go?"

"It is pretty on Bender Creek Road this time of year. I like to drive there all the time like we used to do," Peter suggested.

Tootie bit her bottom lip as she felt completely discombobulated. *The local Amish Lover's Lane.* She wanted to say yes so badly to go for a nice ride with Peter. If he had picked anywhere but there. "I guess not today. I'm needed here to help Hallie. Maybe some other time."

Peter trudged back to his buggy, climbed in and snapped the lines over his horse's back and took off out of the driveway.

Jim scratched a sideburn. "What do you make of that, John?"

John couldn't help the sadness he felt when he thought of the good, hard working man Peter once was. "The poor old man does not know what he is doing anymore. I hope Cooner Jonah can convince him their digger was not stolen. No one would do that."

"No, I mean what do you think about Peter talking to Tootie? Wonder what is up with that? They talked so low I couldn't hear what they said, but they sure looked friendly," Jim marveled.

John shrugged. "Do not know what that was about."

"Guess we better go to the field now," Jim said.

"Jah, mer muss hoi mache, wann die sunn scheint," John said, heading toward the tractor.

Jim stepped faster to catch up. "You lost me there."

John sat on the tractor seat. While Jim climbed up, he grinned at his father-in-law. "I said I need to make hay while the sun shines." As John pulled the corn planter through the field, he said, "So you did not have any trouble with your horse yesterday in town."

"I didn't say that," Jim replied.

John gave him a sharp look. "You did have trouble?"

"Nothing Daniel and I couldn't handle," Jim said with a shrug.

"You want to tell me about it?"

"Might as well as long as Nora doesn't get wind of it. I just hate to admit that horse is smarter than me," Jim said. "Mike untied his lead rope from the hitch racks at the stores and took off without us. We were on foot a couple times until we found him."

"No wonder you were longer coming home than the women thought you should be," John said with a chuckle.

"The first time the sheriff took us to where the buggy was parked on Main Street. He acted like I was peculiar for owning a buggy or something. The horse untied himself again at the grocery store. I was hating to call the sheriff again when Bishop Bontrager happened to come along. He helped us find the horse and buggy that time. Would you believe he stopped in the tree nursery rows?"

"That so?"

"You must have tied the knot different when you tied Mike to your fence. He didn't get away once while he was tied there. Reckon you could teach me a knot to use that my horse can't figure out how to untie? I'd like to go to town and know he's going to be where I leave him. That was embarrassing, being a foot like that," Jim said.

"I can do that," John said, trying not to laugh again.

"Fine, and whatever you do, don't let this slip to Nora. That woman would never let me live it down if she found out. Once she started in on me, Tootie would side with her. They would make my life miserable."

"I will not say a word," John declared.

Chapter 9

That evening, fourteen years old Andy Zook, drove in to pick up Noah, Daniel and their dog. The boys had been watching at the window, more than ready to leave with him. When Daniel placed Biscuit in the back of the buggy with Andy's dog, the older, territorial black hound growled at Biscuit. Daniel snatched up the pup and sat with his back to the growling hound. It was hard to keep Biscuit from wiggling out of his arms, but he wasn't about to turn him loose. Andy's dog acted like he'd whip Biscuit if he could get at him.

They drove down Bender Creek Road and came upon several buggies parked by a small clearing on the edge of the timber. As the three boys and their dogs walked to meet the others, the chilly night breeze carried spring fragrances of dogwoods and wild plum thickets.

A dozen boys stood around with a flashlight in one hand, and a rope tethered to their dogs in the other. The dogs sniffed at each other and growled. When the boys jerked on the ropes to distract the dogs, the hounds leaped and pulled against the ropes. They huffed for breath when the ropes tightened around their necks, eager to run through the timber. Most of the dogs were seasoned hunters wanting to try out their trailing and treeing skills.

Biscuit didn't understand what was going on. He moved close by Daniel's leg, licked his dangling hand and whined for protection.

Johnnie Mast elbowed Benny Gingerich. "Look at the Lapp hound. Ain't the little fellow something?"

"Little young to be coon hunting, ain't so?" Benny said to Noah.

"We know that, but we have to start training him by letting him run with the other dogs," Noah explained.

"Do not make fun of the pup," Jimmie Miller defended. "He is out of my gute hound and will make a gute coon hound."

"So what is the plan?" Andy Zook said to the group.

Johnnie Mast spoke up. "We should spread out in a line, turn our dogs loose and take off after them."

Matthew Stoll stepped out of the group with a twenty two rifle cradled in his arms. "I think spreading out is a gute way to do it. Quite a few of us here."

Noah frowned. "Matthew, why the rifle? This is not open season on coons. We should not shoot them."

"I know it. Thought there might be a reason we would need protection. I heard a mountain lion has been seen in the area. I do not want to walk into one and not be able to defend myself," Matthew excused.

"Just make sure you know what you are aiming at. Like you said there is a bunch of us here in the dark," Andy Zook warned.

They scattered out and turned their dogs loose along Bender Creek. The boys and dogs made a tremendous rustling noise, tramping in the deep leaves. Hidden branches crackled and popped under the many feet.

After they were by themselves, Daniel listened for any noise he couldn't tell what was. He whispered to Noah, "Not much chance of a mountain lion sticking around with all this noise, ain't so?"

"Nah," Noah agreed. "But Matthew was just using that as an excuse to carry his rifle."

With wide eyes, Daniel glanced around their surroundings. "We are sure that a Sneak Upon has not followed Dawdi Jim from up north and is hiding behind a tree, ain't so?"

"Daniel, you should not let your imagination get the better of you, or we will never be able to concentrate on teaching Dog how to coon hunt," Noah scolded. "We better catch up to the pup so we do not lose him."

Biscuit put his head down, trailing in front of them. Occasionally, his head perked up, his ears wiggled and his nose twitched, trying to pick up certain scents in the air.

Noah said, "He sure does act like he knows what he is doing."

Ahead of them and off to the side, a hound bayed loud and clear on the trail of a coon. Soon the boys heard the distinctive bawl of a dog's tree bark off to their left.

"Should we see what's going on?" Daniel asked.

"Nah, we need to keep following Dog," Noah said.

Suddenly, Biscuit woofed and froze in his tracks. He stared straight ahead. His body turned rigid. His head went up, and his nose wiggled as he sniffed the air. Suddenly, he charged the gooseberry thicket in front of them.

As Biscuit fought his way into the brambles, a throaty growl shattered the darkness, warning the dog to stay away. Biscuit was more curious than scared. He dove into the middle of the thicket, bawling a challenge.

Noah and Daniel raced to his aid, whooping for the dog to come to them. Daniel cried in delight, "Dog has already found himself a coon."

"Sure sounds like it," Noah replied. "But a coon can whip that pup. We got to get him out of there."

Too late! The sounds of a fight broke out. Biscuit whimpered and yelped during the loud thrashing in the bushes. Growls and deep hisses came from a cornered animal. By the time the boys reached the edge of the thicket, the dog came crashing out of the bushes and raced at them. He ran into Noah and knocked him down. Biscuit picked himself up. He shivered and whined by Noah's side, licking the boy's face.

Daniel grabbed the dog and held him. "Are you hurt, Boy?" Biscuit whimpered and snuggled close for protection.

"You are not worried about me, ain't so? I am the one that

took a tumble," groused Noah.

"You look all recht to me so get up," Daniel said and put his attention back on their dog.

On the backside of the thicket, the coon crashed out of the gooseberry bushes and rustled dry leaves. Daniel stuttered, "Noah, we – we better run for it. That coon Dog cornered was too big for him or us to handle if it is mad enough to fight ."

"Nah, listen. He is running away from us," Noah reasoned.

"Gute. We better get back out on the road and shine our flashlight on Dog. He is trembling something awful. He may be hurt," Daniel fretted.

In the flashlight's glow, Noah examined the scratches around the pup's face. "Not very deep but those rips in his hide were caused by sharp claws. That is for sure."

"Think that run in will scare Dog enough he will not want to hunt again," Daniel worried.

"Nah, hunting is bred into a coon hound. He will be all right once he gets a little age to him." Noah added, "And wiser. Next time, he might not tackle a coon if he finds one on the ground."

Two of the boys burst out of the underbrush and rushed to them. Andy Zook asked, "That little pup find a coon? We heard you whoop."

Daniel stood taller as he elbowed Noah and whispered, "I'm going to pull one on Matthew for saying there was a mountain lion in these parts." He said to the boys, "We have had a time of it over in that gooseberry thicket. This dog of ours cornered himself that mountain lion."

"Surely not!" Andy looked doubtful.

"Did you see that cat for yourself?" Matthew Stoll asked disbelievingly.

Noah said, "Just shine your light on this dog's face. See the scratches if you do not believe us."

"What happened?" Bennie asked, curious for their story.

"Our dog stood right up to that cat and ran him off. If I was you guys, I would get out of the timber. It was too dark to see which way that old lion went when he ran off," Daniel boasted.

Andy Zook said, "We have made enough racket to scare the

coons into hiding. We might as well call it a night." He turned toward the timber, cupped his hands around his mouth and hollered, "Come on in. Time to go home."

The next morning while the women fixed breakfast, Emma said, "I am going to clean the school for the free will supper and air it today. Anyone want to come along?"

Tootie said, "Not me. I can't breathe when I'm in musky places. Just remember to get all the spider webs down before Mr. Yoder has a chance to see how the school looks. Otherwise, you will be the object of his next church sermon."

That tickled Emma. "Gute idea, Aendi Tootie. I will do that."

"I'd love to go with you," Nora said. "I'd like to see where you teach school, and I'll help clean."

"Gute," Hal said. "You two go do that. Aunt Tootie can go shopping with me this afternoon and help me cook supper. We need to go to the grocery store."

At breakfast, John asked, "How did the coon hunt go last night?"

"Not bad for Dog – uh – uh – the dog's first time," Noah stammered.

"He was ready to quit and come home after he tangled with a coon and got scratched up in the gooseberry bushes," Daniel said before he put the bite of sausage in his mouth. He garbled, "Mama Hal." Daniel chewed and swallowed the food in his mouth with Hal frowning at him "Our dog might need some nursing this morning. Could you look at him?"

Hal frown turned to displeasure. "You took that little dog out hunting and let him get hurt first thing. What kind of nursing?"

"Just some scratches on his face from the briers and maybe the coon's claws," Noah told her. "They did not look real bad, but we do not want the scratches to get infected."

"I'll look at Biscuit as soon as we have the kitchen work done," Hal said.

Daniel kept wiggling as he ate his breakfast and continually rubbed a spot under his left arm pit. He took the last bite of his eggs, chewed and swallowed as he rubbed the area again. "Mama Hal, I have a sore I would like you to look at. I can not see it gute."

"All right. If you are done with breakfast how about you and I go look at it," Hal said. She led the way through the living room to the clinic. "Unbutton your shirt." Daniel did as she directed and raised his arm. "Oh my."

"What is it?" Daniel asked in alarm.

"You picked up a tick in the timber when you were coon hunting. It's infected. The tick's head is still in the bite. You must have broken the body off when you kept rubbing the sore. Sit at the table. I need to get a pair of tweezers and some disinfectant."

Daniel sat down in a chair while Hal gathered what she needed. "Now lift your arm and hold still."

"This is going to hurt, ain't so?" Daniel worried.

"Not much worse then that sore is hurting you now. That tick head has to come out of there, or the sore will become much worse," Hal told him.

She used an alcohol pad on the red area and dug in with tweezers. Daniel puckered his lips and made a sucking sound. "Hold still. Got it." She showed the head to the boy. "Now I'll put some iodine on the sore." She used a Q-tip to swab the area. The boy let out a hissing sound when the cold iodine smarted on the raw spot. "You remind me to look at this at bedtime and tomorrow morning. I'll need to treat it with iodine for a while. From now on if you're going to be spending time in the timber, you and Noah look each other over really well when you get home. Catch the ticks before they make a sore like this. Ticks can make you very sick. If you start feeling bad you let me know right away. Dr. Burns will have to prescribe you some medicine to take.

"All recht," Daniel agreed half heartedly.

"I'm serious, Daniel. You don't want to be sick from a tick bite. Besides, I'd prefer you didn't let them get loose in the house with Redbird and Beth crawling on the floor. Not to mention what would happen to Aunt Tootie if one crawled on her." She put a bandaid over the area. "Now you are gute to go. See you at dinner."

The men went to do chores, and Tootie washed dishes. When Hal came back from doctoring Daniel, she started scraping plates as fast as she could. Tootie smiled smugly. She was sure she wouldn't have any trouble beating Hal this time since taking care of Daniel delayed her.

Emma watched the two of them compete as she wiped. She hated to see Hal fret over Aunt Tootie washing the slop pail. It just didn't seem fair that Aunt Tootie would get out of doing it time after time.

Emma came up with a plan. She scrutinized the dishes and silverware as she dried them. She declared to Tootie a plate wasn't clean and a glass. She put them back in the water for Tootie to redo.

A spoon Emma tossed into the water clattered noisily against the side of the pan. Tootie's lips tightened as she flinched. Emma kept slowing her down, but she didn't want to object and hurt Emma's feelings. After all, she didn't get a good enough look at the dishes and silverware to dispute the girl's claims.

Emma relaxed when she saw Hal rush across the driveway. The back door banged shut. She struggled to keep from giggling when she saw the surprise look on Hal's face. She had beaten Tootie for once.

Hal noted the satisfied expression on Emma's face, but she couldn't figure out what happened to slow Tootie down. It didn't matter at the moment. She marched over to the counter and set the slop pail beside the dish pan. Tootie retained her grumpy silence without one word of objection as she washed the nasty pail.

Chapter 10

"Are we taking the car to go shopping?" Tootie asked hopefully.

"Nah, the buggy works nicely to go to Wickenburg, and using the car is against the Ordnung except in a medical emergency," Hal explained.

"Can't you bend the rules once in awhile?" Tootie asked.

Hal paused, remembering back to the Lapp family outing to The Old Thrasher Reunion in Mt. Pleasant. "Nah, I tried that once and got into trouble. The bishop won't let me get away with it again.

Help me cook dinner first. We will have plenty of time this afternoon to go to Wickenburg. This morning we need to make bread, and my two little girls can stand a bath."

"Oh dear. I'm not sure I'd know where to start giving a baby a bath. I've never had one you know," Tootie said.

Hal grinned. "A bath?"

"That isn't funny, Hallie! You know I meant a baby," Tootie snapped.

"I'm sorry for teasing you. Giving a bath to a baby isn't that hard if you can keep them in the bath pan, but I'll give you a choice. Do you want to make bread or give baths?" Hal asked.

"I'll make the bread. It's been years since the last time I did it, but I think I'll be all right with that," Tootie said without much confidence.

"The ingredients are in the pantry. The bread bowl is in the cabinet next to the sink, and the yeast container is in the refrigerator. You will have to get a cereal bowl to measure the yeast into. Put a little warm water in with the yeast to get it started working since it's cold." Hal placed one of the bath pans on the table and poured in warm water. She had brought towels and wash cloths to the kitchen earlier.

Beth was crawling close by. Hal scooped her up. "Come here, you. You can be first. See nothing to it, Aunt Tootie. I undress Beth, get her wet all over and suds her down. Then rinse her off."

"Sounds a little like doing dishes," Tootie said as she counted out scoops of flour into the bowl she'd set on the table across from Hal.

Beth splattered Tootie a few times when she slapped the water. Tootie flinched, and Beth giggled. Finally, Tootie moved down to the far end of the table to finish mixing the dough. Hal dried Beth off and dressed her. She put the little girl on the quilt on the living room floor and threw the bath water out the back door.

Once she'd poured clean water in the pan, she said, "I'm coming for you, Redbird." Soon Hal had Redbird bathed and back on the quilt beside her sister. The girls jabbered to each other as Hal went back to the kitchen.

"How are you coming with the bread dough?" Hal asked.

"I already put the bowl on the warming oven. What are we fixing for lunch?"

"I'm thinking we can make a light dinner with soup and cheese sandwiches. Cheese should go good with the fresh bread. We'll do more cooking for supper when everyone is here," Hal said. "How about potato soup and toasted cheese sandwiches?"

"Sounds good to me."

Tootie peeled and diced the potatoes. Hal chopped up an onion and watched the clock. "I think it's time to punch down the bread dough and put it in two loaf pans. You do that, and I'll put the potatoes and onion in a kettle to cook."

104

While Hal was busy starting the soup, Tootie kneaded the dough. She greased two loaf pans, divided the dough between them and put the loaves back on the warming oven and covered them with a dish towel.

"Aunt Tootie, how about a cup of tea or coffee while we take a break?" Hal asked.

"Tea would be nice," Tootie decided, sitting down.

They listened to the soup simmer. After a while, Tootie lifted the lid and stuck a potato cube with the fork. "The potatoes are cooked enough to add the milk, salt and butter now."

After the soup simmered a little longer, Hal got out two spoons. She handed one to Tootie. "Taste the soup and see if it needs anything."

Tootie tasted and smacked her lips. "Put in more salt." She stared in the kettle as Hal measured the salt and dumped it in. Tootie tasted again. "The soup tastes sort of bland. Maybe we should add something to it."

"How about sausage? We have patties canned in the basement," Hal suggested.

"That sounds good," Tootie agreed.

"I'll go get the jar while you put the bread in the oven to bake. That way the loaves should be done just before the men come," Hal said.

Tootie watched the bread closely and took the loaf pans out to cool while Hal set the table. When they heard the men's voices, Hal said, "Aunt Tootie, bring me the cheese and butter from the refrigerator." She dumped one of the loaves on a plate. It was only half the size of Emma's, and so was the other one. *Aunt Tootie must not have put enough flour in,* was Hal's thought.

Hal sawed through the crust with a serrated knife. The bread was dense, but she kept going. Something was wrong. She didn't know what, but she didn't have time to figure it out. The men were washing their hands. She had to get dinner on the table. Hal spread the butter on the slices, laid on cheese, and put on another slice. She placed the sandwiches in two buttered iron skillets to brown.

As the men sat down, Hal placed the soup kettle in the middle of the table and the platter of sandwiches beside John. He said the prayer. "I come before you in the name of Jesus Christ our king. Bless this family and the cooks that prepared our food, and bless me so that I can do your will. Amen."

John filled his bowl and pushed his spoon around in the soup, inspecting what whirled to the surface.

Jim wandered why. The boys ate from their bowls as if they hadn't eaten breakfast, but he decided maybe he should do the same thing John did. He leaned over and whispered, "What are we looking for?"

John whispered back, "If you did not find anything that should not be in potato soup it should be all right to eat." John bit into his sandwich. It seemed stale, but maybe Hal had over toasted it. He ate without comment.

After the men left for the field, Tootie and Hal rushed through cleanup so they could leave for town. Hal scraped the dishes and pans and set them beside the dish pan. She reached for a small bowl on the counter to empty it. It was full of a murky brown substance. Hal stared into the bowl. "Fudge! Aunt Tootie, you forgot to put the yeast in the bread dough."

"I did? I wondered why the loaves didn't double in size," Tootie said. "Well, it's all your fault."

"Why is that?"

"You had to give me all that unnecessary information about how to bathe the girls all the time I was trying to mix the bread. It's a wonder I didn't forget to put in more than yeast," Tootie scolded.

Hal opened her mouth to complain but decided it wasn't worth it. After all, this was Aunt Tootie. She set the slop pail back in the mudroom and dried the dishes. She'd add to the pail after supper and empty it.

Tootie stepped out on the front porch and watched for Hal. An open buggy slowed down and turned in. Peter was coming back again. *I hope he isn't going to invite me to take a drive in Lover's Lane again. Anywhere else would be good when I have time, but not today when I'm going shopping with Hallie.*

Peter parked by the house. He slowly stepped down and trudged toward her with a shuffling gait. *He doesn't look happy. Maybe I shouldn't tempt him. I'll go inside out of sight until Hallie comes with the buggy.* Tootie placed her hand on the screen door handle.

Peter said, his voice raised and irritated, "You come here, Dolly. Come down here and stand before me. I want to ask you a question."

Tootie froze in her tracks. Her eyes widened as he stalked toward her. *Is he mad at me because I turned down the ride? He must not be used to taking no for an answer.*

"I said to come here, Dolly," Peter's voice was harsh as he pointed a finger down and jabbed at a spot in front of him.

Tootie walked slowly down the steps and stopped about five feet from him. She didn't want to get any closer. "Wh – what is it you want?" She stammered.

"I want you to tell me if John Lapp stole my horse or not. I know I will not get an honest answer from him or his English wife. My horse is missing. I have been told that the horse was seen tied to the road fence over yonder." Peter thrust his thumb over his shoulder toward the fence. "You, my special friend, will not lie to me. I will know if you do."

"John would never take your horse. He's an honest man," Tootie said defensively. What kind of sense did Peter make? He'd driven past one of John's horses tied to the fence when he came before. Now he has decided it was his horse on someone else's say so. Tootie looked toward the side of the barn where Hal was hitching up the enclosed buggy. She wished Hal would hurry up. "Peter, are you mad at me?"

The man's eyes warmed just a little. "I have no reason to be upset with you, Dolly. It is the company you keep that bothers me."

Tootie relaxed, but she didn't want to deal with Peter herself. He wasn't going to leave until he talked to John. This man confused her. She needed someone else to convince him his horse wasn't here. She yelled, "Hallie!"

"Dolly, it will do you no good to yell like that," Peter said, shaking his finger at her. "Just tell me the truth, and I will leave."

Hal rushed around the side of the barn, saw Peter shaking his finger at Tootie and ran toward them. He heard her footsteps behind him and whirled around.

"What's the matter, Peter?" Hal asked in a calm tone, slowing to a walk.

"Was ist letz you ask so innocently. I want my horse that John Lapp stole from me. I have heard my horse was seen tied to your road fence," he said roughly.

Hal paused. *Great! What do I say? If I tell him truthfully that his horse died a long time ago he isn't going to believe me. If he did, it would be all John's fault that his horse died in our care.* "Peter, you can look at our horses behind the barn and see if your horse is there. If he is, John will bring him back to you. Could be the horse broke loose and wandered over here. John may have him penned up behind the barn with our horses. He's been busy in the field and just didn't mention it to me."

"But, Hallie, ..." Tootie started. Hal held up her hand at Tootie. She pouted. *All I wanted to do was remind her that it was one of John's horses Peter saw tied to the fence.*

"I will do just as you say," Peter said. He stalked toward the barn and around the side to look at the horse herd. Hal and Tootie followed him.

Peter shook his head. "I do not see my horse in this herd, but you make sure that John brings him back to me."

"I will do that," Hal assured him.

Peter gave Tootie a weak smile. "Gute bye, Dolly."

After Peter left, Hal helped Tootie step up into the buggy. She carried the little girls out and handed Redbird to Tootie then Beth. Tootie placed them on a buggy blanket behind the front seat. She wasn't in the mood to go shopping now. With her tightly clasped hands in her lap, she stared unseeingly out the window.

Half way to Wickenburg, Hal asked, "You're awfully quiet. Is Peter's visit bothering you?"

"Yes, I just don't know what to make of that man," Tootie

admitted.

"Peter isn't well. He has Alzheimer's disease," Hal told her.

"Oh my! What can be done to help him?"

"The disease isn't curable. It's taking his mind away," Hal said.

Tootie looked away to keep Hal from seeing the tears in her eyes. "He's like two different people, a nice man and an angry man."

"That's the way the disease works on the mind," Hal confirmed.

Tootie turned her sad eyes on Hal. "Tell me about Peter. The nice one, I mean."

"He has been a hard working farmer his whole life. Peter has always been a kind man, but he can't abide a dishonest man. That's why he seems so upset with John lately when he thinks John has taken something from him."

"I can see that upsets him," Tootie agreed.

"Peter called you Dolly. How did he know that's your given name?"

"I told him when we went for a walk after the church service," Tootie shared.

"What do you think of Peter?"

"He's a kind man that loves animals. He has a gentle voice and warm eyes when he's himself," Tootie said softly. She was quiet a few minutes. Finally, she fretted, "Why did you tell Peter he could look at the horses? You knew that horse tied to the fence was John's horse."

"Because in Peter's mind his horse is alive. He'd have thought worse of me if I said the horse died a long time ago. He wouldn't have believed me," Hal said.

Tootie pictured Peter with his arm out Sunday afternoon and the peculiar way he moved his hand around the top wire on the fence. Now she understood. "Does Peter have a dog?"

"He did. The dog died a while back, but Peter still thinks the dog is alive," Hal said. She glanced at Tootie's miserable face. "Why?"

"No reason. What if Peter had picked out one of your horses

and said that one was his. What would you have done?"

"I told him if he found his horse John would bring it home for him. If he had picked out a horse, chances are he'd forget what he did today by tomorrow."

"But if he doesn't forget then what?" Tootie insisted.

Hal looked worried. "I don't have an answer, Aunt Tootie. I did the best I could on the spur of the moment. I didn't want to upset Peter anymore than he already was with us home alone with two babies."

"Would he ever be violent?" Tootie asked, looking alarmed.

"Maybe. It's something to keep in mind with someone like Peter. Talking to a person with Alzheimer's is sort of like play acting to keep the person from being upset. We should go along with whatever Peter says. It's called living in his world, because he can't live in ours any longer," Hal explained. "For a while, bad times will come and go. Sometimes, he can seem like his old self. The one we all think so much of. That was the Peter you took the walk with." Hal glanced over at her troubled aunt. "Right now try not to think about Peter. We should enjoy our shopping trip and the scenery."

It was a fine afternoon to be riding in the country. A beautiful, sunny day with a mild temperature and not much wind. Planting season was in full swing. Amish farmers were tilling fields with great jangling teams. Tootie pointed out a mule team driven by a farmer across the field and marveled. This farming wasn't anything like what she was used to seeing around her home. So very much different from the large machinery the English farmers used.

On a whim, Hal drove into the Walmart parking lot. Normally, she wouldn't spend idle time window shopping, but today she felt Tootie needed a distraction. Something to do that the elderly woman might consider fun. After all, it was her vacation. They walked around in the store, looking at clothes and jewelry.

As they came to the perfume counter, Tootie paused. "Do the Amish like perfume?"

"Ach, I think everyone likes to smell gute. Mostly that's

done by taking a bath, but in your case, no one would mind if you bought perfume," Hal said.

"Help me pick out a bottle. My perfume is almost gone," Tootie said.

"Sure, what fragrances do you like?"

Tootie thought a moment about when she planned to apply this new perfume. "I want a scent that smells like flowers."

"We have plenty to select from. The small bottles in front of the row of large ones are a sample. You can see if you like the way each one smells," Hal said.

When Tootie carried her small sack out to the parking lot, she felt more uplifted. It didn't hurt that she and her niece both smelled terrific from a mixture of perfume samples. The purchase she made was Delightful Rose. She wondered when the time came if she'd have the nerve to apply the perfume. Had she thrown her money away on a pipe dream?

Hal parked on the edge of the grocery store parking lot. Inside, she pulled a cart out of the corral and started down the first aisle. "Aunt Tootie, if you see anything you would like to eat tell me. I'll buy it for you."

"I'm sort of partial to chicken. I like it fried. Prefer the breast," Tootie said shyly.

"We have that already at home," Hal said, looking in the cheese section.

"You have a deep freezer?"

"Deep freezer? Nah." A light bulb went off in Hal's head. "Oh, I see why you asked. Nah, a freezer takes electricity. When we want chicken to eat we go to the hen house, catch and butcher them. If that's what you want for supper, you and I can do that when we get home. We'd only need two fryers so it wouldn't take us long to butcher them."

Tootie sniffed huffily. "You kill Emma's chickens that she is so proud of and eat them?"

Hal stopped the cart so she could look at her aunt. "Jah, nothing wrong with that Aunt Tootie. We do live on a farm you know. Animals are killed all the time for food."

"Oh well, don't do anything *special* on my account. I'm

partial to many other foods so let's see what else we can find," Tootie said, backing down. Softly, she mumbled, "I'll bet Emma's poor chickens sleep with one eye open."

Hal kept going with the cart, smiling to herself.

"Nora makes a sour cream potato dish that we like. She calls it Party Potatoes. I'll bet your family would like it, too," Tootie suggested, catching up with Hal.

"You know what goes in it. We could buy the ingredients and make it for supper," Hal told her.

Tootie thought for a minute. "It's a very simple recipe with mash potatoes, cream cheese, sour cream, garlic, salt and pats of butter on top."

"Sounds easy. Let's find the cream cheese and sour cream. The other ingredients we have at home," Hal said. "This is wonderful. We can fix something new for my family for supper tonight and surprise everyone."

Chapter 11

Hal put the groceries away. Tootie watched closely what came out of the sacks. She questioned, "You bought a roll of cookie dough?"

"I thought we could have chocolate chip cookies for dessert tonight," Hal said. "Would you rather mix up some cookie dough from scratch for me?"

"No, Dear, I guess that roll is sort of like baking and certainly quick," Tootie relented.

Hal brought five tubes of biscuits from the sack and started for the refrigerator.

"You don't make your biscuits from scratch?" Tootie asked.

"Jah, Emma does for breakfast, but I had something else in mind for these," Hal said.

"Well, they are better than nothing, aren't they?" Tootie replied with disdain.

Once Hal emptied the sacks and put them away, she said, "Maybe I should wash up before I start supper. The perfume smells strong on me yet."

"I thought you said no one would mind?"

"I said no one would mind you wearing perfume. I'm not so sure John will be pleased about this much perfume on me," worried Hal.

"You worry too much," Tootie declared. "Don't wash all that good perfume off."

"Well, maybe no one will say anything," Hal relented. "I'll keep my distance from John until bedtime."

Tootie giggled.

Adam Keim knocked on the front door. Hal hollered out the kitchen window, "Come on in, Adam." She went back to the stove and took the lid off a kettle. As she stabbed a chunked potato, Adam appeared in the kitchen doorway and searched the room. "Emma's not here. She took my mother with her to clean the school house this morning. They should be home soon. Dad and John are in the field. Noah and Daniel are planting in the sweet corn patch. You might as well sit down and keep Aunt Tootie and me company until they come home."

Tootie cut the cookie dough and filled a baking sheet. She was almost done when she stopped to look intently at Adam. "Emma said you are a furniture maker. Too bad business is so slow. Otherwise, you would be working instead of sitting around here with us."

Adam looked like he didn't understand.

"That's all right. You can't help it if you don't have customers. It's just we tend to worry about these things you know. You're going to be the provider for our Emma some day," Tootie prattled as she laid the raw cookies in rows.

Hal watched Adam and bit her bottom lip to keep from stopping Tootie. Adam frowned his dislike and started to get up to leave. She said firmly, "Sit down, Adam."

He plopped back in his chair with his hands up in the air as a sign of surrender.

"Very funny," Hal hissed. She came over close to his ear. "If you're a member of this family, you have to endure everything good or bad. That means no leaving me alone with her."

Adam wrote on his notepad. "Unless you adopted me I am not a Lapp yet."

Hal laughed.

Adam wrinkled his nose like a rabbit and sniffed.

"Aunt Tootie and I went shopping today in Walmart and sampled the perfumes. All of them. All right?" Hal asked, daring him to object.

Adam grinned and put his thumb and finger together.

Tootie stopped cutting cookies and looked from one to the other. "What's so funny?"

"Nothing important, Aunt Tootie. Adam just noticed how gute I smelled," Hal said, patting Adam on the shoulder.

Tootie smiled at Adam. " I smell as good at Hallie. We had fun today. Hallie, I filled the cookie sheet."

"Gute job. I'll put it in the oven. The potatoes are ready to mash. The cream cheese is soft. You need to help me put this potato dish together so we can bake it."

Tootie surveyed the counters. "Have you got a kitchen aid mixer somewhere?"

Hal frowned at Adam as he put his hand over his mouth to hide a smile. "Nah, Aunt Tootie. That kind of mixer takes electricity to operate. Is a mixer essential to make this recipe?"

"No, guess not. We have to mix the soft cream cheese and sour cream together in a bowl. If you had a mixer, we would add the potatoes next, but we can mash the potatoes in the kettle and mix everything together. After that, we add the seasonings and put the potatoes in a baking pan."

Hal put a bowl on the table next to the hot kettle. She pulled a hand potato masher out of a drawer and held it up. "Which job do you want Aunt Tootie? Mash the potatoes or mix the cream cheese and sour cream together."

Tootie looked at the potato masher as if Hal had tried to hand her the garden hoe again. Hal got a fork from the silverware drawer, dropped it in the bowl and slid the bowl over by Tootie. "There you go. Mix."

Hal grabbed the kettle from the stove with a couple of pot holders and drained the potatoes. She had the mashing done by the time Tootie had the other ingredients and seasonings mixed.

"Okay, now what?" Hal asked.

"You mix the potatoes in my bowl and pour the whole thing in a baking pan."

Hal did as she was instructed. Once the potatoes were in the large square baking pan, she asked, "That it?"

"Now you have to put pats of butter on top."

"How much? About like a stick?"

"Sounds right I think," said Tootie slowly, trying to rack her brain for the correct amount.

"We make our own butter so I'll just spoon some little mounds over the top." Hal scattered the butter across the creamy potatoes. "How does that look?"

"I've kind of forgotten for sure. Plenty of butter is good. Maybe add a few more spoonfuls to make sure," Tootie said.

As Hal added the extra butter, her head came up. She sniffed the air. "The cookies! We forgot the cookies. Adam, please rescue them."

Adam shot out of his chair, grabbed two pot holders, opened the oven door and brought the tray out. He hurried to the table and plopped the tray down.

Hal said, "How do the cookies look?"

Adam made a circle with his finger and thumb.

"Gute," Hal said with relief.

Tootie sniffed disagreeably as she inspected the baking sheet. "A little too crispy on the bottom for me, but maybe everyone else will eat them."

"That's gute to know since those cookies are our only dessert," Hal snipped as she put the potato pan in the oven.

The rest of the supper was made up of dishes she could cook on top of the stove; canned corn, greens, tomato gravy and biscuits. While she got the pans and a skillet from the cupboard she said to Tootie, "Open the jars for me. The can opener is in the drawer where I got the potato masher."

Tootie stared into the drawer. She looked helplessly at Hal and said in a tiny voice, "What does it look like?"

Adam came to her rescue. He reached into the drawer and handed the opener, with a stiff pointed end for opening juice cans and a hook for opening jar lids, to her. "Thank you, Adam. I'm used to an electric can opener," Tootie excused.

About a half hour later, Hal said, "I smell smoke."

Tootie added, "Something is burning in the oven. Smoke coming out around the door. Oh my, the oven is making an awful sizzling noise."

116

Hal opened the door quickly. "Fudge! What a mess. The melted butter is running over the side of the pan and burning on the oven bottom. What can we do?"

"How about putting a piece of tinfoil in there to catch the butter." Tootie glanced at the clock. "We still have at least fifteen minutes before the potatoes are done."

Hal went to the pantry after the tinfoil. She tore off a large strip and folded it in half. She opened the oven door to place the foil over the burning puddle. Too late. Most of the melted butter had dripped over the edge of the pan. Dense gray smoke rolled out at her. As she shoved the tin foil in, flames ignited in the butter pool. The volcanic smoke cloud darkened to black as it bellowed out and filled the room.

"Adam, help. The oven's on fire," Hal shrieked as she backed up.

Adam grabbed one of the larger pot holders from Hal's hand and batted at the flames.

"Quick, Aunt Tootie, we can't stand breathing this smoke. Open all the windows and doors," Hal ordered. They scurried to let the smoke out. They came back to the kitchen to find smoke smudged Adam, watery eyed and flushed faced, standing in the murky haze, pointing to the shut oven door.

"Adam, are you all right?" Tootie asked, coughing.

Adam shook his head no with his hand over his nose.

"You burnt anywhere?" Hal looked him over as he shook his head no. He handed her the charred and frayed pot holder. "Thank you, Adam. You're a lifesaver. What about you, Aunt Tootie? You have black smudges all over your face. You should wash that off before anyone sees you."

"Your face is as black as mine and Adam's. You both should wash, too," declared Tootie.

In the living room, the little girls belted out angry cries. John and Jim rushed in from the mud room.

"Where is the fire?" John demanded.

"It was in the oven. Adam put it out," Hal said."

"Good thing Adam was here," Jim declared.

Noah and Daniel appeared behind the men. Noah asked, "Is

it safe to come in?"

"The way all that smoke is shooting out of the windows and doors makes the house look like one big chimney," Daniel exclaimed.

The front screen door slammed. Emma yelled, "Everyone all right in here?"

"Where are you?" Nora asked, coughing and waving her hand in front of her face.

"We're in the kitchen," Hal called.

"Poor babies," Nora exclaimed. She picked the little girls up and rushed back outside into the fresh air.

Emma waved her hand in front of her face as she turned in a circle, inspecting the kitchen. "My clean kitchen. It wonders me how it could have come to look like this in the short time I was gone."

"I'm sorry, Dear," Tootie said contritely as if she meant it.

Hal said, "We're going to clean this mess up. Aren't we, Aunt Tootie?"

"Oh yes, I'd be glad to help if I don't catch pneumonia first from breathing in all this smoke." She had a coughing attack just to prove the point.

Suddenly from the living room came more voices. "Is everyone all right in here?" Stella Strutt demanded.

"Do you need our help?" Moses asked. "Should we call the fire department?"

Hal hissed, rolling her eyes to the ceiling "Just what we need for company right now. Moses and Stella Strutt. How cruel is this?"

"I agree," spit out Tootie.

Stella tromped into the kitchen on her swollen feet, waving her hand in front of her face. "Need help?"

"Nah," John said. "Denki, but the fire is out."

"Denki to God, you have the fire out already." Moses looked around. "Where was the fire?"

John pointed to the stove. "In the oven."

The oven was still making protesting sizzles as the last of the butter burnt on the hot bottom. Only a small trickle of gray smoke leaked from around the door.

"What happened?" Stella demanded, pushing the brim of her black bonnet away from her eyes.

Hal and Tootie looked at each other. Finally, Hal answered. "We were just baking a potato dish Aunt Tootie knew about."

"Holy Buckets! The potato casserole! We better get it out of the oven, or it will be over cooked," Tootie said urgently.

Stella gave Tootie a hard look as she and the others parted so Hal could bring the steaming pan to the table.

Holding both little girls, Nora came back to the kitchen. "Tootie!" She exclaimed.

They forgot about Tootie's slip of the tongue as they stared at the cause of the fire. Hal said, "It looks all right."

Tootie frowned. "Maybe a little browner than it should be."

"Might taste like smoke," Jim said.

"That looks just like my Party Potatoes. Is it?" Nora demanded.

Tootie nodded.

"That recipe may never be the same again. You maybe should change the name to Smoky Party Potatoes," Jim said with a chuckle.

Nora elbowed him and nodded at how dejected Hal and Tootie looked from him teasing.

Hal grumped, "Aunt Tootie, this whole thing wouldn't have happened if you had let me stop with the first batch of butter. That last I added was too much."

"Don't blame me. This whole mess was all your fault. The pan you put the potatoes in was too small. If you had gotten out a bigger baking pan, the butter would have stayed in it," huffed Tootie.

Hal's face flushed as she defended herself. "That is the largest pan we have."

John leaned against the wall and stuffed his hands in his trouser pockets as his eyes darted from his wife to her aunt and back to Hal.

Stella Strutt gave one of her finest, loudest, throat clearing noises. Everyone quieted. She faced John. "This is a miracle,

119

John Lapp. A miracle for sure."

"I hardly think a fire in the oven makes for a miracle, Stella. It did not burn the house down," John said dryly.

Jim chuckled. "Maybe that is the miracle."

"I am not talking about the fire," Stella said, ignoring Hal Lapp's English father. "The miracle is how calm you are, John Lapp, when a calamity like this happens. This sort of thing always happens when *she's* around." Stella nodded at Hal accusingly.

"I figure I might as well accept what happens. No need to question what has occurred that I can not change. It is God's will," John said flatly.

"Amen," Stella Strutt said. "Come on, Moses. Time to go. We have inhaled enough smoke. Enough smoke for sure."

Tootie watched the sassy woman leave. "I'm glad she's gone." Her bottom lip jutted out in a pout.

"Now what, Aunt Tootie?" Hal said in her ear.

Tootie whispered, "I was just thinking you don't have to worry about smelling nice anymore. We both smell like chimney swifts."

Emma patted Adam on the arm. "You are all right?" He had a save me look on his face. "We need to get out of here for a few minutes while the smoke clears. Come for a walk with me before I help with supper."

Once they were out in the fresh air, they both took a deep breath.

"Sorry I did not get home sooner. The school house needed more attention than I thought it would. Gute thing Mammi Nora went along to help me," Emma said. "Did you have a gute visit with, Aendi Tootie and Hallie?"

Adam gave her a nonplused squint and wrote, "Are you kidding?"

"Well, I mean other than you having to save the house from burning down," Emma said offhandedly.

Adam grinned. He held up two fingers and put one down.

"Oh, let me guess which one you did not have such a gute visit with. Aendi Tootie?"

Adam nodded agreement.

"Figures. We all have to endure her. Since you will be part of this family you might as well get used to her," Emma said matter of factly.

Adam wrote on his notepad, "That is what Hal told me."

"I have been thinking about our future. Maybe we should decide soon about the wedding," Emma blurted out.

Adam wrote, "You suddenly in a rush before I meet any more of Hal's relatives and change my mind?"

Emma laughed and slapped his arm. "Jah, that is the reason." She turned serious. "What I wanted to say was I turn eighteen in September. I should take the lessons so I can join the church. After that we can set a wedding date."

Adam clapped his hands.

"Not so fast. I would like to teach school one more year," Emma said, watching him for a reaction. "I did not think I would ever say this, but I really enjoyed teaching last year."

Adam wrote, "You can teach after we are married if you want to do it."

"Really? You would not mind," Emma squealed.

Adam shook his head no.

"That is why I love you, Adam Keim," Emma said, giving him a big hug. "Now I should go help cook supper, before we have a repeat disaster. I don't know how I can ever leave Hallie alone in the kitchen. I am gone a day and look what happened." She gave Adam a quick kiss. "Maybe later we can talk about setting the wedding date."

"You worry too much," Adam wrote. "Hal managed while you were at school all day."

"That is true," Emma agreed.

"It was the combination of Hal and her aunt that was the problem. Aendi Tootie will go home soon," Adam assured her.

"Maybe that was it," Emma agreed.

Adam pointed toward the noisy barn. The frustrated Holstein cows, bawling in the confines of the barnyard, competed with the loud hum of the generator that ran the milking machine. The unmilked cows walked straddled legged to line up at the door, wanting relief from udders swollen with gallons of fresh milk.

Emma said, "Milk time. I know. Go!" Adam rushed toward the barn as she yelled after him, "But before you eat supper with me remember to wash your face."

Supper was what it was after all the excitement. The women set all the bowls on the table. John asked that they bow their heads for a silent prayer. Hal worried about what John was going to pray that he didn't want to say out loud. Maybe he was asking God to send her relatives home soon. He finished out loud with, "Amen."

Everyone started passing the bowls and filling their plates. When the greens bowl came to Tootie, she was still out of sorts. She whispered to Nora, "What is this?"

"Greens. They're good for you," Nora declared quietly. "You know like turnip leaves, spinach and polk. Try a spoonful. You can learn to like it. It will grow on you."

"I prefer that eating weeds grows on you if you want to eat this. I'll pass," sniffed Tootie as she handed the bowl on.

Chapter 12

The women were washing smoke off the kitchen walls the next afternoon when the living room door burst open. That startled all of them. They hadn't heard a buggy drive in. Hal's first thought was Peter Rogies was back.

An ashen faced, Jane Bontrager burst into the kitchen. She spoke frantically in Pennsylvania Dutch to Hal and Emma. Emma's hands flew up to cover her cheeks. The looks on the women's faces were enough to tell Nora and Tootie something was very wrong.

"What did she say?" Nora asked Hal as Emma put her arms around Jane to hug her.

Hal explained, "There had been an accident in a nearby field. Something has happened to young Johnnie Mast. He's just ten years old. Something to do with a team of horses. The boy is hurt bad. Jane said it was a horrible sight. Eldon sent her to tell me to come. Mom and Aunt Tootie, you stay with Redbird and Beth while Emma and I go." Hal said to Emma. "We can take the car. Just let me get my nursing bag. You go to the barn and tell the men what has happened. We need your father's help. Dad and the boys can finish milking."

Emma raced to the barn, yelled at her father and rushed to the car. Hal came out the clinic door, carrying her cell phone and the neon green bag with the words *Life Is A Blast* across the front. The words were faded from the bag's use but still a part of Nurse Hal's identity. She called for the ambulance as she raced to the car. With John and Emma in the back seat, Hal drove passed Eldon Bontrager's farm and turned at the intersection to Butcher Ben and Edna Mast's farm.

As they neared the farm buildings, Emma cried, "Pull in. I see the team with farmers around them."

Hal stopped the car behind a row of buggies by the yard fence. Several farmers milled about with Butcher Ben Mast in the middle of them. The team had been unhooked from the harrow, a wicked looking contraption with curved tines designed to tear through the earth. The men frantically tugged at the harrow, unhooking sections. As Hal and Emma approached, the men lifted a section and flipped it back to free the boy.

Wailing sirens in the distance told Hal the ambulance was on the way. Emergency help would get there none too soon to suit her. Every minute counted if the boy was to live.

Johnnie Mast was sprawled on the ground, covered with dirt from sliding along the field under the harrow. He was flat on his back. His clothes were torn and tattered. His face was dirt caked. His nostrils and mouth clogged with dirt. His eyes were open, staring into space. He didn't move at all. He looked dead. Hal knelt beside him and hooked her finger in his nose and mouth to clear the dirt away. She wrapped her hand around his wrist and in a minute said over her shoulder, "He has a faint pulse."

Hovering close by, Emma's eyes filled with tears, thinking about how much she had liked being this little boy's teacher.

The ambulance wheeled in and braked beside the crowd. EMT medics came running full speed from their vehicles with bags and equipment. The Amish men, who had lifted the harrow off Johnnie, quietly stood nearby, waiting to see what would happen next. Some of them had their heads bent in prayer.

Hal and Emma got out of the way. One of the medics nodded at Hal. "How is the boy, Nurse Hal?"

"Daryl, I cleaned the dirt out of his airways as best as I could with my finger. He has a faint pulse."

Another medic, Steve, knelt by the boy. He felt for a pulse and sliced the tattered clothes from Johnnie's body so they could see the wounds. Daryl asked for the boy's name.

His father, Butcher Ben, said, "Johnnie."

Steve called firmly and sharply, "Johnnie, can you hear me?"

The boy was unconscious. The sorrowful and sickened faces of the farmers gathered nearby told Hal they were sure the boy was dead or would be soon.

Johnnie's mother, Edna Mast, walked through the squeaking house yard gate. She took the time to say to her other children to stay in the yard out of the way. She wasn't running, just walking fast. A robust, buxom youngish woman, her face and arms dark from endless hours of toiling in the sun. Barefoot, in a blue dress and a white apron, she approached and introduced herself to the EMTs. The medics shifted slightly to make room for her. She leaned over the crumpled, broken body of her son to called his name and speak to him in Pennsylvania Dutch. "Johnnie, can you hear me? Johnnie, these men are here to help you. Johnnie, please open your eyes."

Hal marveled at how calm Edna was. She didn't show hysteria or tears. It was as if she'd prepared herself long ago for such tragic moments as this. Hadn't Margaret Yoder told Aunt Tootie when the Amish worked with horses as much as they did accidents were bound to happen? Hal knew exactly what would be said by Edna and Butcher Ben whether Johnnie survived or died. It was God's will.

Edna crouched down briefly and wanted to brush her hand on her son's face, but she thought better of that and pulled back so as not to interfere with the medics. She called his name again. Still no response or movement.

The head medic, Daryl, spoke in curt commands. He told a third medic, Ivan, to call for a helicopter. Two-way radios blared. Hal knew how good the medics were, completely focused and professionally efficient. She'd worked with them before.

Ivan brought a small stretcher and blankets. They slid the

stretcher under the boy and continued working feverishly while they waited for the helicopter.

Edna paced with her hands tightly gripped together to keep them from noticeably trembling. She stopped again a few feet from her son. This time she crouched by him with her hand resting on her knee. She called to him. When the boy didn't respond, she kept trying again, and again. "Johnnie! Johnnie!"

More sirens screamed. Wickenburg firemen arrived and cordoned off the area. Hal and Emma moved out of the way and stood by Samuel Nisely, one of the men who helped lift the harrow off the boy.

Hal asked, "Samuel, do you know what happened?"

Samuel quietly murmured his story. "Jah, I was working in my field that adjoined the Mast farm. I saw Johnnie driving the team, standing on the evener. The last time I looked, I didn't see Johnnie on the evener. He wasn't on the ground behind the harrow. All I saw was just the horses plodding across the field toward the gate hole. I recht away knew what happened and rushed to stop them. By the time I got to the team, they had walked through the gate hole and stopped by the barn. The horses hadn't run away. They didn't realize Johnnie wasn't driving them.

Somehow, Johnnie bounced off the evener and got caught in the harrow's teeth. The horses dragged him probably an eighth of a mile. When I got to Johnnie his left leg was bent backward and snapped in two. Luke Yoder was going by so I ran out to the road. I told him to get some men to help get the harrow apart and to send someone to get you."

With sirens ringing across the land, farmers stopped what they were doing. They were directed to where the action was by the strobe lights and fire trucks parked on the road at the Mast farm. The farmers came to see if they needed to help. The small crowd was cordoned across the road a good hundred feet away.

Hal marveled at Edna and Butcher Ben's composure as they watched the medics work. Their calmness came from the depths of their quiet strength and faith in God. They were from generations of tough independent people born to the land, stoic forthright people who tilled the soil and lived fruitful lives of quiet simplicity. They accepted adversity, affliction and tragedy without question as God's will. They died as they had lived, close to the earth that had sustained them.

While Edna stayed close to Johnnie, Butcher Ben stood silently watching with his oldest son, Eli Mast and Eli's wife, Mary, by his side. Butcher Ben didn't call his son's name as his wife did. From some deep untaught prompting, the two of them knew the boy might hear his mother's voice when all others were lost to him.

Time seemed frozen, but minutes did pass. There was no doubt in everyone's mind that the boy was dead except for his mother. She hadn't given up hope yet. Edna Mast bent slightly forward, and calmly called her son repeatedly. She spoke cheerfully and forcefully, as if rousing him out of bed at sunrise. "Johnnie, Johnnie, speak to me! Johnnie, these men are here to help you. Johnnie, do you want to go on a helicopter ride? The helicopter is coming! Please, Johnnie, wake up!"

Her voice was the only sound, except for the curt, intense voices of the medics, and the occasional jolting blare of the two-way radios. "The helicopter is about to land, Mrs. Mast," EMT Daryl, warned, wanting her to know her time with her son was about up.

Edna nodded she understood and continued to call her son. Somewhere, from the subconscious reaches to where his soul had slipped, the boy heard the echoes of his mother's voice. He stirred faintly. She had called him back.

He had been totally unresponsive. It was probably about thirty minutes, from the time the men reached him and freed him from the harrow's teeth, but it felt like an eternity to all those watching the scene unfold.

The medics realized Johnnie was stirring before anyone else as they knelt beside him. They continued working feverishly to strap him onto the stretcher, placed an oxygen mask on his face and attached tubes.

Johnnie suddenly emitted a piercing wail of pain and terror.

He was awake, and feeling the excruciating pain from his shattered leg and other injuries. His mother crouched down and spoke to him to comfort him.

The throb of the helicopter warbled in everyone ears as it flew from the east, and circled the field. It swooped down and landed, directed by the firefighters who had pushed all the neighbors back some more. The door opened. Two medical personnel leaped out before the propeller blades stopped. They bent low as they braced themselves in the swift air currant and raced to the boy.

As the men transported him to the chopper, Hal spoke to words of comfort to Edna, and asked Mary Mast if she was feeling all right. Stress was not good for this very pregnant young mother. John offered his help to Butcher Ben and Eli if they need work done while they spent time at the hospital. Emma talked to the other Mast children, all students of hers. After that, the Lapps walked to the car to leave as all the others had. Neighbors had done all they could. As Hal, Emma and John got in the car, the chopper lifted off, made a wide circle over them and aimed east toward the Wickenburg hospital.

Chapter 13

On Wednesday evening, John and Jim hitched up their buggies and loaded the family to go to Peter Rogies's birthday party. Tootie stepped up into John's buggy. She sat down in back by Daniel and smoothed out her dark blue dress. It was tempting to take a deep breath to see if she could smell roses, but she resisted. The last thing she wanted to do was call attention to herself. She just hoped she hadn't applied one squirt too many.

Emma smiled approvingly. "Aendi Tootie, that is a pretty fer gute dress."

"Thank you, Dear," Tootie said, pleased that the girl noticed.

Jim invited Noah to ride with him as he tried out his sorrel horse one more time. If all went well tonight, he wanted to somehow or other manage to convince Nora to ride with him again.

Adam and Emma took up the rear of the possession in Adam's buggy. Adam wrote on his notepad. "Tell me about what happened at the Mast farm. He settled back in the seat and tilted his head toward her to give her his undivided attention.

Emma said tearfully, "I could hardly stand seeing how torn up and broken that poor boy was. I pray that he lives so I can teach him another year."

Adam patted her hand. Emma took a deep breath and filled

him in about Johnnie's accident.

The Rogies family, Cooner Jonah, Anna and their five children, came out on the porch and waited for the Lapp family to get out of the buggies. "Wilcom," Jonah called.

As the women went up the porch steps to greet Anna and her four daughters, Cooner Jonah and his son, David, came down to get a closer look at Jim's courting buggy. "You got yourself quite a buggy there," Jonah offered.

"Thanks, I'm sure enjoying it," Jim said, handing the lines to Noah so he could park the buggy behind John's buggy.

"Looks familiar," Cooner Jonah commented.

"Enos Yutzy's son, Eli, owned the buggy," John supplied.

"Sad thing that," Cooner Jonah said. He held his hand out to shake Adam's hand. "Wilcom, Adam. Glad you could come."

Jim said to John, "My sorrel did all right following you."

"I noticed that," John replied. "That is gute."

The night air had a spring freshness to it. The peepers were in full voice, and the bull frogs croaked on the pond bank in the Rogies pasture.

The boys took off for the old brooder house where David kept his coon dog and his father's old red hound, Mose. They conjured up stories about what was in store for them in the late fall when they took their hounds hunting.

"A pleasant evening for a birthday gathering," John said, sitting down in a chair on the porch.

"Jah, that it is," Cooner Jonah agreed as he lit the lanterns attached to the porch posts.

Jim and Adam nodded agreement as they sat down.

The men waited while the women cranked the ice cream maker and cut the cake. As the women chit chatted, men crossed their legs, placed their crossed arms over their laps and stared out into the darkness.

John said, "You hear what happened to Johnnie Mast this afternoon?"

"Nah," Cooner Jonah said.

So John filled Cooner Jonah in on the accident. Cooner Jonah said, "So that is why the helicopter flew over. We must pray for Johnnie to be well soon."

"It will take a lot of praying from the looks of those wounds," John said.

For awhile, the men sat in silence, contemplating poor little Johnnie Mast then Cooner Jonah switched gears. He started chuckling to himself.

John said, "What's so funny? Let the rest of us in on it."

"I was just thinking about what Bill Hershberger told me the last time I met up with him at the salebarn. You ever hear him talk about the good potato crops he raises?"

"Sure, he always boasts more about it than he should. When I asked him once what he put on the ground to get a gute crop like that all the time he would not tell me," John said.

Cooner Jonah said, "He would not tell Samuel Nisely, either. I was close the other day, listening. Actually, he's too boastful for my taste, too. When Samuel asked how his potato crop was last year, Bill said his fields were so chock full of potatoes you could hear them grumbling when you put your ear on the ground. 'Roll over. You are crowding me,' the potatoes said.

Bill stuck his thumbs under his gallouses, reared back and told Samuel, 'Once a greenhorn asked me for a hundred pounds of potato. I set him straight real fast. I do not believe in cutting into one of my potatoes. You buy the whole potato, or you take your business elsewhere."

Jim chuckled.

Adam slapped his knee.

"What did Samuel say?" John asked, grinning.

Cooner Jonah replied, "He was not sure if Bill was serious or not. Finally, he told Bill he'd heard all he needed to know. He guessed he was too much of a weakling to start raising potatoes like that. More power to Bill for being so brave. While Bill looked puzzled, Samuel winked at me and walked away."

The men laughed.

"You have some good story tellers down here. We talked to a fellow the other day at the salebarn that had me convinced he keeps his girlfriend by herself in a room in his house. Turned out to be his horse," Jim said.

Cooner Jonah chuckled. "You met Ben Krayman I take it?"

"Jah," John replied.

Cooner Jonah said, "Ben pulls that joke on every newcomer he can find."

Not to be outdone, Jim had a story of his own. "We got a fellow just about like your potato farmer living in the next county over from me. He's always bragging about raising better corn crops than the rest of us. A farmer that lives next to me said he met up with this guy in town. He made the mistake of asking the man how his corn crop turned out last fall. We had a summer drought so it was a concern to most farmers that the corn might have suffered some.

The guy claimed he sent his son, Wilbur, to check on the growth of their corn. Wilbur wasn't a tall lad, so he took a ladder with him. When he found a stalk of corn that seemed taller than the others, he leaned the ladder against it and climbed up until he could reach the top joint. From there, he proceeded up the stalk to the top and looked out over the field. There was enough corn for a rich harvest Wilbur figured.

He started back down the corn stalk. He realized suddenly that it had kept growing while he was at the top. He stepped from joint to joint, but it grew so fast he never had time to reach the ladder. He froze right where he was, afraid of falling.

Wilbur's father said he wondered what was taking the boy so long to come back. He knew there was no use in hunting for him in that tall corn, so he climbed to the top of the windmill to look. He saw his son's predicament soon enough, and gathered the neighborhood men to help him. They tried to chop down the cornstalk, but the cornstalk was growing so fast eighteen inches separated every chop. Finally, they gave up. Wilbur was forced to stay on the cornstalk until the drought came, and the corn finally stopped growing."

The boys had perched on the edge of the porch, dangling their feet. They giggled at the stories.

Cooner Jonah took the opportunity to say, "I hear tell you Lapp boys have a tale of your own about the coon hunt."

Noah and Daniel looked serious.

John asked, "Something happen I did not hear about?"

Cooner Jonah said, "Heard that coon hound pup of theirs tangled with something bigger than he was, and he lost. Came back all scratched up."

Noah and Daniel turned away as their father said, "Ach, you mean when Biscuit went into the gooseberry thicket. He will learn what to stick his nose into and what not to as he gets more experienced."

"Expect he will," Cooner Jonah agreed with a chuckle.

David, said to Noah, "Biscuit? That your dog's name?"

"That is just what Mama Hal calls our dog," Noah excused softly.

"Right," Daniel said. "We call him Dog."

"Unhuh," David said, grinning at them.

"Go over to the dawdi house and see what is keeping your dawdi,"Cooner Jonah said to his son. "He should be here with his company for his birthday celebration."

The boys took off on the run. Noah and Daniel were eager to get away before John came up with more questions about the coon hunt. The boys came back with Peter shuffling along beside them. The elderly man sat down in the chair Cooner Jonah reserved for him. Without a word of greeting to the company, he crossed his legs and stared into space.

Cooner Jonah whispered to John, "Look at Daed. He has gruddel vullahs woolly lumps in his beard. He forgot to wash his face."

John said, "Jah, but it is gute to know that he is drinking milk which is gute for him even if he did snag onto a few lumps." He leaned around Cooner Jonah. "Nice evening, ain't so, Peter?"

"Sure is, Charlie," Peter replied.

John looked confused.

Cooner Jonah whispered, "He thinks you are his brother."

Anna came to the screen door. "You can come in now. The ice cream is ready, and the cake is cut."

They all gathered around the table. Hal made sure to get the place next to Peter on his right side so she could observe him.

133

While the others were taking seats, he patted the table on his left. "Dolly, here is your chair." Peter smiled warmly at her.

Tootie flushed at the attention as she sat down.

When the elderly man peered in Hal's direction, she smiled. He gave her a blank look. Hal said, "Happy birthday, Peter."

Suddenly, Peter's eyes widened as if he was seeing her for the first time. "Denki, Sara."

Anna set the first bowl heaped with ice cream and a large slice of cake down in front of Peter. She whispered to Hal, "His wife was Sara.

Hal nodded that she understood. It was clear how confused Peter had become. He thought she was his wife, but he selected Tootie to sit on his left which should have been reserved for his wife if she was alive.

Anna and her girls served the cake and ice cream and sat down. They bowed their heads for a silent prayer then they all sang *Happy Birthday* to Peter.

The elderly man surely didn't like icing. It was true a great plenty of the powdered sugar kind was heaped on the white cake. Hal noticed Peter scraped as much of the icing onto his spoon as he could. He stared at his spoon, wondering what to do to clean the it so he could eat his cake. He swiped the spoon under the bottom of his saucer and left most of the icing on the tablecloth.

That's one way to get out of eating sweet icing. Wonder what Anna will say when she picks up that saucer? It ran through Hal's mind as she observed Peter, *Anna's probably used to Peter doing strange things.*

"The cake is delicious, Peter. You're lucky to have a good cook like Anna in your family," Tootie said.

"I am. Maybe we can talk her into baking you a birthday cake, Dolly. Your birthday is not too far from mine," Peter replied.

"We'll see," Tootie said as she took a dainty bite of ice cream. She picked up her paper napkin and waved it in front of her face. "It's a bit warm in here, isn't it?"

Peter agreed, "Jah."

Hal thought about Peter's statement. *Is Aunt Tootie going to have a birthday soon? How would Peter know that? Nah, Aunt Tootie's birthday is months away, I think. Note to self. I need to ask Mom.* As she watched her aunt and Peter, the scent of roses suddenly came to her. Strange. It's a little early for roses to bloom. Besides, she couldn't remember ever seeing a rose bush or trellis close to the Rogies house.

Everyone chatted and laughed, having a good time as they ate. John said to Cooner Jonah, "Did you ever find your post hole digger?"

Cooner Jonah looked stumped. "I did not know it was missing. David, the post hole digger is in the shed with the other tools, ain't so?"

David said slowly as he tried to recall the last time he saw the digger. "I think so."

Peter's intent eyes focused on the men as he strained to hear their conversation. One of the girls must have said something that was funny to the other children. They all burst out laughing. Suddenly, Peter's fist hit the table as he snapped, "Silence! Why are you all laughing at this old man?"

Cooner Jonah stared at his father, flustered. "We are not laughing at you, Daed. We are enjoying our visit with our friends."

Anna said in a quiet tone, "These are your friends at this table with your family, Peter."

Peter grabbed Hal by the arm just above her wrist so quickly she didn't have time to dodge him. His strong grip squeezed her arm. The demented look on his face and in his cold eyes kept Hal from resisting him as she waited for what would happen next. The sun darkened patina on his skin flushed a red tint. "Sara, I'm tired of you making fun of me."

Hal bit her lower lip to keep from crying out from the pain. John jumped up to come to her aid. Hal put up her other hand to stop him. "Nah, John, sit back down."

"No one is making fun of you, Peter," Anna said in despair. "Turn loose of Nurse Hal's arm. You are hurting her."

"I intend to teach Sara to do the right thing. She should not

135

laugh at anyone let along her husband," Peter argued.

"But," John began. He wanted to correct Peter. Hal wasn't the elderly man's wife. She died eight years ago. Peter knew Hal very well. He visited with her at the service meetings all the time.

Hal shook her head slightly at John. "Peter Rogies." The elderly man focused on her as she said obediently, "I am forlornly sorry for having offended you. I promise not to do it again, and I pray that you will forgive me."

"That is better," Peter said sternly.

Tootie patted the table by his left hand. "Peter, have you finished eating?"

He focused on her. "Jah."

"How about you and me go for a walk? It's awfully warm in the house, and I could use some fresh air," Tootie said.

Peter released Hal's arm. An angry welted ring of finger marks swelled up on her arm. He seemed not to notice he'd hurt her as he focused on Tootie. "A walk sounds like a gute idea, Dolly."

When Tootie glanced at her, Hal said softly, "Don't go."

Tootie stood up. "We'll be fine. We're celebrating Peter's birthday after all."

Peter followed Tootie. She took his hand that now offered a gentle touch, and they went outside. Hal massaged her arm gently as she watched them leave. She was aware that beside and across from her were empty seats and lingering over them was the scent of roses in full bloom. *Roses! Fudge! Aunt Tootie bought rose perfume. She had something with Peter in mind all along. Oh, please, Lord, don't let anyone else figure this out. That woman is going to get us in trouble for sure, and it won't be her that has to stand before the member council for fornication.*

Anna had tears streaming down her face as she came around the table and hugged Hal. "I am so sorry. Did Peter hurt you much?"

"Nah, I'll be fine," Hal said. "Don't worry about me. I understand what Peter is going through."

"I wish I did," Anna said, feeling frustrated.

David put his arm around Daniel's shoulder. "I'm sorry my dawdi ruined the party."

"It is all right. He really did not ruin much. We had the gute cake and ice cream and a gute visit," Daniel said.

"We will do something fun together soon. Maybe go coon hunting again to train the dogs," Noah added.

David brightened up. "Jah, that would be gute."

Cooner Jonah said in a hushed voice to John, "I sure am sorry this happened. My daed comes and goes like this all the time. There is no way of getting his mind back when he's doing something wrong. The change happens so suddenly it takes us by surprise. I never thought he would hurt Nurse Hal of all people."

Hal said, "Your father is sick. He has Alzheimer's disease. If there's a time you could come by the clinic and talk to me away from where your father can hear us, I'd be glad to explain the disease to you. Maybe I can help you figure out how to talk to Peter when he's upset."

"Jah, Anna and me would like to learn about this disease," Cooner Jonah said. "John, why did you ask about our digger?"

"Your father stopped at our house a couple times before he caught me home. He asked me to return the digger I borrowed from him. I told him I didn't borrow his digger and showed him mine in the shed. He was very upset. He said someone must have stolen his," John explained.

"That's not so," Cooner Jonah declared.

Anna studied the screen door. "Will your aunt be safe with Peter?"

Nora looked worried. "Hal, I was wondering that myself."

"I'm not sure why, but he seems to like Aunt Tootie. I think she will be all right. I can tell she likes Peter, too," Hal said.

"It sounds odd to hear Peter call my sister Dolly," Nora said. "We haven't used her given name in years."

"He is reminded of a special friend named Dolly he dated before he married my mother," Jonah shared. "The way I heard it they almost married. I do not know what happened, but he

137

wound up marrying my mother instead."

"John, perhaps we should think about going home," Jim suggested.

"Maybe so." John said, "Noah, will you go find Aendi Tootie. Tell her we are ready to leave."

Noah shot out the door. He rushed back a few minutes later and leaned against the door frame, panting, "I have looked everywhere, but I can not find Aendi Tootie."

"Did you see my father?" Cooner Jonah asked.

"Nah, not him, either. I checked in the dawdi house. Peter and Aendi Tootie are not there. That is not all. Dawdi Jim's courting buggy is missing," Noah said, mystified.

"Peter and Tootie have disappeared? My buggy is gone? How do you like that? She wouldn't go for a ride with me, but she will with a strange … ." Jim paused when Cooner Jonah's head came up. "A stranger," Jim finished politely.

"We need to figure out where Peter would take Aunt Tootie," Hal said.

"He drives around Bender Creek Road often like it is the only place he knows where to go now that he will not get lost," Cooner Jonah suggested.

"That is right. That road seems to hold pleasant memories from years ago for him," Anna remembered.

"How about that. Tootie wouldn't go down Bender Creek Road with me, but she went with Peter in my courting buggy," groused Jim.

"You asked your wife's sister to go to Bender Creek Road with you in that courting buggy, and you have the nerve to call my father strange," Cooner Jonah said harshly.

"I didn't intend to take Tootie there for any other reason but a ride to try my new buggy out. A short ride at that. A very short one." Cooner Jonah continue to stare in a distrusting way at him. Jim turned to Nora. "Tell him, Nora. I wouldn't do what he's thinking, would I?"

"Jim is telling the truth, Mr. Rogies," Nora said. "He's not that kind of man."

"He's a gute man, Cooner Jonah," Hal defended.

"We better be looking for those two instead of talking. Cooner Jonah, how about you and I search for Peter and Aendi Tootie. Jim, you take the women and kids home," John planned.

Daniel sat in quiet contemplation all the way home, looking off into the dark night. He leaned against the barn with his hands in his trouser pockets, staring at his bare feet while Jim helped Noah unharness Ben.

Jim asked, "Daniel, you're too quiet. Is what Peter Rogies did tonight bothering you?"

Daniel nodded. "He scared me. Looking mean at all of us and hurting Mama Hal like that. I do not understand. He has always been such a nice man."

"The poor old fellow isn't well. He might just get worse," Jim said. "If you are around him from now on, you need to be mindful of that fact and keep some distance between you and him."

Noah came back with the harness. "That is not gute to know now that Aendi Tootie is alone with him."

"All we can do is wait and see. Hope for the best," Jim said.

"How come Mama Hal told Peter she was sorry. She didn't do anything wrong. Peter hurt her. He should have told her he was sorry," Daniel said.

"Jah, Mama Hal lied to him," Noah added.

"No, not really. You see sometimes to tell a person something they want to hear when they are sick like Peter isn't considered dishonest. Peter thought he knew the truth so he might have hurt Hal worse if she had tried to reason with him," Jim explained. "Remember that if you're ever around him or someone like him. Telling them what they want to hear is better than getting hurt or making it worse for the person who is sick. In a few minutes, right or wrong, they won't remember what you said to them anyway. On top of that, what Hal did was to show respect and kindness for a fellow human being who has a horrible illness."

It was Tootie's intention to calm Peter down and remind him it was his birthday so he could go back and enjoy what was left

139

of the party with everyone.

The plan seemed to be working until they walked past the Lapp's enclosed buggy. Peter stopped by the courting buggy. "Remember when we used to go on dates in that buggy."

"I don't think it would have been that one," Tootie said.

"Let me take you for a ride now," Peter urged.

"Now! It's dark. I thought maybe we could take a moonlight walk right here."

"I'd rather go for a ride," Peter insisted.

"It's getting late," Tootie excused.

"We will not stay gone long. Please go for a ride in my courting buggy with me," Peter coaxed.

Tootie looked toward the house. She didn't see anyone watching them to get help from. What was it Hallie said? This was like play acting. Peter was happy again. She should go along with whatever he said. She wanted him to enjoy her company and not be mad at her. "All right, let's go. Just don't make it a long ride. We don't want our families to worry about us."

Peter relaxed once they were in the seat. He dangled the lines over the horse's back and let Mike walk. Peter looked like he wouldn't mind if this ride lasted all night. Tootie felt uneasy about taking Jim's buggy, but what else could she do? Hopefully, she could talk Peter into turning around soon and taking the buggy back before Jim noticed it was gone. "Where we going?"

"Just around the Bender Creek Road," Peter said.

Tootie suddenly felt jittery. She didn't think it was proper to be on Lover's Lane with Peter, but she didn't have a choice now. She should have ask Peter before they started. Too late. She was along for the ride now.

She'd read about teenage dating in her All You Need To Know About Amish Customs book. She racked her brain for what was written in the book. It finally came to her what she should say as they turned onto Bender Creek Road. "Peter, I mean to stick to the no touching policy on this date."

"No touching? Oh, you mean a Hands Off Courtship." Peter

chuckled heartedly. "It is a little late to ask for that between the two of us, ain't so?"

"Holy Buckets!" Tootie exploded and felt a tight lurch in her stomach. Peter and the real Dolly must have been closer than she realized. Now what was she going to do?

"Young lady, that is no way to talk. Have you forgotten the teachings? I will remind you scripture states, Now ye also put off all these; anger, wrath, malice, blasphemy, and filthy communication out of your mouth.

You know if it had not been for my responsibility to Sara I would have followed you when you moved away. I wanted to marry you that bad." Peter pulled the buggy over to the side of the road and stopped. He twisted in the seat and took her hand. "We need to talk. I want you to know I did not want to let you go all those years ago. I checked with your brother as often as I could without getting caught to see if you were all right after you left. When I found out you married, it was no use anymore. I had to give up."

"I see," Tootie said quietly.

"I can tell you do not really see. You were not around when I was wishing things could have been different. Ach, I loved Sara, but I loved you more, Dolly." Peter leaned over and pressed a light, very gentle kiss on Tootie's cheek. It was such a tender kiss she couldn't ignore it. "Now do you see?"

The gesture was so sweet it brought tears to Tootie's eyes and a load of quilt to her insides. She shouldn't have let this mess go as long as she did. Peter needed to know she wasn't his Dolly. She was just a fill in even though she wished she had been the real deal back when they were young. "I'm beginning to," she whispered as she wiped tears rolling down her cheeks with her fingertips. "Now that you've told me don't you think we better go back to your place. We've been gone long enough."

Peter's gaze didn't budge from her face as he took her hand in his. "Jah, but only after you make me a promise."

"I'll try. What is it?" Tootie asked.

"You will come back here with me again soon. I've spent a

141

lot of time traveling on this road by myself over the years with just the memory of you to keep me company. Now that I have the real thing, I want you to come here with me again," Peter said.

"It's a date for sure," Tootie agreed solicitously. "As late as it's getting maybe you should take me to the Lapp house."

"Jah, I can do that. It is getting late so this is all I will make you promise for now, but we have to talk again soon. We have had too many years go by. We can not let what is between us go unsaid or not acted upon." Peter flicked the lines and turned the buggy around in the road.

The pale light from the gas lamp lit up the Lapp's living room window. Tootie sighed. Someone must be waiting up for her. She steeled herself for the chewing out Nora and Hal were going to give her for taking off with Peter. Worse yet, Jim was really going to be mad about them using his old buggy without asking.

Tootie let Peter help her down. They climbed the porch steps and entered the house. Her family stared at the door, wondering who would be coming through it when Tootie opened the door.

"Where have you been?" Nora barked.

Tootie shrugged, "We went for a ride."

"My buggy all in one piece?" Jim snapped.

With an offended sniffle, Tootie said, "Yes, it is, and so are we. Thanks for asking." She patted Peter's arm. "Peter needs a ride home now."

"I'll take him," Jim said begrudgingly.

Tootie excused softly to Jim, "Peter thought the buggy was one he used to own."

Jim went over to stand at the door by Peter, ready to leave.

Hal said, "Wait, Dad. She said softly to Noah, "Go along with Grandpa in case Peter gives him trouble. You will make sure Dawdi finds his way back home. See if you can find your father on the way. Tell him and Cooner Jonah that all is well. They can come home."

Noah put his hand on the elderly man's rounded shoulder. "Come on, Peter Rogies. It's bedtime. Time to go home."

Chapter 14

"That quilting frolic at Jane Bontrager's house is this afternoon," Hal said as she helped her mother clean off the table after breakfast. "Eldon stopped John down by the road and told him to pass the word on to us."

"Do they live close?" Tootie asked as she put a glass in the rinse water.

"Jah, they live just down the road," Hal said. "We'll leave right after lunch, and it won't take long to get there."

Tootie frowned. "We didn't bring needles and scissors to quilt with."

"That's all right," Emma said. "We will give you some of ours to use."

Nora gazed out the window. "I haven't been to a quilting bee since we were children. We went to them with Mama."

"I haven't, either," Tootie said.

Nora turned to her. "You're always telling me you quilt with women in the church basement."

"Sure I do if you call sewing squares of material together and tacking with different colors of scrap yarn quilting. Hardly the same thing as a good old fashion quilting bee," Tootie declared.

On the short ride to the Bontrager house, Nora pointed out to Tootie a farmer with eight snorting horses pulling a plow. The jangling harness sounded like music accompanying the farmer's loud shouts to keep moving as the rich gumbo rolled from the gleaming plowshares.

At the Bontrager house, Jane met them at the door. They sat down in empty chairs between the other ladies already working around the quilting frame. Tootie hesitated when she saw the only empty chair left by Stella Strutt, but she didn't have a choice. Sallie Gingerich and Jane were on the other side of Stella. Nora and Hal were seated across from Tootie with Linda Yoder and Margaret Yoder beside them.

As the three women threaded needles, put on their thimbles and started stitching, Linda Yoder asked, "Wonder how Mary Mast is getting along now?"

Hal said, "She's doing fine. She's not far away from delivery. We're praying for a different outcome this time."

"We will all pray for her," Sallie Gingerich said in her soft squeaky voice.

"Sure did not help her any when Johnnie had his accident," Margaret said. "Johnnie must be coming around by now, ain't so?"

"He's doing better, considering how badly his leg was broken," Hal said.

"Always something bad happening to someone," Jane Bontrager said. "Did you hear Jonas Bender broke his leg yesterday morning?"

"His son, Mark, came for me. I called an ambulance for him while I stabilized the leg," Hal said, pulling her needle through the cloth. "He needed surgery on the bone to put a pin in the break."

"That poor family always has struggles of one thing or another with that farm," Margaret said.

Jane added, "Elton is organizing a work bee so the men can help the Benders out while Jonas's leg is mending."

Displeased, Stella Strutt yanked her needle through the quilt, puckering the material. "Moses says Jonas Bender never gets in a hurry on a gute day. In any hurry at all. That is why he always has too much left to do by bedtime. His own fault. Really his own fault. He does not get an early start like most men.

Appears to me it is his own fault his farm is struggling when he gets hurt."

"Perhaps, but we should help Brother Bender in his time of need just the same, ain't so?" Jane said, looking at each of the other women to take her side.

"Is so," Linda Yoder agreed.

The others nodded that they agreed.

Tootie looked at the quilt and contemplated, "The farmers around us help each other when one of them is sick or hurt. It's what you do as your Christian duty."

Stella looked stern down her nose at Tootie. Tootie glanced at Stella then concentrated on her needle and thread.

Changing the subject, Katie Stolfus asked, "Have any of you noticed the sad shape Peter Rogies is in?"

"Yes," Jane said. "He is failing."

"I do not know how to talk to the poor man anymore," Linda Yoder said. "I tried at the last meeting service, and he called me by his late wife's name."

"Just answer him in such a way that makes him feel all right with himself," Hal told her. "He has Alzheimer's disease. His family has their hands full trying to keep him calm."

Stella Strutt grunted. "With the shape the man is in not much any of us can do for him. Not much we can do but leave him alone."

Jane said, "Des verschtehn ich, but we can keep him in our prayers. God understands even if we do not and will be by Peter's side."

"Peter needs understanding from all of you," Tootie said gently as she cut the thread.

"We understand very well. The man has lost his mind," Stella Strutt said bluntly as she brought her needle back up through the material.

"Peter is a kind man that isn't well. You would do good to remember that." Tootie was vex. She knotted the end of the thread and rammed her needle through the quilt. While Stella glared at her, Tootie busied herself feeling for the needle to retrieve it under the quilt. She made a wide sweep with her

145

hand, found the needle and tugged on it when the needle resisted. Whatever it was caught on gave way, and Tootie stuck the needle back through the quilt bottom and brought it to the top.

Sallie Gingerich said, "Anna Rogies told me the birthday party did not go well. Peter grabbed Hal by the arm and was angry with her."

"Nurse Hal probably stuck her schnuppich nose too close to where it did not belong. Did not belong at all like she has a habit of doing," Stella said snidely.

"What happened wasn't my niece's fault," Tootie defended sharply, glaring at Stella. "You would have had to be there to understand, and you weren't invited."

Stella stopped her needle in mid air and got into a staring match with Tootie.

Jane intervened before things escalated between the two women. "We can see Hal is right here, and she is all right. Stella, we know she knows how to take care of herself and is a great help to those in need."

Tootie settled down and went back to stitching.

Stella was spoiling for a fight. "Have you cleared the smoke smell from your house yet, Nurse Hal?" She rubbed in.

Margaret worried, "Smoke? Did you have a fire?"

"Nah! Well, just a little one as a result of a cooking mishap," Hal explained. "Jah, Sister Stella, our house is fine now."

Stella leaned close to Sallie Gingerich and whispered loudly for all to hear, "It wonders me who is really the oddest one in that family."

Tootie's head shot up, but Hal shook her head in a let it go warning. Tootie took the hint and went back to stitching energetically. The women managed to keep the rest of the conversations on neutral subjects.

Finally, Hal said they should go home. Jane walked with them to the door. "Nora and Tootie, come back and visit anytime."

"We will. This was such a treat." Nora said to the other women moving away from the quilting frame, "We've enjoyed quilting with all of you."

Hal started to respond likewise when Stella stood up. The quilting frame tilted away from Stella and toppled over, scattering chairs. Stella did a nose dive on top of the frame. Her black dress billowed out over the quilt as she floundered with her arms and legs treading air. She squalled for help. The women rushed to her. It took several of them to help her onto her feet. When they succeeded, the quilting frame followed her into an upright position.

"That's odd," Jane said.

Linda Yoder peeked under the frame. "Stella's apron is sewn to the bottom side of the quilt. I need scissors." Margaret handed her the scissors, and Linda squatted down under the frame to cut the threads.

Hal asked, "Are you all right, Stella?"

"I think so, but I could have been hurt because of your dummkopf aunt," Stella sputtered.

"Me? I wasn't even close when you fell down," Tootie said innocently.

"Never mind, Aunt Tootie. If Stella isn't hurt, we're leaving," Hal said as she pushed Tootie toward the door. She turned and whispered to Jane, "I am so sorry to leave you now. Can you calm Stella down?"

"I can manage," Jane said, her eyes twinkling. "See you soon."

The buggy ride home started out in silence. Suddenly, Tootie blurted out, "If I said something wrong to that mean old witch I'm sorry. I was tired of her picking on Peter. Besides, my Pennsylvania Dutch may be bad, but I think she called me a dummy for the second time."

"It's all right, Aunt Tootie," Hal said. "Stella says lots of things like that when she's angry. She was really mad, because you sewed her apron to the quilting frame."

"Me? How do you know she didn't do that to herself?" She's not much of a quilter. Did you see how she puckered that pretty quilt when she jerked her needle through the material," Tootie sputtered.

Nora shrugged. "Might as well let it go. What is done is done I guess."

Tootie sniffed haughtily. "You're beginning to sound more Amish every day, Nora,"

"Aendi Tootie," Emma said, trying not to smile. "We have a saying. Keep your words soft and sweet just in case you have to eat them. I might add, keep your needle in front of you when you sew at a quilting frolic."

"I'll remember that the next time," Tootie grumbled. Under her breath, she said to Emma, "Unless I have to be at a quilting bee with that old bat."

Nora leaned over to Hal. "There will always be a next time for my sister. Maybe not at a quilting bee, but there will be a next time. Sorry, Hal."

Emma added, "No need to worry, Aendi Tootie. I doubt Stella Strutt will let you sit by her again."

Hal rolled her eyes toward the buggy roof and kept driving.

Tootie grumped, "Oh, you girls."

Hal didn't know what Stella Strutt would spread about her sassy English aunt, but this time she was pretty sure Tootie had it coming to her.

When they arrived home, Emma thought it might be a good thing to get Tootie away from Hal and Nora for a while. "Aendi Tootie, come with me to the hen house while I gather eggs. I'll show you my hens. I have the best laying flock around here." She hoped that didn't sound too boastful, but she had to have a good reason to get Tootie out of the house.

"No, Dear, hen houses are smelly and dusty. They make me wheeze," Tootie said.

"All recht, you do not have to come inside. Stand outside the door and watch," Emma said.

"Oh, I don't know. There's probably something in here I should be doing," Tootie stalled, hoping Nora or Hal would come to her rescue. The women didn't seem to be listening.

"I wanted you to see my rooster, Abraham? He's a pretty fellow," Emma enticed.

"Don't care to get close to a rooster. I got pecked by a mean one once. It hurt," Tootie complained.

"My rooster will not hurt you. He is not mean," Emma wheedled.

Tootie kept eyeing Hal and Nora. They didn't say a word in her defense. Finally, Tootie ran out of excuses. "All right, I'll go with you."

As they crossed the back yard, Tootie fretted, "I'm in trouble with your mother and Nora, aren't I?"

"They will get over it. We have always had to endure Stella Strutt and her strict ideas. Sometimes, it does her gute to be confronted with someone who puts her in her place. Mama Hal would agree with that."

"I don't think Hallie wanted it to be me that put Stella in her place in front of all those women at the quilting bee of all places," Tootie worried.

"Probably not, but I will tell you a secret. Usually it is Hallie that gives Stella a hard time. They have never gotten along," Emma said, giggling.

"Really? That makes me feel a little better," Tootie said. "Thank you for telling me that."

Emma pointed to a setting hen, racing across the dusty chicken yard, followed by her brood of fluffy chicks. The hen stopped and scattered the dirt, looking for bugs. When she found some insects, she clucked to her chicks to eat. She spotted the women coming and squawked as she bristled at what looked like danger. Her chicks fled under her and huddled in a pile beneath the protective shelter of her cradling wings.

Emma said, "Stand at the door and watch me gather the eggs. That way you get to see my gute flock."

"Okay," Tootie said half heartedly. She focused on the too close for comfort setting hen growling at her.

Inside, a hen cackled her displeasure when Emma stuck her hand under her, looking for an egg. The hen flew off the nest just as Tootie looked to see what the trouble was in the building. The hen sailed at Tootie in the doorway.

"Oh, my!" Tootie slid against the wall in time to get out of the hen's way. Only her head reappeared in the door so she'd be less likely to get assaulted by hens and could still watch Emma.

The hen cackled loudly, scaring the other hens on the floor. They raised their heads and joined in a chorus of noisy cackles. They didn't know what they were upset about, but when one of them set off the alarm, they all joined in.

"Ouch!" Tootie felt a sharp pain in the back of her hand. She looked behind her and screamed. In the next breath, she wailed, "Emma, get him away from me."

Emma appeared in the door. "What is wrong?"

"I shouldn't have come out here. I told you roosters bite. Your big rooster just bit my hand," Tootie shouted, flattening herself against the building as Tom peered closely at her. "You said your rooster wouldn't hurt me."

"This is Tom, our turkey. I forgot about him," Emma admitted sheepishly. "I am sorry, Aendi Tootie. Shoo, Tom. Go away." She fluttered her apron at the turkey. He fanned his tail feathers out and chirped as he stared at Tootie.

"Please get me away from him. He's eyeing me like he plans to bite me again." Tootie gave a tragic sniffle while she held her hands together up against her chest.

"Tom does not like strangers very well," Emma admitted.

"Now you tell me," Tootie said with a haughty sniff. "I wouldn't have come out here if I thought I'd be attacked."

"Just stay with me. I am done gathering eggs. We will go to the house," Emma said, putting her arm around the elderly woman's shoulder. Hallie and Nora were on their own from now on. She was pretty sure there wouldn't be any way to talk Tootie into going outside with her again after this run in with Tom.

On Friday evening, Jimmie Miller picked up Noah and Daniel so they could run the hounds again in the timber. They turned down the dirt road behind two other buggies and stopped at the same place the boys gathered the first time.

Noah noticed Matthew Stoll had his twenty two rifle cradled in his arms again. "You should leave that gun in the buggy."

Matthew shrugged his shoulders. "Ain't hurting anything?"

"Noah is right. No need for a gun out here. You should leave it home," Andy Zook told him.

Matthew walked over to his buggy and laid the rifle on the floor in front of the seat. All the while, the dogs barked at the air, lunged on their ropes and rumbled at each other. They were ready to hunt.

"Too bad Johnnie Mast can not be here this time. He is missing all the fun," Jimmie Miller said sadly.

"He will be well by the time we go coon hunting for real. Johnnie can go all he wants in season." Daniel had Biscuit's rope shortened so the dog stayed right beside him, but he was excited. The pup leaped up and bounced off Daniel's leg, causing him to stagger.

Noah said, "It's time to let the dogs go."

The dogs took off and scattered through the trees, sniffing for coon scent. The boys were right behind the dogs.

Biscuit whined and licked Daniel hand. "Now can I let the dog go?"

"Jah, we will just wander around here. We should be careful not to let Dog get into a fight with the other dogs. Mama Hal would want us to stop training him if he came home hurt again," Noah said.

The mummer of Bender Creek was loud as the water twisted through the hickories and oaks. Biscuit picked up a scent near the creek bank. He raised his head, sniffed the air, bawled a challenging bay and trotted off. His long ears flopped, keeping time with his loping stride. The boys raced after him.

Biscuit picked up speed. His deep bays rang loud and clear. The boys whooped at him to encourage him as the dog disappeared. They heard his tree barks before they saw him. He was racing around a large oak tree. He leaped up on the trunk and bounced off to make another lap.

Noah shone the flashlight up in the tree and made contact with two yellow eyes shining through the leaves. "He found a coon!"

When Biscuit saw the boys, he came tearing back to them. The coon decided it was a good time to move. Biscuit heard the rustle of branches as the animal jumped from one limb to another. The dog's body went rigid. The hairs on his back bristled His eyes bored into the darkness above him, and his black shiny nose wiggled as he tried to catch the coon's scent again.

"Gute dog," Daniel said as he patted the dog's head.

In the distance, they heard other voices whoop and dogs baying. Noah and Daniel listened to the voices to see if those dogs were successful.

Suddenly, a rifle report echoed through the woods. A shrill, pain filled scream followed. A boy's voice yelled, "Help! Matthew shot himself."

Noah said, "I better go see what happened?" His excitement turned to a sickening dread. His knees shook, and his heart pounded. "Daniel, catch our dog and bring him." He took off running toward the voices.

His rustling footsteps blended in with the other boys as they all converged on the cries and moans coming out of the darkness.

David Rogies was on his knees, trying to hold the boy still as Matthew Stoll thrashed in the dried leaves. Noah got down beside David and shone his flashlight on Matthew. "Where is he hit?"

David's voice trembled. "In the side of his neck. See the blood. So – so much blood."

Noah pulled Matthew's shirt away. "I see. The vein is open. He will bleed to death." Noah picked up a handful of leaves, wadded them together and packed the wound to slow down the bleeding. He pulled his blue handkerchief from his back pocket and bound Matthew's neck to hold the leaves in place. "We need to get Matthew to Nurse Hal quick. Put him in a buggy, and let's go."

Four boys grabbed an arm or leg, and they took off back to the road. When they got to a buggy, they laid Matthew on the back seat and turned the buggy around to head for the Lapp farm.

The procession of buggies came down the road at a fast clip. Tootie heard something and looked out the window. She saw the headlights and knew from the black shapes it was buggies. "Are you having a party here?"

"Nah, not that I know about," John said. "Why?"

"A bunch of buggies are pulling in the yard fast," Tootie said.

John came to the window with Hal. "What's happening, John?"

"I do not know." John opened the door and went out on the porch.

Noah yelled, "Tell Mama Hal Matthew Stoll is hurt. He needs her help fast."

Jim, Nora and Tootie stayed on the porch as Hal passed by John on the steps. She raced to the front buggy. "What kind of injury?"

Andy Zook said, "A bullet wound in the neck."

Hal grabbed Noah's flashlight and shone it on Matthew. His pale face was stained red. Hal pulled the handkerchief back. Blood trickled out around the leaves in the wound, soaking the handkerchief. "Don't move him," Hal ordered. She clambered into the buggy and pressed against the leaves to slow down the bleeding. "Stay still, Matthew. Mom, go get a blanket from the clinic for this boy. He's going into shock. Emma, call 911 for an ambulance. Tell them we need an aircare copter to light as close to the Lapp farm as they can get. Explain that the boy's jugular vein is open from a bullet wound. John take the boys up on the porch out of the way." As an after thought, Hal asked, "Who put the leaves in the wound?"

Noah spoke up. "I did. The blood spurted out. I wanted to slow the flow down."

The screen door banged as Hal said, "Gute job, son."

Nora unfolded the blanket and handed it to Hal.

Emma came running back. "The copter is going to light at the intersection on the highway with our road. The ambulance will be here soon." She grabbed a corner of the blanket and helped Hal cover Matthew. Gently, she placed her hand on the boy's forehead. "Hang in there, Matthew. Help is coming." Her voice trembled as she said, "Mammi Nora, that is one of my students. Makes two in so many days that I have seen badly hurt."

John went to the porch and sat beside Jim and Tootie in the swing. The boys sat down on the porch floor. "When Matthew gets to the hospital, the shooting will be reported to the sheriff. I need to hear from you boys what happened before the sheriff comes to talk to you."

Noah said, "Matthew had a twenty two rifle with him in the timber. I told him to put it back in his buggy. He did put the gun away before we started to run the dogs."

"Matthew just waited until Noah was out of sight and got his rifle again. He said Noah was a sissy," Andy Zook said. "I told him he should listen to Noah."

David Rogies said, "We were running after Matthew's dog. He treed a coon. Matthew tripped and fell. He must have had the safety off. The rifle fired and hit him in the neck."

"All recht, I will tell the sheriff this," John said. "He will want to talk to each of you to get the story from eye witnesses. Tell him what you know when Sheriff Dawson stops by."

The ambulance screamed in and parked by the buggy. The EMTs came running with a stretcher. Daryl said, "Nurse Hal, what's up?"

"Matthew accidentally shot himself in the neck with a rifle. He hit his jugular vein. He's lost a lot of blood. I've been pressing against the wound. It's filled with dried leaves and bound with a handkerchief." She looked behind Daryl. "Hi, Steve. I'll get out of the way and let you guys take over."

Soon they loaded Matthew into the ambulance and raced down the road with strobe lights flashing.

Hal stared at the last of the buggies leaving.. "I don't suppose those boys are going to get a wink of sleep tonight. I'll check at the hospital in the morning to see if Matthew made it through the night."

"The boy that bad?" Jim asked.

"Jah, Dad, he's that bad," Hal said. "He has lost a lot of blood already."

The next morning, John wanted to talk to the sheriff about

154

the shooting accident so Hal rode in with him to the hospital. Lucy Stineford was the nurse on duty at the emergency room nurse's station. "Hello, Hal. Seems like I've seen a lot more of you lately."

"Don't you ever go home?"

"Supposed to be there right now. Filling in for someone. You know how that goes," Lucy said.

"I do. I'm just checking on one of my patients," Hal said. "Matthew Stoll came in last night with a gun shot wound in his neck."

"I just looked in on him. He made it through the night. Vitals aren't too strong yet, but he lost a lot of blood," Lucy said. "He's in ICU. Want to go see him?"

"Nah, I don't want to disturb him," Hal said. "I imagine his parents are with him."

"They are," Lucy confirmed.

"Think he will make it?"

"Could go either way, but the boy is healthy otherwise so he stands a good chance to come through this," Lucy said.

After John stopped to talked to Sheriff Dawson, they went home. Hal explained Matthew's condition to the boys and told them to spread the word to the other boys. Matthew made it through the night. They should pray for him to get through the coming night. With each day he survived, he would grow stronger.

Chapter 15

Saturday afternoon, the sheriff's cruiser pulled into the Lapp driveway. Sheriff Dawson knocked, and Hal answered the door. "Hello, Sheriff. What can I do for you?"

The sheriff removed his hat. "I want to talk to your sons about the shooting that happened during the coon hunt over on Bender Creek."

"Of course. The boys are with their father in the barn," Hal said. "Want me to go get them?"

"No need to bother. I can go to the barn and roust them out. Thank you, ma'am," he said, tipping his hat brim. Hal stood at door, watching the long legged lawman. With his long strides, he was across the driveway and peeking over the barn open half door in no time. "John Lapp, are you in here?"

John came to the door. Above the rumble of the generator, he asked, "What can I do for you, Sheriff?"

"I'd like to talk to your boys about the shooting if that's all right with you."

"Jah, it is." John called for Noah and Daniel. "Step outside and talk to the sheriff where you do not have to shout to be heard," John told them. "Sheriff, this is Noah, and this is Daniel," he said, patting each boy on the shoulder.

"Daniel and I met when I helped his grandfather find his buggy," the sheriff said. The boys fidgeted from one foot to the other. Not liking it at all that they were the center of attention.

"This won't take long. You boys aren't in trouble. I just need to make out a report about Matthew Stoll's accident. I'm talking to all the boys that were training their hounds in Bender's timber to get the story straight. That all right with you?"

Noah said, "Jah."

Daniel nodded.

"Good. Noah, tell me where you were when the shooting occurred."

Noah cleared his throat. "Daniel and I were following our pup hound. He seemed to be on a trail, but we are just training him so we let him go off away from the other dogs. He really does not know what he is doing. We heard the shot, and Matthew screamed right after that. David Rogies yelled that Matthew had shot himself. We heard the other boys all running toward where they heard the shot. I told Daniel to chase down our dog, and come as soon as he could. Then I ran in the direction of the voices."

"What did you find?"

"Matthew was on the ground with his hands over his neck. The boys had flashlights on him. Matthew was in a lot of pain, moaning and wiggling around." Noah's face paled as he described the scene.

"I know this is a hard thing to talk about for you boys. I understand that. Bare with me," the sheriff said kindly. "What happened next?"

Noah swallowed hard and continued. "I got on my knees beside Matthew and peeked under his bloody hands. I saw the bullet hole in his neck. Blood came out in squirts when he moved and breathed. I picked up a hand full of leaves and poked them into the hole to slow the bleeding down then tied my handkerchief around his neck. It looked like he might bleed to death really quick. I told the other boys we had to get him in a buggy and take him to the clinic for Nurse Hal to tend him."

"You saved Matthew's life. Your folks must be real proud of you," the sheriff said. "How did you know to do that with the leaves in the wound?"

Noah shrugged as he thought. "I think I picked the idea up

while I listened to some of the men talk about hunting accidents."

"It's a lucky break for the Stoll boy that you knew what to do. That's for sure," the sheriff said. "Did you know he had a rifle with him?"

"Jah, he took it out of his buggy when we were ready to follow the dogs," Noah said reluctantly. "I told him to put it back in the buggy. We could not use guns until open season. There were too many of us in the dark timber, and he might cause an accident."

"Obviously, the boy didn't pay any mind to what you said," the sheriff replied.

"Matthew did lay the rifle back in his buggy while Noah was watching him," Daniel said. "We saw him do it. He must have picked it back up after we left."

"I see," the sheriff said. "You boys have been a big help. From now on if you're out at night with other boys training your dogs, you remind them about what happened to Matthew Stoll. I don't want to hear about any guns. I sure don't want to have another shooting accident to investigate. Looks like Matthew is going to pull through. The next time this happens the boy who shoots himself or someone else may not come out of the accident alive. When Matthew is up to talking to me, I'm going to tell him the same thing I just told you."

"Jah, Sheriff," Noah said.

"You have anything else to add, Daniel, or is what Noah said all you know about this incident?" The sheriff asked.

"Noah told it all," Daniel said, studying his bare feet.

"All right, just try to be very careful from now on and do the safe thing," the sheriff stressed.

"Jah, I agree," John said, coming forward. "We have an old saying. You can not help it if a bird flies down and sits on your head, but you can help it if a bird is making a nest on your head."

The sheriff thought about that a second. He grinned. "I believe you have something there, John Lapp. Oh, your father-in-law keeping better track of his courting buggy these days?"

John grinned. "Jah, he found out what the problem was. The horse knows how to untie a slip knot and take off on his own."

"Well, isn't that something?" The sheriff chuckled. "You men have a good afternoon. I got to get back to the office and write out that report."

The women cooked for the school fund raiser all afternoon. They prepared potato salad, a large bowl of canned peas, and three white cakes.

Nora sat down at the table with a cup of hot tea. "This reminds me of when I was about Emma's age. What fun the box socials were when we had fund raisers for our country school. Weren't they, Tootie?"

"Yes, especially when we had a beau we were struck on." Tootie giggled as she sat down across from Nora.

"A beau?" Emma asked, pouring a cup of tea for Hal and herself.

Hal said, "That was a boyfriend in their day."

"I see. What were those socials like?" Emma asked, sitting down beside Hal.

"Oh, you probably wouldn't care about our stories," Nora said.

"Jah, we both would," Hal urged. "So tell us."

"Those box suppers were events of great importance in our teenage years. There wasn't many events to take a girl to for a date," Tootie said, her eyes sparkling. "The mothers and daughters prepared lunches in boxes decorated with ribbons and bows.

We filled the boxes with the most delicious foods our mother could cook for us. In those days, it was chicken, duck, goose, venison, beef, pork quail or rabbit. There would be salads, canned, pickled and preserved foods, vegetables of all kinds, homemade bread slices with jellies, pieces of pies and cakes arranged in the boxes to catch the eyes and stomachs of our beaus. Isn't that so, Sister?"

Nora said in a far away voice, "It is. The box socials took place at the schoolhouse usually on a night in early fall. A fire roared in the cast-iron potbellied stove to warm the place up.

We didn't have electricity in those days. Kerosene lamps set on shelves high around the room. One lamp was on the teacher's desk by the stacked boxes, waiting for the auctioneer to sell them to the highest bidder."

"Having a date was so romantic," Tootie said dreamily.

Hal winked at Emma, and she responded with a bashful smile.

Nora said, "A great to do had been going on with each boy who was sparking. That's what we called it when we dated a boy. I believe English teens call it going steady these days.

Each girl's beau was trying to get her to talk about her box. He hoped to get her to make a slip so he'd find what her box looked like. That would help him recognize it."

Tootie butted in. "He wanted to bid the highest on her box, to the exclusion of all others for the sweet privilege of sitting and eating with the girl of his choice."

"Were the boys supposed to do that, Aendi Tootie?" Emma asked.

"No, they were supposed to bid on a box and eat with whom ever the box belonged to," Tootie said.

"That was cheating then," Emma stated.

"The girls didn't want to sit with someone they hadn't been dating," Tootie enlighten her. "Now with the older women, married and old maids, it didn't matter who picked their boxes. They were usually happy with ever which man they got, young or old. The money was going for a good cause, and it was just an evening to socialize for them."

Nora said, "I remember some amusing and some embarrassing situations. Some girls had younger brothers and sisters that passed out the wrong description about their older sister's box to her boyfriend. That would caused him to bid sky-high on a box that didn't belong to his best girl. Remember the time, Tootie, when Ima Jean Sandersfield's beau, Steven Heckter, got the wrong information."

"Remember it? We laughed about that for days." Tootie giggled at the thought. "I'll never forget the look on that boy's face. Steven got stuck with plain jane Hector Cozy. She was delighted since she rarely had a date, and he was real cute in those days."

"I remember that happening to you once, too," Nora said with a mischievous smile.

Tootie frowned. "You can forget that story right now."

"Nah, she can't," Hal said. "Mom, what happened?"

"Tootie thought she was going to be eating supper with the best looking boy in the room, Art Klinefeld. I was there with Jim. For a joke, Jim told Art which box he saw Tootie carry in. Turned out to be the old maid school teacher's box.

When Tootie's box came up for auction, Oscar Donner bid until he got it. The old man had lots of money and liked to help out the school fund. He didn't care whose box he bid on. Tootie wasn't a bit happy to have to eat supper with that old man. Ruined her whole evening."

"Well, who wouldn't be upset at my age. He was about eighty years old. That old potbellied grandpa man wasn't nearly as much fun as Art, and here I was stuck with him until he finished eating," Tootie groused. "I thought he was never going to get to the bottom of the box so I could get away from him. He acted like he was eating slow just to aggravate me. All I could think about was hunting up my beau, before some other girl stole him."

"You worried for nothing. The spinster school teacher wasn't any competition for you," Nora said.

Tootie smiled. "She sure wasn't. That was the only good thing about that evening. The other girls had a hay day out of me being stuck with that old man. I didn't speak to Jim for months, because he pulled that prank on me and ruined my evening."

Nora said, "Sometimes, we young folks had a hilarious time watching as a couple, very much in love, would be separated, because of the boy bidding on the wrong box. Another boy spent the high point of his evening with that boy's girlfriend. Oh my, the looks that crossed from one young person to another were as hot as the fire in the stove."

Tootie giggled. "Boys were so busy watching to see how

close their girl sit to the other boy they couldn't even enjoy their supper. Some girls completely ignored the boy they were with while they worried their boyfriend bid on another pretty girl's box lunch on purpose."

"Business was lucrative for the smaller boys and girls with sisters and brothers older than them," Nora said. "They were able to pick up a little cash by telling their older sister's boyfriend exactly how her box was decorated. He was glad to pay to be able to bid and buy her lunch.

Same with the ones who misinformed the boys about the boxes. The tricksters took their money and hid out for a few days until everyone cooled off. That included your father, Hallie."

"Remember how husbands attempted to buy their wives' lunches?" Tootie grinned as she went on, "Remember when some bullheaded husband bid higher and higher, finally to be awarded a box that wasn't his wife's but one belonging to a woman who wasn't even a friend of his wife.

Worse of all was when it was an old gossip or trouble maker, like Stella Strutt, that the wife couldn't stand. The hour the husband spent with that woman provided great amusement and glee to the rest that knew about the ill feelings between the two women. The poor husband knew he was going to be in the dog house when he got home even if he couldn't help what happened."

"It was a great time to visit, swap news, gossip and gather information since most of us didn't socialize much except to go to church and school," Nora said. "Especially for our folks."

"Our visiting at the fund raiser gathering is the same, but this fund raiser will be different from yours. We all bring food and eat together in fellowship. The only fee for the meal is the free will donations placed in a box on the end of the food table," Emma explained.

Chapter 16

That evening, almost all of the Plain people in the community filed into the school. The women placed their casseroles, salads, meats, bread and other dishes along side desserts on the cloth covered planks at the front of the room. Styrofoam plates, glasses and cups were stacked beside plastic silverware. The large thermos jugs of tea, juice and coffee were lined up after the box at the end of the table for the free will donations.

Bishop Bontrager said a prayer of thanks for the delicious food and the cooks that prepared it. He praised God for sending such a good turn out to help fund the school house needs for their children.

The line formed in the manner as Sunday meeting dinners. The men first, the teenage boys, the women, small children and the girls.

Peter Rogies sat in the back of the room with the old men, watching and listening to the hubbub around him. His confused face showed he couldn't make heads or tails out of all the talking. So many different voices mingled together that the words blended into sentences that didn't make sense.

A man who seemed to know him approached and shook his hand. "That food sure looks gute. Better get in line with me, Peter."

Peter studied the man's face. "Do you know me?"

The man took it as a joke. He laughed. "Now how many years has it been that we have lived on neighboring farms, Peter Rogies?"

"Many years," Peter managed. He hoped he said the right thing. He must have, because the man left him to get in line. All the other men on his bench left him by himself.

Peter studied the women, looking for a familiar face. Some were serving men from behind the table, and others were bustling around, tending to their young children and talking to other women. He searched for Sara among them. He didn't see her. Perhaps, she stepped outside to go to the outhouse or for a breath of fresh air. He should go find her and tell her it was time to eat.

Peter stood and was uncertain which way to go. He looked up and down the aisle and noticed the open door. The cool night air drifted his way. He peered out the door into the darkness. Sara was out there somewhere. He'd find her and tell her -- tell her ... . His mind went blank. He wasn't sure what he meant to say to his wife, but he had to find her. He slipped away without notice and wandered around the school yard.

"Sara, Sara," he called toward the shade trees and the outhouse. He heard horses stomping and snorting, disturbed by his voice. A whinny answered him once. Perhaps that was a horse named Sara.

Tootie came outside. As bad as she hated to be in the dark, she had to go to the bathroom. She heard Peter call his wife's name. She followed his voice and found him in the grove of trees behind the horse barn. "What are you doing out here?"

He asked, "Dolly, that you?"

"Yes, you should be inside eating your supper," Tootie scolded gently.

"Why are you out here?" Peter asked.

"I have to go to the outhouse," Tootie said bluntly.

"Will you do me a favor and look inside to see if Sara is in there? She is out here wondering around," Peter said.

"All right, I'll look." Tootie opened the door and felt her way inside the black space, shut the door and managed to find the bench hole. When she came back out, Peter was pacing in front of the door. "Sara, isn't in there."

"Sara," Peter called. When he stood still and listened, he didn't hear a reply. All that reached his ears were the tree frogs harmonious song, chatter from the school and the gentle breeze moaning through the tree limbs. He grew anxious. "Sara is lost. Dolly, I have to find her quickly. Sara must be so scared. She doesn't like the dark."

In the distance, screaming yips stopped Tootie. She grabbed Peter's arm. "What was that?"

Peter listened. "Coyotes on the run."

"Really? Let me tell you, Sara isn't the only one scared of the dark. So am I with wild animals like that loose around here," complained Tootie.

As if he didn't care, Peter's stooped shouldered form shuffled away from the building until he was out of range of the yellow glow flowing from the door and windows.

"Wait for me." Tootie darted a look into the darkness and hustled after him.

By that time, Peter was at the fence line. He bumped into the barbed wire. His jacket hooked on a barb. Peter backed up and heard the rip made in his snagged jacket. He didn't have time to pay that any mind. Not with Sara missing. He stared at the timber.

"Peter, why don't we go back and get some of the men to help us look for Sara. We would find her faster with help." Tootie thought, *That sounds like good reasoning to get Peter back into the school. Let his family talk him out of looking for his wife.*

"Sara is my only worry right now. She wasn't in the school yard so she must be out in those trees." Peter nodded across the fence. He was sure of it. He could feel it. No place else she could be. He pushed the top barbed wire down and stuck one leg over. He balanced for a second on that foot then raised the other leg up and brought it over the wire. When he planted his foot, he stepped on a limb which off balanced him. Peter staggered backward, but he regained his footing.

"You shouldn't hunt for her by yourself," Tootie said. "It's too dark out here to see what you're doing."

"You want to go with me. I'd like you to go with me, Dolly," Peter coaxed.

Tootie debated. She'd be crazy to go out in that dark wilderness with this man and no telling how many spiders and for sure coyotes. She should run back and get the men. They could make Peter go back to the school house. Only he'd be mad at her, and there was no way he'd stay put long enough for her to return with help. No way he'd believe Sara was dead if she tried to tell him. *Oh dear, more play acting. I will just have to go with him and see if I can't get him to turn around soon.* "You have to help me over the fence. I'm not as agile as I once was."

Peter lifted the top wire and lowered the bottom wire so the space for Tootie to squeeze through was larger. Once, she was through Peter took her hand. The leaves crunched under their feet. The deafening snap of a dry stick hidden under the leaves echoed through the timber. The sounds their footsteps made were loud in the quiet darkness as they wondered around the trees.

Peter stopped. He listened intently. "Hear all that noise. Is there someone behind us?"

"I think it was our walking you heard," Tootie said, wishing he was right.

Peter look behind them. "Who is there?" He sighed with a great measure of relief when he recognized his brother coming to them. "Charlie, what are you doing out here?"

"I came to help you find Sara," Charlie replied.

"Come along. I can use your company."

"Who is Charlie?" Tootie asked, looking at the empty space beside Peter.

"Forgive my manners. Charlie, my brother, this is my special friend, Dolly. I'm sure you remember when Dolly and I dated," Peter introduced. "Charlie, we may have a ways to walk. Sara is in this timber somewhere, and she is lost." Peter took off fast, making it hard for Tootie to keep up. He acted as though he was listening to a voice beside him. Peter replied to the empty space, "I know Sara is not going to be happy to see Dolly with me. It can not be helped. We are worried about her." Peter grabbed his upper arm with the other hand and rubbed it. "My arm where I hurt it pains me. I can tell there is going to be a change in the weather."

"Maybe a rain coming. No moon or stars this dark evening. All the more reason to find Sara soon," Charlie said.

"I know it is not gute for Sara to be in the timber during a storm," Peter declared.

"How did you hurt your arm?" Charlie asked.

"Charlie, your memory is growing old like we are if you have to ask. You should know since you were there. Remember that unbroken horse Daed thought he bought so cheap. Me and you said we were going to break that horse. Daed didn't want us to. He said it wasn't safe. We would get hurt.

We waited until he wasn't home to give it a try. That old horse bucked me off on my arm and broke it. Daed was really mad when he saw I was hurt. Remember he said to me foolishness like that after I disobeyed him should be driven away with the rod. I was not sure which hurt worse when he got done with me, my bottom or my broken arm. I must have been about fifteen at the time, wasn't I?"

Peter didn't get a response from his brother. "Charlie?" He stopped to search around him. Charlie was gone. Peter shrugged. "He sure did not stay long, Dolly." He trudged on. "Is not the first time Charlie has come to see me and left as suddenly as he came. Sara does that a lot lately, too." *So many others in my family come to visit and leave just as sudden. I should be used to it by now. They always come back.* "Sara, Sara, I'm coming," Peter called as he struggled forward with faltering steps. "Where are you?"

"We'll find her," Tootie assured him.

"When we do, Charlie was right. She is not going to be happy to see you with me after all these years," Peter warned. He halted quickly. "Dolly, I need you to promise me something."

167

Whatever Peter wanted surely couldn't be any worse than to take her on another buggy ride. She'd gladly agree to go for that ride with him if she could get him out of this timber.

"I'll try," she assented.

"You will probably live longer than me given you are some younger. I want you to tell our son the truth about who his mother is," Peter said.

Tootie felt as if Peter had punched her in the gut. "What truth?"

"I want you to do for me what I did not have the nerve to do myself. When I am gone I want you to tell Jonah you are his real mother so he knows Sara wasn't," Peter said.

Holy Buckets! Tootie put her hand over her mouth. She was so surprised she wasn't sure if she spoke the words out loud or thought them. How could he ask her to do such a thing?

In the school, Anna Rogies filled a Styrofoam plate with the food she was sure her father-in-law liked to eat. She took it to the back of the room. Peter wasn't there. Only an empty space on the bench where she had last seen him.

"Did you see where Peter Rogies went?" She asked Elmer Swartzendruber. The man was eating his supper from the plate in his lap.

"He went outside about the time I got in line to fill my plate. He did not say where he was going," Elmer replied.

"How long ago was that?" Anna asked, trying not to sound concerned. Their family had tried to hide the peculiar way Peter acted for as long as they could, but word had a way of spreading. She was pretty sure everyone knew by now that Peter was sick.

Elmer thought a moment. "Long enough that he should have been back by now if he was just going to the outhouse."

Anna set Peter's plate on the bench and rushed to Cooner Jonah. She bent down by his ear. "Your father has left the school some time ago and hasn't come back."

"I will go find him. He probably went to the outhouse and can not figure out how to get back in here," Cooner Jonah said. "Do not worry. Not yet."

In a few minutes, Cooner Jonah was back. He shook his head no at Anna and searched over the crowd until he saw John Lapp. "John, my father is missing. I can't find him outside. I looked in the outhouse and called around the school, but he did not answer."

"We can get the men together and all search. That will be faster," John said. He walked to the front of the room. "Can I have your attention, everyone?"

The room quieted down as the Plain people looked curiously at John in front of the food table.

"Peter Rogies is missing. Cooner Jonah thinks he has wondered off and got turned around. We need the help of all the men to look for him," John announced.

"Jah, we can do that," Eldon Bontrager said.

"Go together in groups so you do not get lost in the dark. We need to check the timber and the road in both directions," Cooner Jonah said. "I have not an idea which way my father would go."

Hal stood up. "Most of you know that Peter has not been well for a while. Please approach him carefully if you find him. He may not remember you. If he doesn't understand that you are trying to help him, he might become angry or fearful. Talk to him softly and speak slowly when you find him so he will come back with you willingly."

Nora looked around her. "Hallie, when is the last time you saw Tootie. She isn't here, either."

"Oh no! John while you're looking for Peter watch for Aunt Tootie, too," Hal said.

"You are not serious?" John asked disbelievingly.

Hal nodded.

Jim snorted. "Figures! All of a sudden, where one of them two is the other is sure to be."

The hunt lasted through the night. The women and children waited at the school, singing hymns with the hope that Peter and Tootie might hear their voices and come back on their own.

The hymns and prayers gave the Plain women and children strength to endure the long night. While they were within

169

hearing, the men listened to the lilting voices praising God. It gave them energy to go on when they grew weary.

Some of the men had lanterns in their buggies, and others had flashlights. For awhile, Hal stood in the doorway to watch. All around the school, the wobbling glow of bright lights, like giant lightning bugs, dimmed and faded from sight. Men's voices called for Peter. Some of the voices were close. Distant voices faintly echoed with calls of their own.

At day break, the men trudged back empty handed to the school. The women uncovered the food and let them eat from what was left on the table. Regrettably the farmers had to give up the search long enough to go home and do chores.

John threw his paper plate in the trash. "Hal, I hate to stop looking, but I have to milk. I'll be back as soon as I can."

"I'm going to look for Peter and Aunt Tootie while you're gone," Hal said.

"I do not think that is wise after the way Peter treated you at the birthday party," John objected.

"Peter won't always act the same from day to day. By now I don't think he can remember what happened on his birthday. I'm not afraid," Hal said.

"All recht, take Noah and Daniel with you. I do not want you out in that timber alone. Jim and me will get back here as soon as we can," John said. "The timber is a big area to cover. We have taken way too much time looking for Peter and Aendi Tootie already. If we do not find them by noon, we will ask the Wickenburg fire department to send out a search party to help us before another night comes on us."

Hal searched for Noah among a group of boys in the yard. "Your daed is going home to do chores."

"Does he want me to go with him?" Noah asked.

"Nah, Grandpa is going to help him. I want you and Daniel to come with me to search for Peter and Aunt Tootie. Are you too tired to keep searching after a long night?"

"Nah," Noah said.

"Daniel, are you too tired?" Hal asked.

"Nah," he said.

Anna Rogies heard her. "All the women and older children can scatter out and hunt. We have dozed off and on through the night so we are more rested than the men. I can not stand this waiting and doing nothing."

"All recht, let's do it," Hal said.

"I'll go tell the women. Someone will have to stay with the smaller children," Anna said, heading back to the school.

David Rogies suggested, "My daed has a tracker hound. We should go get him."

"That's a gute idea," Hal said. "Noah, take your grandfather's buggy and go with David to get the dog."

When they drove in at the Rogies farm, David said, "I need to find a piece of Dawdi's clothing to let the dog sniff so he knows what scent to track." The boy ran to the dawdi house and came back with a pair of dirty socks. "These have plenty of scent in them."

"I will say they do," Noah said, waving his hand in front of his nose.

David grinned. "Dawdi forgets to change his clothes until Daed makes him."

Cooner Jonah came out of the barn. "What are you boys up to?"

Noah explained the plan while David put a rope loop around the red hound's neck and lifted him up into the buggy. When they arrived at the school, the women had already scattered out. Hal, Emma and Daniel were the only ones waiting with Nora and Stella Strutt inside the school with the small children. Most of them were still asleep.

The boys jumped from the buggy, and the dog leaped down. David tried to hold the hound back as he lunged forward and tugged at the rope.

Hal was watching at the window. "Noah and David are back. We can start now."

Stella Strutt fanned her worried face. "I do not think I will be very gute at trying to keep up in the timber."

Hal said, "That's all right. You stay here and help my mother take care of the little ones. Why don't you sing hymns. It will

171

calm the children. If Peter and Aunt Tootie come back you can keep them here. Peter would like hearing songs if he's wandering close by."

"Boys, get the dog started," Hal said. "When you take the rope off roll it up and bring it along for later to lead the dog back."

Noah held the socks down for the dog to sniff. Hal wondered how old the hound was. His body was so thin she could count his ribs. He looked as old as Peter.

David took the rope from around the dog's neck. "Find Dawdi Peter, Mose."

The dog took off in a clumsy ambling gait that made his long ears flop up and down. His front end looked to be going one way and his back end the opposite direction. He hunkered down and slid under the fence. The boys climbed over and waited for Hal and Emma.

Hal had to fight her skirt while she lifted one leg over and then the other. She said under her breath, "I wish I had on a pair of slacks. Fence climbing would be so much easier." After she finally made it over, she said, "Okay, your turn, Emma. Let me tell you that was not easy."

"Never is," Emma acknowledge with a grin. "But the bible says in Deuteronomy, The woman shall not wear that which pertaineth unto a man, neither shall a man put on a woman's garment for all that do so are abomination unto the Lord thy God." By the time she was done reciting, Emma had mastered the fence.

Hal watched, hoping she'd learn the technique before she had to go back over the fence. "Jesus wore a robe, but he didn't have a reason to complain. There were no barbed wire fences in his day to get his skirt hung up on."

"Hallie," Emma warned and looked around to see how close the other women might be. She didn't want them to hear her stepmother make such remarks.

The boys whooped at the dog, but Mose was almost out of sight in the underbrush, sniffing the trail and baying his find. Suddenly, the dog stopped, giving them time to catch up. He

172

bayed deeply, raised his head to sniff the air and took off again. He had Peter's trail.

After an hour in the timber, Hal said, "I swear I remember seeing that snarled oak tree more than once."

Noah agreed, "You did. The dog has been circling the same area."

David said, "Dawdi Peter and your aendi must be wandering in a circle."

"Sounds like they are," Hal said.

From off in the distance, Mose bayed a tree bark.

Daniel grabbed Noah's arm. "Listen, Mose has something treed."

"Let's just hope it isn't an old coon," Emma said.

Daniel grinned. "Maybe Barabbas. He might have stayed in this timber after we turned him loose here."

"Oh, please, do not let it be so," Emma cried.

Noah said, "Do not worry, Sister. He would be glad to see you again."

"He gave you a big hug before we turned him loose. Remember?" Daniel asked and teased, "He liked you."

As Hal made her way through the underbrush she said, "Keep moving, boys. Peter and Aunt Tootie have been out here through the chilly night. It is not gute for them. We need to hurry."

David cupped his hands around his mouth and called, "Dawdi Peter."

Hal reached over and grabbed the boy's arm. "Maybe we should not call out. It might frighten Peter into walking away from us if he heard us call for him. He's confused."

David nodded he understood.

Mose's bay grew louder and longer as they closed in on the dog. Finally, they entered a small clearing. Tootie was limply propped up against the rough bark of a hickory nut tree with Peter's head in her lap. Mose was licking first the elderly man's face then Tootie's.

Peter said weakly to the dog. "Gute to see you, Pet."

Hal put her arms out to stop the others. "Be very quiet and

stay back. I'm going to them, and see how they are." She knelt down in the leaves. "Gute morning, Peter and Aunt Tootie."

"I'm glad you found us, Dear," Tootie said wearily, pushing the dog out of her face.

For a moment, Peter puzzled about who she was as he focused on Hal. As recognition came to him, he broke into a smile. "Sara, I found you. I looked for you for so long I had to give up and rest. It turned cold out here. Are you all recht?"

"Jah, I'm fine. We need to find a place where it's warm for all of us," Hal said softly.

Peter breathed with a rattling wheeze as he spoke, "I am so stiff I am not able to move."

"I brought some boys and Emma to help." Hal said, "Boys." She kept her attention on Peter as she stretched her arm out slowly and wrapped her fingers around his wrist to feel his pulse. "We will need a litter made to carry Peter. Have you all got a pocket knife?"

"Jah," the boys said in unison.

"Go get two sturdy limbs longer than Peter and cut enough small ones to space along the carrying poles so we can tie them on. That will be the litter," Hal instructed.

"What are we going to use to tie the sticks on with?" Noah asked.

"Our shoe strings," Hal said.

"How is he?" Emma asked.

Peter's head bobbed over toward his left shoulder, and his eyes went shut. Hal looked doubtful. "Pulse is very weak. Lungs are congested. We get him and Aunt Tootie to the hospital as soon as we can. Aunt Tootie, how do you feel?"

"I'm fine."

"Are you able to walk?"

"I will be glad to walk to get out of here. This timber has been a nightmare," the elderly woman whimpered.

The boys scattered into the underbrush. After the sound of snapping twigs, Noah said, "The sticks are cut for the litter."

"Everyone take out your shoe strings." Hal unlaced her strings and handed them to Noah. "Make sure to bound the sticks gute and tight. Cover the litter with pine boughs and leaves to cushion it for easier riding."

Mose ambled up and sniffed at Peter, expecting another greeting. "David, catch the dog and tie him to a bush so he can't bother your grandfather." Hal stuck her arm out in front of the dog to keep him away.

David scrambled to the dog and put the loop around his neck and secured him to a nearby gooseberry bush.

"We have the litter ready, Mama Hal," Daniel said quietly.

"Gute, now bring the litter here and lay it beside Peter." Peter opened his eyes at the mention of his name. "Peter, these boys and Emma are going to help you onto this bed." She stood up and turned to the boys. "Say very little to him. Take hold of him under his arms and legs and lift him onto the litter gently. He thinks I'm his wife so let him think that." Hal got middle ways of the litter and knelt again. "When you have lifted Peter, I'm going to put my arms under his middle to support him until we get him centered. Now on the count of three."

Swiftly, the children lifted and placed the elderly man over the litter and held him up until Hal removed her arms. She stood up and backed out of the way. "David, do you want to lead your dog or carry your grandfather?"

David looked confused.

Hal said, "The job you don't want I'll take."

"I can help lift my dawdi if you want to lead the dog. Dawdi Peter will be heavy," David offered.

Hal put her arm under Tootie's arm and lifted her to her feet. "Can you stand all right?"

"I'm fine, Dear," Tootie assured her.

Hal went over to the bush to untie Mose. He bounded ahead of her, thinking he was free. She had to give a hard tug on his rope to slow him down. She put her free hand under Tootie's arm and supported her.

The four children took an end of the litter and lifted. Hal cautioned, "Try to balance Peter and watch where you walk. It will not help him if you trip and drop him."

When they got back to the school, the children helped Hal

transfer Peter to a bench. They scattered to round up all the other women hunting in the timber. Nora and Stella went to the remaining buggies for blankets to cover Peter. Nora put one around Tootie's shoulders, but she took the blanket off and rolled it up tight. She stuffed it under Peter's head for a pillow. Then she sat down across from him on a bench and held his limp hand. His eyes were shut, and he was very still except for wheezing when he exhaled. The women all gathered around, knelt down and prayed for him.

The boys scattered in buggies to tell the men the search was over. Hal sent Emma to the nearest phone shed to call an ambulance. "Emma, when the ambulance gets close to the school tell them Nurse Hal requests no sirens. I don't want the patient to become upset by the noise."

When Cooner Jonah parked his buggy in the yard and started for the building, Hal was watching out the window. Peter had his eyes open. She said, "Peter, here comes your son. He has been worried about you."

Peter's face was blank as he looked at the man in the doorway. "That is not my son. My son left home a long time ago and turned English. He is never coming home again."

Cooner Jonah's eyes filled with tears when he heard his father's words.

Hal said to the old man, "My mistake, but you do live with this man and his wife, Anna. They're going to go with you to the doctor in Wickenburg." Hal told Cooner Jonah, "I had Emma call an ambulance. Your father is in poor shape from exposure."

The ambulance emergency crew pulled up in front of the school. Daryl and Ivan carried in a stretcher and placed Peter on it. The elderly man became more alert after they moved him. He said, "I am very tired and cold." Ivan pulled the blankets over him and buckled the stretcher straps. Peter held his hand out to Tootie. "Dolly, you are coming with me, ain't so?"

"I want her to be checked by the doctor in ER," Hal told Daryl. She asked Cooner Jonah and Anna, "Will it be all right with you if Aunt Tootie rides with Peter?"

Cooner Jonah said to the EMTs, "Please, let her go with my father. It might keep him calm to have his friend with him."

Tootie took hold of Peter's limp hand. "I'm going to the doctor with you."

"Remember your promise. You will tell the truth," Peter urged.

"Yes, I will take care of it," Tootie said. "Now rest."

The elderly man closed his eyes and let the EMTs transfer him. Hal rode up front with the driver, Steven. The Rogies followed the ambulance in their buggy.

In the hospital, Peter was put in one emergency exam room and Tootie in another. Hal explained Peter's condition and her findings to Doctor Christensen. While he did an extensive exam on Peter, Hal sat with Tootie.

Nurse Lucy redressed Peter, while the doctor went next door to examined Tootie. He asked, "How do you feel?"

Tootie said, "I'm fine. Just tired and cold."

Dr. Christensen patted her on the shoulder. "I shouldn't wonder with all you've been through. You go home, take a hot bath and get into bed for a long rest." He turned to Hal. "Now I have to talk to Peter Rogies family. Want to go with me to the waiting room?"

"Sure," Hal said and turned to her aunt. "I'll be back soon."

"I'll explain my findings on the way." By the time Hal was updated on Peter's condition, they reached the waiting room. Hal introduced Peter's son and his wife to the doctor. Doctor Christensen shook hands with them and got down to business. "Your father has many problems right now. Alzheimer's disease is taking its toll on him mentally and physically. The exposure last night while he wondered around in the timber weakened him. I seriously doubt Peter is ever going to be able to get out of bed again. From what I know of your customs, I expect you're going to take Peter back to your home. Is that right?"

Cooner Jonah said, "Jah, that is recht."

"He's going to need nursing care around the clock. He will not eat very much from now on, and his appetite will decrease to nothing in time. I don't know how long it will take, but your father is going to die soon," the doctor said to Cooner Jonah.

"Denki for telling us, Doctor. It is God's will. We will take gute care of him," Anna said.

"In that case, Peter can go home with you now. Do you want him to ride to your house in an ambulance?" The doctor asked.

"Nah, we will make a bed for him in the floor of the enclosed buggy. That will be gute enough until we get him home," Cooner Jonah said.

The doctor started for the door. "I'll get some help to bring Peter to the buggy on a stretcher."

Hal went to tell Tootie about Peter.

"Can I see him before we leave?" Tootie asked.

"Sure, come with me," Hal said.

Tootie walked over to the bed and patted Peter's hand. His eyelids fluttered and then he focused on her. She said, "I'll be over to see you as soon as I'm rested up."

He gave her a weak smile. "You remember to keep your promise."

Tootie sighed. "Yes, I'll remember. You rest easy."

Hal and Tootie met Jim and Noah coming through the emergency room exit doors. "We thought maybe you two needed a ride," Jim said. "Tootie, are you all right?"

"I just need some rest. A ride with you might not do it," she replied. "You aren't going to fit all of us in that courting buggy."

Jim grinned. "Ah, Tootie, stop worrying. I brought my car."

Hal slid into the back seat with Tootie and thought she caught a faint hint of rose perfume. Once they were settled, she said, "Aunt Tootie, what did Peter want you to promise to do for him."

Tootie studied her hands in her lap a moment. By the time she looked at Hal, she'd came up with a reasonable explanation. "I promised to visit him after he gets home."

Chapter 17

The next morning, Nurse Hal made her first visit to the Rogies farm. When Anna took her to Peter in the spare bedroom, their voices woke him up. His eyes followed Hal as she came around the bed. "Gute Morning, Peter. I'm Nurse Hal. I stopped by to see how you're doing this morning."

"Guder Mariye," Peter said weakly.

"Would you like to sit up in bed? I can prop the pillows behind you," Hal said.

"Jah, sit me up."

"Anna, hold him upright while I place the pillows against the bedstead."

Once Peter was sitting, Nurse Hal took his vitals. "Did you rest well last night?"

"Jah, I did," Peter replied, disappointed as he looked around the room. "I was hoping my special friend would be with you. The young woman that stays with you."

"Ach, Dolly?" Peter nodded. "She is still resting up. Do you want her to come visit?" Hal asked.

"Jah, I want to have her come be with me," Peter said.

"All recht, I will see what I can do," Hal told him. "Now I must leave to finish my rounds. See you soon, Peter." She patted his frail hand. He gave her a weak smile and closed his eyes.

Anna followed Hal out of the room. "I was surprised that

your aendi was not along."

"We talked about it. Truthfully, with her being English, we didn't know if you would want Aunt Tootie to come see Peter now that he's so very weak."

"Ach, it is not a matter of what Jonah and I want. We want to fulfill Peter's wishes now. What is important to him is to have your aendi be with him as much as possible. He has asked for her every time he wakes up," Anna said. "Would Tootie be willing to come sit with Peter, knowing that will help him die happy?" Anna's eyes filled with tears.

Hal gave her a hug. "Aunt Tootie very much wants to be here. Her thoughts are with Peter all the time. If Jonah and you don't mind, I'll go home and get her. She will feel so much better if she can be here."

Each morning from that day on, Hal left Tootie by Peter's bedside. She checked Peter's vitals and received a condition report from Anna. Each time she made the visit, she knew that Peter was declining. He slept more and took less nourishment.

Hal worried about Peter's family and mentioned that at home. "Anna, Cooner Jonah and their children look tired from lack of sleep. Aunt Tootie should get more rest, too. The caring process is hard. The waiting and worrying about Peter is taking a toll on all of them."

John said he'd go over to sit with Peter that night. Jim offered to go along. Hal sent Emma to spread the word so others in the community could take turns helping. That gave the family time to rest at night and get the daily chores out of the way.

One morning when Hal and Tootie made their visit, Tootie patted Peter's shoulder. "It's Dolly, Peter."

He opened his eyes and smiled as he always did when he saw her. "Sit down and stay a while."

"I intend to. Is there anything I can get you. A drink or something to eat."

"I'm starved," Peter replied. "I would like a plate of dippy eggs."

"Good! Wait a minute." Tootie rushed to the kitchen. "Peter

is awake. He's hungry, and he wants dippy eggs. Whatever that is."

"It's just eggs flipped over easy and served runny," Hal told her.

"What should he have?" Anna asked Hal.

"It's been so long since he last ate, we should be careful. Have you some chicken broth he can drink. The dippy eggs is okay for sure if that's what he's hungry for," Hal suggested.

Anna set to work, and soon she handed Tootie a tray. Hal plumped up the pillows under Peter's head. "Now enjoy your meal," Hal told him as she left Tootie feeding him.

Anna and Hal listened from the other room. Anna said softly, "It wonders me that Peter wants to eat and seems more alert."

"That happens sometimes. Don't get you hopes up," Hal cautioned. "Sometimes, a person will have a bright moment like that and die soon after."

Peter said, "You smell like roses again today. Nice smell that is."

Tootie giggled. "Thank you. Want to know a secret? I bought this perfume just for you."

"Denki, Dolly, for telling me. We were never very gute at keeping secrets from each other, were we? Ach, but the biggest one of all we did keep from everyone else and did it well." Peter had a sad hitch to his voice.

"You shouldn't dwell on that right now," Tootie soothed. "Take another bite. You don't want these eggs to get cold."

"I will let it go now that I know you are going to help me. You promised." He gave her an intense look.

"Yes, I did," Tootie said reluctantly. "Take another bite."

Peter sighed. "I am full now and tired."

"You should rest," Tootie said.

As she helped Peter slip back down in bed, he pleaded, "Dolly, you do remember your promise? Please help me."

"I said I would. Now rest," Tootie appeased.

Peter closed his eyes and fell into a deep sleep. One he didn't wake up from again. John, Cooner Jonah and Samuel Nisely were with him through that night. His emaciated frame hardly made a movement except for his chest rising and falling.

The next morning, Hal and Tootie came back.

Anna met them at the door. "Peter is not breathing gute."

In the bedroom, Tootie stood at the foot of the bed, watching Peter's long wispy beard rise and fall slowly with hesitation between breaths.

Hal said to Anna, "The doctor needs to come. Did Peter doctor with Dr. Burns?"

"Jah," Anna said.

"I'll call him for you," Hal offered.

Dr. Burns drove in close to dinner time. Cooner Jonah met him at the door. "Wilcom, Dochtah. I'll show you to my father."

Dr. Burns examined Peter and said, "It will only be a matter of hours Peter has left. Call the family in now."

By eleven that evening, Peter's bedroom was lit by two kerosene lamps. The room was full of family, standing around the bed. Their focus stayed on Peter's pallid face. His mouth gaped open, and every breath took effort.

Before morning, Peter's raspy gasps stopped. Everyone in the room stopped breathing with him. After a few seconds, Peter's chest started to rise and fall again. That happened several times. Then came the time Peter didn't start breathing again. After a minute transpired, Tootie went to the kitchen for Hal.

Hal checked for his pulse and told Anna and Cooner Jonah, "Peter ist todt."

"Hal?" Tootie whispered.

"I just told them that Peter has died."

Cooner Jonah patted his father's hand and in a choked voice said, "It is God's will. My father is at peace now."

Anna wiped tears before she hugged Hal and Tootie. "Denki and God bless you both for helping Peter."

Peter's extended family and grandchildren clung to each other for a few minutes. Finally, the family moved from the room into the living room. Hal and Tootie went home. Cooner Jonah hitched up his buggy and went to the phone booth to call Doctor Burns. When he came back, the family worked out the funeral plans.

It was not quite daylight when the doctor parked behind the buggies in front of the house. As he entered, he looked around at all the family. Someone directed him to the bedroom. Dr. Burns made all the checks for signs of life. He asked Jonah and Anna some questions, made some notes, filled out some papers and left.

John and Samuel Nisely washed Peter's body and dressed him in long johns. Cooner Jonah and Anna left to make arrangements at the funeral home in Wickenburg. The funeral director followed them home to pick up Peter's body, driving his horse drawn hearse.

The men helped the funeral director lift the body on a covered gurney and into the back of the hearse. The next day just before noon, the funeral director brought Peter back in a pine coffin. John and Samuel helped Cooner Jonah and the funeral director place the coffin in the middle of the living room. John and Samuel dressed Peter in his funeral clothes, a white shirt and suit, and covered his face with a white cloth that went down to his waist.

When they had Peter ready for the visitation and the funeral, Cooner Jonah pushed the roll away walls out of sight to make the room bigger. Moses Strutt drove in with the bench wagon. The men carried benches in and set them in rows. Chairs were placed around the coffin for the family and three for the ministers.

John and Samuel went home to get their families for the visitation. Buggies came a few at a time all afternoon to pay their respects and bring food. The coffin's top double doors were laying to the sides of the coffin. Cooner Jonah asked each visitor if they would like to view Peter. If they said yes, he pulled the cloth back so they could see Peter's face and say their good byes. After people stopped coming, Peter's family sat with his coffin that night.

The next morning was the funeral. The possession was long. John drove his buggy in the middle of it, and Jim followed with Noah beside him to pay their respects.

They parked as they would for a Sunday service meeting and walked among the other Plain people to the house. They left the horses hitched to the buggy since the service usually lasted only an hour and a half. That time would go quickly, and they would stay lined up to follow the hearse to the cemetery.

People went past the family seated facing the coffin. A woman ahead of the Lapp family said to Cooner Jonah, "I was so sorry to hear of your father's passing."

Cooner Jonah nodded. She moved on with sympathetic words for Anna and the rest of the family.

An old friend about Peter's age said to the family, "Let us hope Peter Rogies is walking close with God now."

Cooner Jonah nodded solemnly "I am sure he is already."

The three ministers sat in chairs at the front of the room, waiting for the mourners to assemble. After awhile, no one else came through the doors. Everyone quietly waited. The ministers removed their hats and all the other men did likewise.

Luke Yoder stood up and read Peter's obituary, starting with the birth and death dates and listed his family from his son and wife to grandchildren, his parents, siblings and their children. When he finished the obituary, he quoted the scripture from Matthew. "Come unto Me all ye that labor and are heavy laden, and I will give you rest. Take my yoke upon you and learn of me; for I am meek and lowly in heart, and ye shall find rest unto your souls. The only way to find rest from our sins and our work is to come to Jesus Christ in faith and repentance. We need to submit our will to Him. Only then will we find rest."

Luke sat down, and Enos Yutzy stood up. He read the hymn, *Amazing Grace,* and sat down.

Bishop Eldon Bontrager stood up to give the sermon. He raised his voice for all to hear him. "Thank God! The answer is in Jesus Christ our Lord.

While we do appreciate celebrating the life of Peter Rogies today, we are also reminded that as death is, it is the only thing that rescues us from sin. Our lives will end some day like Peter's life has ended, and if we have faith in Jesus Christ our freedom will come as Peter's has now for him. Our story is not about what we achieved on earth but rather about what we allowed Jesus to achieve for us and in us in this life and in eternity. Let us pray."

Bishop Bontrager bowed his head. The mourners followed his lead. "Dear heavenly Father, sometimes I think only of the pain of death. Today I thank you for the freedom death has brought Peter Rogies. I thank you Jesus who made a sinless eternity after death possible for Peter to find peace in. Amen."

The bishop sat down, and Luke Yoder stood up. "In Romans it tells us, For we know that the whole creation groaneth and travaileth in pain together until now. And not only they, but ourselves also, who have the first fruits of the Spirit, even we ourselves groan within ourselves, waiting for the adoption, to wit, the redemption of our body." He spoke to the Rogies family. "Whereas Peter has experienced physical rest, and the spiritual rest of sins were forgiven, we will experience that perfect rest only when we get to Heaven as Peter has found. Now the reading of the hymn, *The Old Rugged Cross*." When Luke finished the song reading, he said, "Now we will file out and go to our buggies. Wait for the coffin to be brought out, and the hearse to leave then all of you follow."

On the gravel roads to the cemetery, the rattle of the carriage wheels on rocks crunched loudly under so many buggies. In the short time Hal had been a member of the Plain community, she had come to recognize that funeral sound. She connected it with a feeling of loss and sadness that came with death.

As buggies parked, the four pallbearers carried the pine coffin across the cemetery over to the open grave. They set the coffin gently down on the two boards laid across the opening. The ends of two ropes stretched over the hole and into the grass beside the boards.

After everyone gathered, Bishop Bontrager read the hymn, *In the Sweet By And By*, in German in a slow litany which seemed to hang on forever.

When he finished, he bowed his head. "Now together we pray." Everyone chanted, *The Lord's Prayer*, in German. "Unser vater der du bist im himmel." While they prayed, the coffin was lowered by the four pallbearers. They picked up shovels from the mound and tossed dirt into the hole. Each shovel of dirt hit the coffin and scattered with a thunk until the wooden coffin was covered.

As everyone prayed, Tootie felt a tickle on her ankle. She gave a startled gasp as she opened her eyes wide and stepped sideways, thinking she might be on a snake or have a spider crawling up her leg. With a measure of relief all she saw was grass blades waving in the breeze, tickling her ankle bone. As she looked around on the ground, she thought, *At least it wasn't something that would bite. Not yet anyway.*

The long neat rows of the same size and shaped granite headstones were a strange sight. She was used to seeing all shapes and sizes of stones in the cemetery where her family was buried. She glanced at the stone beside the open grave. The stone didn't have Peter's wife's name on it. She would have to ask Hal about that. *Why wasn't the man's wife beside him?*

A nervousness about what creatures might be in this country cemetery made her keep her eyes open. She intended to be very watchful until she was out of this lonely, grassy terrain. If there wasn't a snake lurking nearby, it was only because the creature was scared off by horses and human feet tromping the ground. The crawling serpents came back to their den when they could. She looked for slick holes around her. The only one she saw was near a small mound of dirt where gophers lived.

It took more than people walking in the grass, and buggies making noise to scare off spiders. She sure didn't want a spider going up her leg. If she caused a scene at this solemn occasion, Hallie would be mad at her forever.

When the service ended, Hal noticed Mary and Eli Mast wandering down the row of headstones. Mary lumbered along beside her husband, weighed down by her pregnancy. They reached the grave they wanted and stopped to pray.

Mary slipped a bouquet of red peonies from under her cape and laid the flowers on the grave. Hal remembered the words on that headstone all too well. Hallie Mast, infant daughter of Eli and Mary Mast.

This was a baby lost before she had a chance to begin life. Hal was honored by the baby's parents. They named the stillborn baby, Hallie, because Nurse Hal helped Mary with the delivery. Perhaps, the honor resulted because Nurse Hal took it so hard that the baby was lost on her watch.

While Plain people had to be at the cemetery for the funeral, some wondered around the rows, stopping at certain graves to reminisce and say prayers for loved ones and friends. It was the way of Plain people not to cling to grief when they lost a loved one, because they thought their loved ones were in a better place. On a sad day like this when they had to be in the cemetery anyway, they felt the need to connect with the ones they had lost.

In an orderly fashion, the Plain mourners climbed in their buggies, turned around in the road and headed back to the Rogies farm for the dinner. By the next day, life would go on as usual for all of them. Peter would only be a memory to summons up once in a while. Maybe with a story about him someone remembered fondly. Hal hoped that the stories wouldn't always be about Peter in his last days when the elderly man talked to family, his horse and dog that had died long before him.

Chapter 18

For the next couple of weeks, one day blended into the next for Tootie. Hal wondered what Tootie must have promised Peter for him to bring it up so many times. Did the promise have anything to do with the depression Tootie seemed to be in.

Tootie certainly didn't have much to say. She washed the dishes and even stuck around long enough to wash the slop pail. That uncharacteristic move was enough for Hal to be worried about her aunt. She asked her mother if she thought Tootie was acting troubled. Nora said perhaps Tootie was mourning the loss of her friend.

One Sunday morning, Tootie sat down at the breakfast table. "Where are we going to church this morning?"

John said, "This is the in between Sunday. No worship service today. It is a day of rest or to visit with friends and family usually."

"At home, we have church every Sunday," Tootie said quietly. "It's comforting to go to church. I forgot about this in between Sunday."

"We thought today would be a perfect day to have a family picnic," Hal said. "You know a better way to cheer everyone up?"

"No, Dear. I guess not if anyone needs cheered up. That's why you bought all those packages of hot dogs and potato chips when we went shopping the other day," Tootie said.

"That's right. Emma baked extra bread yesterday. We can

build a fire and roast hot dogs and marshmallows."

"I didn't see you buy any marshmallows," Tootie said.

"That's because I already had a package."

Daniel asked, "Dawdi, do you like to fish?"

"Fishing just happens to be my middle name," Jim said with a wink. "But I didn't bring a pole."

"We will loan you one so you can fish in the pond with us," Daniel said.

Hal asked, "Noah, could you and Daniel put Molly in the horse pen for the day? I think we would have a better time in the picnic grove if she's caught."

Jim's head came up. "That's the horse I used on my buggy, isn't it? Why do you have to pen her up?"

"Molly likes to come to picnics. She has a way of annoying Hal and Emma when she does," John said, smiling at Hal. "I'll tell you about it later."

After breakfast, the women packed bundles. Emma brought the red wagon up by the back door to load. The men finished the chores. They hunted up their fishing poles and walked to the pond.

Biscuit scampered to Emma and jumped on her, leaving two paw prints on her apron. She let out a long, "Ach!"

Daniel grabbed the puppy and pulled him away from her. "He just wants you to pat him."

"Why is he loose?" Tootie wrinkled up her nose in disapproval.

"We thought he would like to go on the picnic with us," Noah said.

"I see," Tootie said as she lined up on the far side of Nora and Hal as they placed bundles in the wagon.

The puppy trotted over by the chicken house and sniffed. A hen cackled and flew out the door to light in the grass near the puppy. He stood still. Every muscle quivered, and his nose twitched. Suddenly, he raised his head to the sky and let out a loud bay. The hen stretched her neck high and cackled again. The pup slinked toward her.

"Noah, do something with that dog now!" Emma ordered.

"He is going to catch that hen."

The boys ran to Biscuit. Daniel put his arms around the dog's neck. "Come on, Dog."

"Biscuit," Noah corrected in a hiss.

"Biscuit, you get away from Emma's chickens," Daniel scolded loudly so Hal could hear him use Dog's given name.

Shortly, the boys sat down one on each side of a multi flora bush on the pond bank and concentrated on their red bobbers. Biscuit was beside Daniel, stretched out with his head on his front paws.

The women strolled down the lane between the pasture and the cornfield. They were in the pasture by the time a covey of quail whistled bobwhite near a lone mulberry tree. Biscuit stood up and listened to the quail. He took off on a dead run toward the tree, scattering the sheep flock.

Tootie watched the dog rushed the tall grass in front of them. The covey soared up and didn't stop until they were over the hay field fence. She slowed down. This picnic was the last thing she wanted to do. She'd rather just stay home by herself.

Nora looked back. "Keep up, Tootie. You're a slow poke this morning."

"Where's this picnic going to be?" Tootie asked, looking around.

Hal pointed toward the picnic grove. "Over there."

"That far away? I thought we might have the picnic under that big tree in the yard," Tootie sniffed disapprovingly.

"The grove is where we always have picnics," Emma said.

"It's the perfect place. Plenty of shade and far enough from the house to make the picnic special." Nora added. "I know. I've been on a picnic there before."

"We have to walk through all this tall grass clear over there. A picnic in the house yard would do fine," Tootie complained. "I don't think I'm going to like this."

Nora twisted around with her hands on her hips. "Well, aren't you a ray of sunshine this morning. You wanted to go on the picnic. Just come along and enjoy the day. We'd rather you didn't rain on our good time."

Tootie ducked her head. "All right." The elderly woman took one step at a time in the thick spring grass and checked around her feet. She fell behind again.

"Stop everyone and let Aunt Tootie catch up. Aunt Tootie, are you having trouble walking in the grass?" Hal asked.

Tootie complained, "How will I ever know if I step on a snake or spider if I don't check the grass in front of me first. I don't know how you Amish people can be brave enough to walk in this grass barefoot."

"Oh, for goodness sakes," Nora said, clearly exasperated. "You are the last one to walk on the path. Do you really think a snake or anything else would still be in that spot?"

"Oh, guess not," Tootie said sheepishly.

"We can't keep waiting on you," Nora told her. "We have the wagon to unload and firewood to gather. Just get there as soon as you can."

Tootie watched the three women take off without her. Redbird and Beth waved at her and tried to say good bye. She hustled along and caught up to them.

When they entered the grove, Hal handed Tootie one of the two quilts she carried. "Unfold this and lay it on the grass so we can sit on it. I'm going to sit the little girls on the one I have."

The women relaxed as they watch the men and boys fish in the pond. Finally, Emma said, "I am going to go fish."

"Gute luck. See you later," Hal said.

"Emma fishes?" Tootie asked.

Hal nodded. "She loves to fish, and she's gute at it."

When it was close to dinner time Hal was ready to build the fire. "We should go get wood."

"Where?" Tootie demanded.

"Where do you think? Under the trees where sticks fall," Nora said, pointing at the underbrush.

"Oh, I don't know about that," Tootie cried. "I won't be able to see where I'm walking in that jungle."

"How about you watch the girls while we go get the wood?" Hal suggested.

"That sounds good to me. I can do that." Tootie knelt beside the girls. They crawled over by her and grabbed her arms so they could stand up. Tootie put her arms around them and gave them a hug as if she wanted to protect them from unseen dangers.

When Hal brought an armload of sticks back, the little girls were jabbering to each other, and Tootie had the saddest look as she stared at the ground. Something was still bothering her. Tootie hadn't been eating much lately, and she had been too quiet. What she went through with Peter had been a drain on her. Hal knew that, but Tootie wasn't bouncing back. Maybe she was still sad about Peter dying like Nora thought, but was there something else she wasn't sharing with her family? Hal decided the day would come she'd catch Tootie alone and ask what was wrong" That is if the woman didn't perk up on her own.

After lunch, the fishermen went back to the pond, and the women relaxed. Redbird and Beth napped. The grove was peaceful except for the rustle of leaves high in the trees. Tootie spotted the wooden crosses in a patch of tall grass. "There's a cemetery? Whose buried there?"

Hal smiled. "The Lapp's pet dog, Patches, and a tea box."

Tootie's nose wrinkled as she tried to understand the significant of such a weird cemetery. She couldn't. "Oh," she said softly. *That must be a weird Amish custom. I wonder if it's mentioned in my book.*

It had been the longest day ever for Tootie. She was so glad to get out of that wilderness the Lapp's called a picnic grove. That night, the bed felt so good when she laid down. Before she closed her eyes, she noticed a flicker of lightning lit up the room. A soft, summer breeze stirred the transparent sheers at the open window. Maybe the storm was going around. No need to get up in the dark and close the window just yet. The breeze felt good in the stuffy room.

She closed her eyes and dozed off only to toss and turn. This happened often to her since Peter died. Images raged and floated through the thunderstorm in her mind. Peter faded in and out, glaring at her and shaking his finger. He was impatient with her for not going to see his son. He wanted her to keep her promise. A promise she shouldn't have made.

Tootie's eyes shot open at a loud rumble of thunder. Must be that was what had startled her awake. The curtains flapped wildly out into the room. She should get up and close that window. Sounded like a real sky buster coming. She rubbed her eyes, hating to get out of bed. There the noise was again. It wasn't thunder that woke her. Someone knocked on the door.

"Go away," Tootie snapped. "We're all in bed."

"Please open up," a woman's voice begged. "I need to see Nurse Hal."

Tootie slid out of bed and felt for her housecoat on the foot of the bed. She put it on and got down on her knees to feel under the bed for her fuzzy house shoes. She didn't come up with them. She must have flung them back too far when she kicked them off.

The knocking was more impatient this time.

Tootie stood up. Hal left a flashlight on the table. She had to make due with it to get across the dark room. No way was she going to mess with trying to light the lamp. She made Emma or Hal put it out at night once she laid down. She wasn't about to light the lamp herself. Be her luck she'd burn the house down.

Again, the next rapid knocking. She snapped, "I'm coming."

Tootie opened the door a crack and peeked outside. Rain poured onto the porch's tin roof and fell in sheets to the ground. All she could make out were two black figures. She shone the flashlight in their faces. "What do you want?"

"I have to see Nurse Hal. Please let me in," the woman said, putting her hands in front of her eyes.

"Why?" Tootie demanded.

"I am having a baby," she said.

"Come back tomorrow when Hallie is up." Tootie started to shut the door.

A hand slammed into the door to keep it open. The man said, "We have to see Nurse Hal now. My wife is having the baby soon."

193

The woman cried out in pain and grabbed her protruding stomach.

Tootie opened the door wide. "Oh dear! I'll say soon. Come in quick." She grabbed the young woman by the elbow. "Come over here, Dear, and get in bed. I'll go get Hallie right away."

The woman laid down. Tootie covered her up and ordered the man to close the open window before she hurried from the room. She went up the stairs carefully, not wanting to miss a step. At the top, she looked from one closed door to the next.

"I don't know which one is Hallie's room. Guess I'll pick the first door and find out," Tootie mumbled.

She turned the flashlight off and opened the door slowly. As she eased across the room to the bed, she could make out a snoring man on this side. She made her way around the bed and leaned down close to see who was on the other side. *This is Hallie*. Tootie reached out and patted Hal's arm.

Hal let out a gasp.

"Hallie," Tootie whispered. "It's me, Aunt Tootie."

"Are you sleepwalking?" Hal asked groggily.

"No, I'm awake. I just came to tell you something," Tootie said.

John rolled over. "Was ist letz?"

"The matter is Aunt Tootie is standing over us," Hal said.

"She must be sleepwalking," John mumbled. "Take her back to bed."

"I'm not sleepwalking, and I'll have you know, John Lapp, I'd like to go back to bed," Tootie said impatiently. "But I can't. We have a problem."

"What kind of problem?" Hal asked groggily.

"A woman is having her baby in my bed."

"What?" Hal cried, sitting up.

"I'm sorry to have to wake you. I told her to go home. She demanded I come get you. She says she can't wait until morning to give birth," Tootie complained.

"Who is it?"

"I didn't ask her name. I was too upset when she screamed," Tootie said.

"I've got to get to the clinic fast," Hal said urgently.

Her arm came out to move Tootie aside so she could get out of bed. She slipped into her robe, grabbed a flashlight, and turned it on in John's face.

He threw his arm over his eyes and groaned.

"I'm so sorry, John. Go back to sleep. I have to deliver a baby," Hal said as she rushed for the door. Tootie was right behind her.

"I heard," John said sluggishly.

When they were in the hall, Tootie turned on her flashlight. She asked in a put out voice, "Just where am I supposed to sleep?"

Hal turned around. "What? Oh." She pointed to Emma's door. "Go sleep with Emma."

"All right," Tootie grumbled to Hal's back as she started down the stairs. Tootie slowly opened the door and eased in. The room was so dark. She walked slowly and leaned over to squint at the bed. Emma was sleeping on this side. Tootie went around and pulled back the covers. She sat down, put her feet in bed and covered up.

The draft from fanning the covers woke up Emma. She rolled over fast. "Was ist letz?"

"Don't get mad at me. Hallie said I could sleep with you," Tootie whined.

"Aendi Tootie! I am sorry. You scared me. Are you sleepwalking?"

"No, I'm wide awake unfortunately," Tootie complained.

"Why are you supposed to sleep with me?" Emma asked.

"There's a woman in my bed having a baby," Tootie explained with a put out sigh.

"Really! I have to go," Emma said, vaulting up.

"Why?" Tootie demanded.

"I assist Hallie. I have to build a fire in the cookstove and heat water," Emma explained as she put on her robe and fumbled for her flashlight on the side table.

"Oh," Tootie said. She pulled the covers up to her chin. "See you in the morning."

After Emma left, Tootie felt wide awake. She grumbled, "Nora told me coming here was going to be a relaxing vacation. She was wrong, wrong. Just all wrong. I wash a pickup truck load of dishes three times a day. Emma is always trying to talk me into hoeing her old garden. Hal makes me hang up laundry.

We go, go, go all the time in that old dusty buggy. No wonder they need so much help when they're home. They spend too much time running around. The only person I had fun with up and died on me. Since then I can't even get a decent night's rest in this place, thinking about what Peter wants me to do for him. How could he die and leave that burden on me?

Holly Buckets! A woman has to be in my bed to have her baby. What was wrong with messing up her own bed? I'm going to tell Nora in the morning I'm ready to go home. Maybe once I'm home in my bed, I'll not feel so burdened with Peter's secret. I have no intention of keeping my promise to him. I just want to go home right away."

Hal entered the dark clinic. She could make out two figures, one on the bed and the other standing by it. "We need some light in here, don't we?" She lit the lamp and turned back to the bed. Until then she didn't have a clue which one of her patients she'd find. "Mary Mast, you're doing it to me again! You aren't supposed to be ready to deliver for a month yet. I should call an ambulance and send you right to the hospital."

"I don't think you have time to do that," Eli Mast said. "She is ready to have the baby now."

"I'll be the judge of that, Doctor Eli. Let me check," Hal said, giving him a half smile.

Eli's usually twinkling eyes were dim with worry. He nodded solemnly.

Hal's visual assessment saw Mary's usually pale face was flushed. Her fair hair was damp with sweat, leaking from under her prayer cap and plastered along her face. Her blue eyes were pain filled.

Emma stuck her head in the door. "I put the water on." She

looked at the bed. " Ach nah, it is Mary. What else do you need?"

"Bring clean bedding. We need to change the bed with Mary in it," Hal said, and Emma left. "Eli, you go sit in a chair. Rest until I need you." When Eli moved out of the way, Hal pulled the top covers back at the foot of the bed. She checked Mary for dilation. Mary was in labor all right, but Hal found the umbilical cord coming down before the baby. That was a bad sign.

"Eli and Mary, the umbilical cord is coming out first. A prolapsed cord means when the baby's head gets in the birth canal the head will press against the cord and shut the baby's oxygen supply off. Chances are great that the baby will be born dead if that's allowed to happen."

Both parents looked frightened. They lost their first baby. They didn't want to lose this one, too.

Mary's voice trembled. "What can we do?"

"First, I need to call that ambulance. You're going to have to have a cesarean section. Until we get you to the hospital, I'm going to insert my hand and keep the baby from entering the birth canal until we get you a doctor's help."

Mary blushed. Her shy nature bothered her at the thought, but her brave response was, "You do what you need to do."

Hal looked at Eli for his approval. The muscle in his jaw bunched as he responded, "Jah, we want this baby."

"That's right. We all do," Hal agreed. "I don't want a repeat of what happened to the last baby. I want to save this baby."

Mary looked at Eli and back at Hal. "We would be very sad if this baby does not make it, but Nurse Hal, God makes no mistakes. He does all things well. We only see right now in our life, and he sees our whole life."

Eli nodded. "That is right. God would see our tears. He would know what we are feeling when we look at the empty crib in our bedroom just like last time. God gave up His only Son when he sent him to earth to die for our sins. He is our help and our strength in time of need. That help is for you as well as Mary and me. Just do your best. That is all we ask. All three of us will have to accept what happens, good or bad."

As Hal pulled her nursing bag out of the cupboard, she knew what the Masts said was supposed to make her feel better but it didn't. Only being in action now and hoping for a successful outcome was going to make her less anxious. She rifled through her bag for her cell phone, praying the battery was up enough to make the 911 call.

The phone had bars. Hal made the call and explained to the dispatcher the problem. She asked for an ambulance. She told the dispatcher to alert ER so the nurse on duty could get a doctor ready to take over when Mary arrived. They needed an operating room prepared quickly for the cesarean section. Since she'd begin holding the baby in right away, she didn't have time to make the calls herself. The dispatcher said she'd take care of everything.

Hal assigned Eli and Mary tasks to make the wait go easier. "Eli, go find Emma and tell her to come here so I can explain what's happened. In the morning, she will need to tell my family where I disappeared to. We won't be needing warm water or bedding anymore." As soon as he left the room, Hal put on a glove and covered it with lubricant. Mary's painful modesty showed on her face when Hal said, "I'm ready to insert my hand now so you pray that what I'm about to do is successful to save your baby, and that my arm and hand hold out until we get you to the hospital."

"Do what is necessary. Eli and I want this baby to survive," Mary said in a strained voice.

Hal took a deep breath and inserted her hand until she felt the baby's head. She threw the blankets back over Mary with the other hand until only Mary's bare feet were sticking out. Mary groaned and her back arched as she pushed, causing Hal to strain to keep her hand in place.

It seemed forever until the ambulance came roaring into the drive, the siren a warbled blare and strobe lights pierced the darkness. Hal said, "Mary, stay in the buggy now. The move to the stretcher is not going to be easy for either of us."

"Hi, Nurse Hal," EMT Daryl greeted. "What we got going

this time?"

She explained to Daryl, Steven and Ivan what the situation was to make sure they understood the problem. "Now you have to somehow keep the two of us together and covered up as we move from the bed to the stretcher."

The emergency workers managed to get Mary on the stretcher and keep Hal in place by slowly moving as one unit. Her hand slipped once when she stepped off the porch steps, but she managed to get her hand back in place before Mary's next contraction

Hal told Eli on the way to the ambulance, "Go to the hospital waiting room. I'll find you as soon as I can and wait with you. When all is well with Mary, you can give me a ride home when you leave." By then the emergency workers were putting Mary's stretcher into the ambulance.

"Jah, I will," he called into the ambulance as the door shut.

The drive to the hospital was bouncy. Hal told herself ambulances weren't built for the comfort of the sick people they carried. Each bounce sure made it hard for her to do her job at the moment.

Getting out of the ambulance was another precarious procedure, but they made it inside the Emergency Room. Lucy Stineford was on duty that night. "We have a room ready for your patient." She giggled when she got a close look at Hal. "Had you planned on finding a bed to spend the night in?"

"Very funny. I was sleeping when this emergency occurred," Hal said. "There wasn't any time to change clothes."

The Operating Room team was waiting. A nurse put a hospital gown on Mary. She told Hal to remove her hand, and they rushed Mary to the operating room. Hal scrubbed her hands and massaged the right one to get rid of the numbness.

She went to the waiting room and sat with Eli. The cesarean section procedure went fast. A nurse came back about twenty minutes later to tell them Mary had a baby boy. Both were doing fine.

Hal took Eli to the window in the surgery room door so he could see Mary. The doctor held the tiny, blood streaked baby up for them to see. Eli and Hal breathed a sigh of relief when they heard the baby's mewing cries.

Hal said, "Mary will have to stay here for a few days. The baby will probably stay in the nursery for a while since he's small. The nurses will have Mary and the baby ready for you to see soon when Mary is taken to a room."

"Denki, Nurse Hal," he said, patting her shoulder. "You look as tired as I feel."

"I am so while you are with your wife and baby I'm going to the break room and have me a cup of coffee. You want one before they call you back? You can always take the cup with you to Mary's room."

"Jah, maybe I better have one to stay awake," Eli said.

"Gute idea. I don't want you so tired when you leave this hospital you forget you're supposed to give me a ride home."

Eli chuckled then he turned serious. "You are one person I would never forget. Bless you, Nurse Hal."

Hal glanced at the waiting room clock. An hour and a half had passed. It must have been about fifty minutes, she held the baby back as Mary contracted against her hand. Her arm felt achy yet. Her hand was slightly numb from the experience, but she'd be all right with some rest. Even better, Eli and Mary were going to be floating on cloud nine now that they had a successful start to their family.

As Hal brought Eli a cup of coffee to the table, he said, "I've been thinking Nurse Hal. Life is a mixture of sorrow and joy. We sorrowed when we lost our baby girl, and now we are filled with joy because we have a baby son denki to you. God is gute. He moves in mysterious ways His wonders to perform, ain't so?"

"Jah," Hal said wearily as she sat down to wait for the nurse to come.

Meanwhile that night at the Lapp farm, the ambulance siren pierced the quiet. The strobe light flashed red and yellow across the covers and brought Tootie upright in bed. She felt a panic attack coming on. She shouted, "Fire, Fire! Get out of the house, everyone! It's on fire!"

By the time she rushed into the hall, the rest of the family gathered, looking around.

Nora said, "Mercy, Jim, Tootie's been sleepwalking again. She just came out of Emma's room."

"I'm awake. Emma said I could sleep in her room," Tootie retorted. "I saw the flicker of flames flashing on the walls, coming through the open bedroom door.

John and Jim rushed downstairs. Nora, Tootie and the boys followed.

Jim sniffed the air. "I don't smell smoke anywhere."

John said, "I do not see flames."

Emma was coming from the clinic with an armload of bedding. "Was ist los? What are you all doing out of bed?"

Nora said, "Your Aunt Tootie screamed fire. She woke us all up."

"There is not a fire," Emma said calmly.

Nora frowned at her sister. "I might have known this was another one of your nightmares."

"I tell you I saw flashing lights from the flames and heard the sound of a siren like a fire truck was already here," Tootie said. "I'm sure I did."

"Actually, Aendi Tootie did see and hear something like that," Emma defended. "Hallie sent for an ambulance to take Mary Mast to the hospital to have her baby. The ambulance siren was loud, and the lights strobed as they usually do."

John wondered, "Why didn't Hal let Mary have her baby here?"

"The baby was coming early. Mary Mast needed more care than Hallie could give her. Hallie is on the way to the hospital in the ambulance with Mary. Eli is following. When it is safe to leave Mary and the new baby, Eli is going to bring Hallie home."

"In that case, all of us are going back to bed for what is left of this night," John said as he motioned for everyone to move up the steps.

Tootie looked uncertain about where to go. Emma said, "Go back to my bed, Aendi. I will be coming as soon as I take this bundle of dirty bedding to the mudroom. I'm not cleaning and making that bed this time of night."

When Emma slipped into bed, Tootie made a weak sniffle. "Emma, I've been thinking. Hallie is really needed around here, isn't she?"

"Jah, everyone depends on her for help all the time, including this Lapp family. I do not know what we would do without her."

"That makes me sad." Tootie sounded maudlin.

"Why?" Emma asked.

"If I was to die tomorrow, no one would miss me or even remember me down the road," Tootie said.

"Do not fret, Aendi. You would be missed by this family. We have enjoyed your visit here and getting to know you. We love you. We want you to come visit us again. Believe me when I tell you we will remember you always."

"Honest?"

Emma giggled. "Honest! I am very truthful. You are a gute Christian woman who loves her family and is loyal to family and friends. Just look at how kind you were to Peter Rogies."

"Thank you, Dear. I'll sleep better knowing that. Good night," Tootie said.

In her mind, Emma listed the memories probably brought up at gatherings later on when Nurse Hal's English Aunt was mentioned; swatting Stella Strutt on the bottom in a meeting service, daring to sew the woman's apron to the quilting frame and taking off in Dawdi Jim's courting buggy to Lover's Lane with Peter Rogies. Emma smiled. Aunt Tootie wouldn't be forgotten by anyone. Nurse Hal's English aunt had created some lively moments to be relived in the minds of Plain people for years to come.

Chapter 19

As the summer days went by, Tootie spent much of her time by herself, sitting in the porch swing or at the clinic table where she could look out the window, contemplating Peter and her promise. Emma told her she was loyal to her friends. If Peter were here, he wouldn't think she was very loyal. She hadn't kept her promise to him.

She'd chickened out about asking Nora if they could go home right away. It was selfish of her to make Nora and Jim leave just because she wanted to go home in the worse way. Anyway, Nora would just stare her up and down, realize something was wrong and demand to know what her hurry was. So Tootie decided to stick it out. They would have to go home soon anyway. They had visited long enough. At least to suit her.

When Jim was around, he was on a mission to get her or Nora to go for a ride in his old buggy. Nora continued to turn him down which upset him, but Jim didn't stay miffed for long. He was back soon, asking Nora to go with him. When Nora said no, he asked her. She kept refusing, too. Jim had become so insistent Nora barely spoke to him. When they did talk it was usually in short huffy sentences.

When Tootie's mood didn't change, Hal was sure something was troubling her aunt. She didn't know any other way to get to the bottom of it except to come right out and ask.

"I want to go for a walk. Come with me, Aunt Tootie," Hal

said. "While Mom helps Emma pick the green beans, we can get some of that exercise we're always talking about." As they started down the lane, Hal said, " It's a perfect summer day, isn't it?"

"It's a lovely day. As Peter would have said, Praise the Lord," Tootie replied.

"You miss Peter, don't you? You do understand that you weren't the Dolly he'd been in love with years ago?" Hal asked.

"Yes, I knew the way he saw me was because he was sick. I wasn't the Dolly he once loved, but I didn't see any reason to explain that to Peter. You said he wouldn't believe the truth anyway. So I went along with him, because I liked him."

"No harm in that. Peter had some very comforting times in his last days because of you," Hal said.

"I enjoyed being his Dolly. I admit that," Tootie confided.

"Is that all there was to it? After you went on that ride on Bender Creek Road and was lost in the timber with Peter, you haven't seemed the same since."

"What do you mean?" Tootie stared at Hal. "Are you thinking there was more between Peter and me then just a friendship?"

"I don't know what to think. Something has been bothering you for some time now. I didn't say anything before, because I thought you were just grieving for Peter. Time has passed, and you still seem so down in the dumps. Now I think there's more. What don't we know?"

Tootie shrugged. "I kept thinking if I could just get away from here and go home I'd put what happened behind me. I would feel better and just forget it all."

"Sounds like you would be running away from the problem. I get it, but what is the problem? You need to tell someone just to get it off your chest. If you don't want what you say repeated, I promise not to tell a soul."

"I wish I'd been able to say that to Peter. It didn't work that way for me. He made me promise to tell a secret, and it's simply none of my business," Tootie declared vehemently.

"Oh my! Now you really should tell me before this burden

eats you up," Hal said.

Tootie walked over to the pasture fence and stared off toward the picnic grove. Her voice was hollow as she spilled what was wrong. "Don't worry about anything other than friendship between Peter and me. That's all there was. All Peter did was talk about the past most of the time. He told me how much more he loved Dolly than his wife. He was sneaking around with Dolly after he married Sara. They met on Bender Creek Road often. That's why Lover's Lane meant so much to him."

"Peter Rogies did that! Cooner Jonah said something happened between Dolly and Peter that broke them up. He said Dolly just disappeared, but he thinks it was before Peter married Sara," Hal told her.

"Dolly didn't leave Peter until after he married Sara. She finally grew tired of him always going back to his wife after he had been with her so she moved to Fremont. Peter asked Dolly's brother about her every chance he got. Dolly worked at house cleaning jobs to support herself."

"Wonder who her brother was?"

"His name was Rudy Briskey."

"Oh," Hal said. "I know him well. I delivered some lambs for him once."

"Months later, the brother told Peter that Dolly had a baby boy, and the baby was his. Peter told Sara he was spending the day at the salebarn. Actually, he went to see Dolly and his baby. She couldn't support herself and take care of the baby so she wanted to find a good home for him. Peter and Sara were sure by then that Sara was never going to get pregnant so Peter asked Sara if it would be all right to adopted a baby. He said he'd heard at the salebarn about an unwed mother that had given birth to a boy a few weeks before. Sara agreed. Peter brought the baby home. He said the mother had named him Jonah so they stuck with that name."

"Uh oh," Hal said softly.

"I don't think Peter ever saw Dolly again, but he didn't stop asking her brother about her until the brother said she had left

205

the Amish faith and married an English farmer close to Fremont. She had been on shaky ground with the Amish, because she was an unwed mother. When she married an English man, her family and the Amish community shunned her. Peter didn't dare bring her up to Mr. Briskey again.

He didn't stop loving Dolly, and he felt guilty. He tried hard to make it up to Sara for the way he felt about Dolly. No one knew where the little boy came from. It was just an adoption as far as the Amish neighbors were concerned. I find it hard to believe that Sara didn't suspect something. When Jonah grew older, it would be hard to miss how much like Peter he looked.

You told me that Peter was a very honest man that couldn't abide dishonesty in others. I suppose that's why he was so torn up for years over keeping this secret from Jonah and Sara."

"That explains why in his mind he wanted to be close to Dolly again. He loved her so much," Hal said.

"Yes, he didn't want to ever hurt Sara or have it get out in the community what he'd done. He reasoned he couldn't say anything as long as Sara was alive, but he wished Jonah knew the truth. After Sara died, Peter lost his nerve. So he picked me, his Dolly, to tell Jonah the truth for him. He made me promise several times before he died. I kept saying I'd do it to ease his troubled mind, but Hallie, I can't. It's none of my business. I don't want to be the bearer of such news to a man who has just lost his father."

Hal let out a big whoosh. "I understand. The only reason to be truthful, I can think of, is Jonah might want to look up Dolly. He might want to see if his mother is alive and get to know her. On the other hand, if the Amish shunned her that might stop Jonah from wanting to see her. So telling him would be unnecessary.

I can't tell you what to do. You have to be the one to decide. You give it some thought. Like I told you, I won't say a word to anyone. This secret is safe with me, but you should make a decision soon. Dad is making noises about going home."

"Thank you, Dear. It really has helped to get this off my chest," Tootie said.

"We've walked far enough. We should go back and raid the refrigerator for some of Emma's gute lemonade. Emma and Mom are probably done picking green beans and could use a gute drink by now, too."

A few mornings later, Tootie caught Hal alone, dusting in the clinic. "I've decided to go visit Jonah and Anna. Peter stands over me every night in my dreams, shaking his finger at me. It doesn't look like he's going to let me have a good night's rest even after I go home. Could you take me today?"

"I'd be glad to," Hal said. "Would you mind if we used Dad's buggy?"

"Right now I'm so upset about this whole mess I don't care what we ride in," Tootie said forlornly.

Hal went to the garden to tell Nora and Emma she was taking Tootie for a ride. Nora was squatted in a row of green beans. She stopped picking and studied her daughter intently, but she didn't ask where or why. She just said okay. Emma nodded and kept picking. She always seemed to sense when saying less was better.

Hal hunted her father up in the barn with John. "Dad, would you mind if I borrowed your buggy today?"

"Of course not. I'll get Mike hitch up for you."

John asked, "Where are you headed?"

"I thought I'd take Aunt Tootie for a ride. Maybe a ride would cheer her up," Hal excused.

Jim turned around at the door. "Really? More power to you if you think you can get either one of those Petermeyer sisters in my buggy," Jim growled.

"Aunt Tootie has already agreed to ride with me," Hal said timidly.

Jim grunted as he went out the door and grumbled, "Must be the driver they object to then."

Hal looked helplessly at John. He stuffed his hands in his trouser pockets and leaned against the barn wall. Hal rolled her eyes up at the cobweb covered barn ceiling. "Lord, give me the strength to smile when I don't feel like it. Honestly, John, sometimes I just want to hide under the bed and stay there until

207

everyone in this family can get along."

"Don't do that," John said.

"Why not?"

He kissed her cheek. "I'd miss you."

When Hal came to the Bender Creek Road, she turned onto it. "This really is a pretty area in the daylight."

"It is," Tootie agreed. "I couldn't tell much about it in the dark with Peter. I didn't give the scenery much thought. Peter sure didn't have his mind on scenery." She giggled like a school girl. "He said he drove around this road often, thinking about Dolly. He used to bring her here a lot where he thought no one would see them. Why did you pick today to come here?"

"I thought you might feel closer to Peter. Maybe that feeling would help you when you talk to Cooner Jonah."

Hal followed the road until they reached the intersection stop sign and drove toward the Rogies farm. Jonah was coming out of the barn when they drove in. Hal helped Tootie down, and they went to meet him.

"Come on in. Anna will be glad to see you," Jonah greeted.

They all sat down at the table while Anna poured coffee and set out a plate of chocolate chip cookies.

"I had a reason for stopping by." Tootie licked her lips nervously. "You might be sorry I came, but we're going home soon so I couldn't wait much longer to talk to you, Jonah."

His head came up fast. "Me?"

"Yes. You see your father and I confided in each other. Of course, the intimate things he shared with me he thought he was sharing with the Dolly he loved long ago. I didn't mind until he told me a family secret that he made me promise to share with you after he was gone. I was for letting sleeping dogs lie, as they say, but my conscious has bothered me so much I decided I should tell you what your father wanted you to know."

Tootie took a drink of hot coffee to wet down her throat and told the story as Peter had told it to her. Jonah and Anna were surprised that Peter had loved two women at the same time. Maybe it happened more than they knew, but they didn't think that love was always acted on, especially not in their family.

Tootie assured them that they were the only two that knew the story besides Hal and her. What they chose to do with the news was up to them. No one else need know as far as Hal and she were concerned. Tootie stood up and declared the visit over. Anna and Jonah gave her a hug and thanked her for sharing.

On the way home, Tootie worried, "Everyone is going to wonder where we went today? I'd just as soon not get into where with Nora and Jim. They would ask too many questions. I'd be sure to say the wrong thing, and before I knew it, they would know more than I want them to know."

"What should we tell them?"

"Take me by the cemetery if you have time. I'll say I wanted to visit Peter's grave," Tootie said.

"I'll make time. That sounds like a gute reason to go for this ride," Hal replied softly. "But only if you will do something for me in return."

Tootie snorted. "Is this what you call blackmail for helping me?"

"Nah, I'd call it one hand washing the other. The next time my father is going to take this buggy somewhere I want you to volunteer to ride along with him," Hal said.

Tootie looked put out.

"Aunt Tootie, you're hurting his feelings. You take the fun out of his owning this buggy by turning him down when he asks you to ride in it. It's about time you and Mom acted like you enjoy riding with Dad. Besides, have you ever thought that Dad is dragging his feet about going home? He's hoping Mom and you will give in to liking his buggy first. The quicker you act like you like this buggy the quicker you could be going home," Hal scolded.

"I did like riding in the buggy with Peter. Why don't you tell your mother to go with Jim? She's his wife," Tootie retorted, pouting.

"Ach, don't worry. Mom's going to be the next one to hear from me. Now do we have a deal?"

"All right, but when is this ride going to take place?"

"When you see me nod at you. You wait for the signal," Hal told her.

That morning, Emma had done a fair amount of baking. Hal asked her to bake a coconut cream pie for the Bontragers. After lunch, Hal said, "Dad, will you do me a big favor?"

"Sure thing," he said agreeably.

"Emma made a coconut cream pie I want delivered to the Bontragers this afternoon. Can you deliver it for me?"

"Sure, be glad to."

Hal gave Tootie a nod and nodded toward Jim. Tootie cleared her throat. "Jim, could I ride along with you? I'd like to visit with the Bontragers. They are the nicest people."

"Of course, you can," Jim said with a pleased smile.

After they left the house, Nora stood at the kitchen window, staring at Jim and Tootie climbing in the buggy. "What do you suppose got in to that sister of mine? I didn't think she'd ever get in that buggy with Jim."

"Guess she just decided to be nice for a change. You saw how happy it made Dad to take her for a ride. You should volunteer next. Dad has had his feelings hurt a lot lately. You and Aunt Tootie have been so unkind to him about that buggy. You really should make it up to him," Hal said.

When Tootie came back from her ride with Jim, she was all smiles. "Hal, I apologized to Jane for what happened at the quilting bee. She has forgiven me. Isn't that great?"

"It's very gute news. I'm glad you did that," Hal said.

"Jane even invited me to come visit again when we're down this way. I promised to be on my best behavior next time so I wouldn't spoil her quilting bee. You should have heard her laugh."

Later that afternoon, John appeared in the mudroom door. "Hal, clean up. You and me have some place to go."

"Where?"

"Just come upstairs with me and get your fer gute clothes on so we can take a ride," he said, smiling at her.

"Are you sure? It's so close to supper time and chores," Hal worried.

Nora winked at John. "Hal, just do as John says. Tootie, Emma and I can handle supper tonight."

"Go on," Emma insisted, pushing Hal out of the kitchen.

Jim said from the living room doorway. "The boys and I will milk. Get out of here. The buggy is waiting out front."

Consumed with curiosity, Hal did as she was told. She put on her newest lavender dress and cape. John changed into his white shirt and black trousers. When John opened the screen door for Hal, she stepped out on the porch and stopped. "I thought Dad said the buggy was waiting."

"It is," John said, pointing to Jim's courting buggy.

"We're taking Dad's buggy?"

"Jah, he does not mind. Seems only recht to use it since we are going on a date," John said, grinning at her.

"A date? Really? A real date."

"Jah. Now go get in that courting buggy," John ordered.

Hal studied him as Mike started off. "Why all this?"

"Because you need a night off to get away from this mad house. Because I can't take care of this family without you if you really do decide to hide under the bed. Because I love you. Need anymore reasons?" John asked.

"That will do for starters. Where are we going?"

To the Gingerich sisters for supper and for a long moonlit ride," John said, grinning at her.

"Uh huh. Would this ride happen to end up going down Bender Creek Road?"

John chuckled. "How did you guess?"

That later evening, after a wonderful supper prepared by great Amish cooks, John turned onto the Lover's Lane. With a full moon glowing down on them, Hal's senses livened up. She felt the heat of the breeze on her face and dampness coming off the creek. A sweetness from the timber leaves scented the air. She reminded herself places like this was the reason she loved this part of the country. Most importantly, she loved the man beside her on the courting buggy seat as they enjoyed this place together.

The next morning, Jim announced at breakfast they should head for home the next day. They had been gone long enough. It was time for Nora and Tootie to pack their bags.

"I'm going for one last ride around the countryside in my buggy this morning," Jim announced.

Hal caught her mother's eyes and nodded at her father. She mouthed the word go.

Nora licked her lips and swallowed hard to keep from choking on her words. "Sounds like a nice ride. Can I go with you?"

"You sure can," Jim said, smiling from ear to ear. He hurried outside to hitch the buggy to Mike and waited for Nora to climb in. They rode down gravel roads now as familiar as the country roads around their home. As they passed each farm, echoes of the Lapp farm, they chatted about what they saw happening. It was as if the Plain people had always been their neighbors.

After awhile, Nora realized she didn't mind riding in the buggy as much as she once thought she did. "I've been thinking, Jim. If you really want to take this buggy and horse home, why don't you hire a truck to haul them?. That would be the safest thing to do."

Jim asked, "You really think that would be all right?"

"Yes, taking the buggy home is what you want, isn't it?"

"Well, I thought it was, but before you know it, winter will be here. I'd have to get out on cold, snowy days to take care of the horse or pay for his board somewhere. Then when we came back here to visit I'd have to haul the buggy and horse back down here where I really like using the buggy. I think I'd rather leave the rig here and dream about using it next year."

"Whatever you think is best," Nora said.

When they arrived back at the house, Jim stared out the living room window at his courting buggy and horse parked by the barn.

Nora asked, "Jim, are you sure you've decided what you're going to do with that buggy? You look as if you hate to leave it behind."

John said, "We will be glad to store the buggy here and keep the horse for you. When you come visit you will have it to use, Jim."

"There you see. That sounds like a good idea," Nora added.

"That's what I'd like, but I don't want John stuck with feeding my horse on my account, and the buggy just parked, gathering dust and not being used. I've decided I want to give it to Noah to use when I'm not around," Jim said.

"Really, Dawdi Jim," Noah said excitedly.

Hal intervened, "But Dad he's only fourteen."

"I've seen how he can drive and take care of a horse. He will take good care of my buggy and horse," Jim defended.

"I know Noah would, but he's a little young for a courting buggy. We have an open buggy he uses," Hal insisted.

"Time goes fast. He and Daniel can use it to go to the singings. Before you know it, Noah will have a girl in the seat with him," Jim said.

"That's what worries me," Hal said dryly.

"What do you think about this, Noah?" John asked.

"I would like to have the buggy to drive," Noah said. "I will take gute care of it."

Jim said, "Three things you need to know if you use my buggy to cinch this deal. So you better think about this a minute, Noah."

"Jah, tell me, Dawdi Jim."

"One is I want the buggy well taken care of and my horse, too. I already know you can handle that. Next, I get to use the buggy when I come back on vacation like it's still my buggy. Third, when you don't need the buggy anymore Daniel gets his turn to use it. He can pass the buggy on to whoever is next in line," Jim said.

"I agree," Noah said eagerly.

"Maybe I should have said four things. I want to pay for the horse's feed," Jim said to John.

"That is not necessary," John protested.

"That's nice of you, but if I took Mike home with me, I'd have to buy his feed or pay to board him. I think I owe you that much for the pleasure I'll have when I'm here," Jim insisted.

The next morning, Jim, Nora and Tootie left early, hoping to make it back to Titonka that evening. After they left, the house was quiet. Too quiet without the extra people around.

After dinner, Hal stared at the dish pans. "Emma, which one of us is going to wash and which one wipe this time?"

"I have wiped for a long time. I do not mind washing dishes if you wipe. Just one thing. I am not sure I want to wash the slop pail. This morning, my Aendi Tootie warned me I should offer to dry dishes from now on. Washing the slop pail was a bad job to have," Emma said and broke out in a smile.

Hal giggled. "Aunt Tootie is one of a kind."

"That's why we're going to miss her," Emma said sagely. "She had a way of livening things up around here."

Hal laughed. "Ach, nah! You think?"

After supper, the Lapp family formed a circle in the living room so John could read devotions. Hal said, "I have something that's been bothering me that I want to bring up before you start, John. Before our company left this morning, my father said I should as he put it let Noah and Daniel off the hook about their dog's name."

"He said that?" Noah asked, surprised.

"Jah, he told me that Biscuit is not considered a gute name for a dog," Hal said as she looked from Noah to Daniel. "I told him I already knew that. I've watched the two of you struggle with the dog's name to please me. You should know I picked the name Biscuit because you were bribing me by giving me the privilege of naming the dog so you could keep him. Your father said I was being mean. I said I meant to be. Now I'm feeling less mean. I'm willing to let you pick a name for the dog that suits you on one condition. From now on when you want a pet or anything else, you just say so instead of worrying about what I will think. Deal?"

"Jah," Daniel said sheepishly.

"That is a deal, Mama Hal," Noah agreed.

"Now your turn, John," Hal said, winking at him.

For bible devotions, John finished by reading, "All ye have

214

done for the least among you, you surely have done unto me."

Hal declared, "John, I can't think of a single reward we received from hosting Aunt Tootie."

Emma defended Tootie. "Hallie, Peter might have disagreed with you."

John grinned, "Who knows? Maybe your Aendi Tootie was an angel in disguised sent to teach us the patience of Job."

Hal snorted. "I don't think so. If that was so, it didn't work on me."

"Do not be so hard on, Aendi Tootie," Emma scolded playfully. "I think she was busy being Peter's angel not ours."

Hal gave that a moment's thought. "Great, Emma! Whose angel is she going to be the next time she come?"

About The Author

Hello! I'm Fay Risner, and I go by booksbyfay online. I enjoy writing about the life of Nurse Hal while she struggles to understand Amish life. My books are designed to offer some humor along with the serious moments.

As well as these books, I write a historical mystery series set in Iowa and westerns. Also, I've written two books about Alzheimer's disease. I worked for many years in a local nursing home and helped my mother care for my father which gave me insight about what caregivers deal with. Switching genres, when an idea comes to me, gives me flexibility as a writer.

I write in 12 font to make reading my books user friendly. My husband and I live on an acreage with chickens, rabbits , cats and through the summer months a flock of goats. We enjoy raising a large garden and flowers. For fun, we go fishing in the summer and read a lot in the winter.

Fay Risner's books sold by her at her bookstore at www.booksbyfaybookstore@weebly.com, on Amazon, B&N, Smashwords and Kindle

Nurse Hal Among The Amish Series

A Promise Is A Promise
The Rainbow's End
Hal's Worldly Temptations
As Her Name Is So Is Redbird
Emma's Gossamer Dreams

Amazing Gracie Historical Mystery Series

Neighbor Watchers
Specious Nephew
The Country Seat Killer
The Chance Of A Sparrow
Moser Mansion Ghosts
Locked Rock, Iowa Hatchet Murders
Poor Defenseless Addie

Westerns
Stringbean Hooper Westerns

The Dark Wind Howls Over Mary
Small Feet's Many Moon Journey

Tread Lightly Sibby
Ella Mayfield's Pawpaw Militia

Christmas books

Christmas Traditions - An Amish Love Story
Leona's Christmas Bucket List

Children Books
My Children Are More Precious Than Gold

Nonfiction
Alzheimer's disease
Open A Window - Caregiver Handbook
Hello Alzheimer's Goodbye Dad-author's true story